AARDVARK

TWO GENTLEMEN, TWO WARS

For Wolf Harris and Sir Percy Harris Bt

ABOUT THE AUTHOR

Paul Ashford Harris was born in Lower Hutt New Zealand in the last days of WWII, the son of an English Baronet and an Australian actress. Paul attended Cambridge University where he studied law and had a front row view of the machinations of the English class system at work. Since childhood he has always had an interest in the two world wars and their dramatic impact on his homeland New Zealand, on Australia and on Great Britain. Paul currently resides in Sydney with his wife and four children.

Aardvark is Paul Harris' first fiction novel. He has previously published five children's books highlighting the potentially terminal threat to Australian native wildlife and the unique habitat that sustains them.

A NOTE FROM THE AUTHOR

This book is a story loosely based around the remarkable life of Admiral Wilhelm Canaris, the chief of the Abwehr, German Military Intelligence, in WWII.

It is not history: for history there are many books and articles exploring his life and tragic death. Some of the major characters names will be easily recognised but the rest is invented, including the many meetings and discussions.

The part of the story involving New Zealand and New Zealanders is also invented, although the story of the Douglas family roughly follows the history of my own family.

The purpose of this book is no more than to provide some enjoyment to readers for whom the subject holds interest and to pose some questions for which there are as yet no definitive answers.

CHAPTER 1

First Sea Lord Jacky Fisher was short and pugilistic. A round face was topped by spiky hair, which looked as if it had been cut by a midshipman in a hurry, as it probably had. His yellowish colouring, legacy of early dysentery and malaria from his time in the Far East, enhanced his justified reputation for a choleric temperament. He glanced out the window at the low clouds. Rain belted against the glass and ran in rivulets down to the sill. It was a glum, grey November day in London, winter coming and little flakes of sleet landing with the rain. In the street below people scurried along, their raincoats pulled tight. Water ran along the gutters and puddled opposite the bus stop. A young woman struggled with an umbrella and finally disappeared from view still trying to fix the canopy. The foul weather matched Jacky Fisher's mood, which was more than usually belligerent. The silence in the room was interrupted by the chiming of his antique clock on the mantelpiece. It was 10am and he was already behind in the demanding program he had set himself since taking over as First Sea Lord from Prince Louis of Battenberg less than a week ago.

The phone rang insistently. Admiral Fisher looked at the ceiling for a few seconds and then took a deep breath before lifting the handset. As he had expected, it was his boss, Navy Minister and First Lord, Winston Spencer Churchill. There was no time to waste on niceties; if anything he was in a worse mood than Fisher.

"You've seen the headlines, 'Disaster in the Pacific'. I'll come straight to the point, Jacky. *The Times* is right. Coronel is an absolute disaster for us; the most humiliating defeat for the Royal Navy ever. Ever. What is the latest situation?"

Fisher knew this was not hyperbole. The brutal analysis was essentially correct.

"We were out-gunned, out-thought and unprepared. The loss of life has been considerable. As you are aware, Admiral Cradock went down with the *Good Hope* along with the entire crew, and then the *Monmouth* was also sunk with all hands. We have lost 1700 men. With the war only days old, we must react with all forces available otherwise we will be a laughing stock."

Churchill interrupted, "I want every ship within range deployed in the South Atlantic. The Kaiser's cruisers must be destroyed, every one of them. Tell Sturdee, every one of them." There was a pause. "Where on earth were *Canopus* and *Defence*? They were supposed to be with Cradock."

"I have already given the orders to Sturdee," replied Fisher, ignoring this embarrassing question. He knew perfectly well that there had been a major communication failure during the period between Battenberg's departure, Churchill's instructions and his own arrival at the Admiralty. *Defence* had been sent to reinforce Cradock but was then diverted, with *Canopus* ordered to replace her but had not arrived on time. And why had Cradock attacked without *Canopus'* 12-inch guns? This was most definitely not the moment to debate the issues with Churchill, and potentially severely embarrassing both of them. "We're still piecing the facts together. There have been some very poor decisions but I will await more detailed information before commenting further. In the meantime, Sturdee has very clear instructions."

Churchill was well aware of the antipathy between Fisher and Sturdee going back some years to Sturdee's participation in plans to get rid of Fisher in his previous stint as First Sea Lord. This antagonism was unhelpful in a situation where co-operation was essential, especially with Fisher back in the job for such a brief period. Churchill had needed to appoint Fisher at very short notice, Prince Louis of Battenberg having been forced to step down following the furore over the British Navy at the outbreak of war with Germany being under the command of a German Prince, however anglicised. The Coronel fiasco could not have come at a worse time for Fisher and Churchill.

"When can *Invincible* and *Inflexible* sail?" asked Churchill. The two battle cruisers, equipped with 12-inch guns and capable of 25 knots, had ample capacity to exact revenge on Vice Admiral von Spee's German cruiser squadron, but were refitted in Plymouth.

"My latest information just an hour ago is one week."

"They must be able to improve on that; time is critical, critical," pressed Churchill.

"I think they will be sufficiently resourced to sail in two days if the shipyard works around the clock," replied Fisher. "I'll give the order immediately that they will sail by midnight Tuesday. Like you, I want every German cruiser hounded down and sunk."

"I would be astounded if you held any other opinion, Jacky. Go after them."

Both men had ample reason to be concerned. The British Navy was still without doubt the most powerful afloat. Its reputation was sufficient to make any adversary hesitate before taking on Britain. But if the first significant naval event of the war was to result in the annihilation of the British fleet, however ragtag, it would raise the possibility for potential adversaries that perhaps the British Navy was not as formidable as it seemed.

It had been only a few weeks after the war started in August 1914 that Vice-Admiral Sir Christopher Cradock was cruising in the South Pacific on the lookout for German raiders, and in particular von Spee's cruiser squadron. Prior to the outbreak of war, the Kaiser had been determined to build up the Imperial Navy's strength so that Germany could offer some competition to the giant British fleet. Part of his efforts had resulted in the construction of a fleet of modern fast cruisers more than competitive with similar sized ships owned by the British.

These fast German cruisers, accompanied by single armed raiders disguised as merchant ships, had been creating havoc with Allied merchant shipping since the outbreak of war, with regularly occurring losses in the Atlantic, Pacific and Indian oceans. To cover more ocean, Cradock had approval to split his squadron into two, an Eastern (Atlantic) fleet and a Western fleet to remain in the Pacific. He was left with only the armoured cruisers *Good Hope* and *Monmouth*, the light cruiser *Glasgow* and the armed merchant cruiser, *Otranto*.

Cradock looked out at the seas breaking over the bow of his flagship, *Good Hope*. He inched his way across the heaving deck to the starboard point on the bridge and saw a young sailor rush to the rail and vomit. Yellow flecks blew back all over him. Cradock smiled to himself. First lesson of sea sickness, vomit down wind. He paced back to the other end of the bridge to find a more agreeable sight. Off the port bow he could see *Good Hope* had the company of a huge wandering albatross. Its grey wings must have been more than 10feet from tip to tip. It seemed to hover motionless, its wings scarcely moving as it effortlessly kept up. He could see the bird's pink beak in the sunlight as it rotated its head to inspect the ship and the ocean below. He thought of Charles Darwin, and his book *On the Origin of Species* that he kept in his cabin. Darwin had traversed these seas in *Beagle* and here was this bird, a perfect example of evolution, totally at home in one of the most inhospitable corners of the world.

The wind had moderated a little, down to Force 7 but it was still whipping the spume off the tops of the waves. The previous night's storm had pushed up a lumpy swell so that the *Good Hope* was barrelling off the peaks and burying its nose into long deep troughs, throwing white water in a cloud over the bow to smash against the bridge. Every now and then the ship would kick sideways, its propellers out of the water, so that they would cavitate and the ship would shudder before the props bit again and drove it forward. Cradock decided to ease off a few knots. Speed was not really the issue. The issue was what to do in the face of the enigmatic order from Admiralty to "be prepared to meet the enemy in company". With his fleet split, Cradock had only four ships and the quality of his crews were quite poor. They were young and inexperienced, many were hopelessly seasick and their gunnery skills were below requirements. Worse, he had been forced to leave *Canopus* and her 12-inch guns behind because, although a battleship, she was old, unreliable and could manage only 12 knots. Cradock faced a dilemma. If he met the German cruiser force without *Canopus* he would be out-gunned, but if he rejoined with *Canopus* and then engaged them, the Germans would simply speed out of range if the 12-inch guns on *Canopus* posed too much of a threat. The Admiralty favoured attack and the cruel reality of the comparative number of ships in each navy meant Britain would win that if each side lost tonnage at an equal rate.. So, should he go after the German cruisers or turn back to *Canopus* for protection? It depended on what he might be facing; perhaps only one German cruiser on a raiding mission but perhaps two or more.

Cradock tried to put himself in von Spee's position. If he were von Spee, he would know very well that there were British ships in the area, given the carnage his ships and the raiders had been inflicting. He would not want to risk meeting them alone. Cradock's intelligence was contradictory, but then there was the fate of his good friend Rear Admiral Troubridge to consider. Troubridge, who was now before a court martial for "failing to engage the enemy", had allowed the *Goeben* and *Breslau*, a superior German force, to slip by him in the Mediterranean and escape to Constantinople, considerably embarrassing His Majesty's Government which was engaged in desperate attempts to enlist Turkey in the cause of the Allies. The British Admiralty was not amused. Troubridge's honour and name were now impugned, regardless of the outcome of the court martial and Cradock had no intention of suffering a similar humiliation. Whatever the consequences, he must press on without *Canopus*,. He decided to leave *Good Hope*'s speed where it was and head towards the small port of Coronel, south of Valparaiso, on the Chilean coast.

As he neared Coronel, his lookouts spied smoke that could only come from the enemy, but it was smoke from three ships not one. Cradock found himself confronting a German Cruiser Squadron which included *Scharnost* and *Gneisnau* with 16 8-inch guns against his two 9-inch guns plus numerous outranged 6-inch guns. For a moment he considered making a run for it towards *Canopus*, but *Otranto* was too slow and would be left behind. He pulled his cap down a little tighter on his head. He knew he had gambled and lost, but without missing a beat gave the order to turn his ships to attack.

The Germans had gained the favourable inshore position, the battle-grey of their ships hard to distinguish against the grey-green of the Andes rising behind them. The British ships by contrast were starkly outlined, haloed by the golden rays of a setting sun. Firing began at a range of ten kilometres with salvos every 15 seconds. *Good Hope* was soon ablaze and *Monmouth* severely damaged. Though straddled by shells, somehow *Glasgow* and *Otranto* escaped, but within a few hours the other two were gone.

Fisher's reputation could suffer and so could the First Lord's unless immediate action was taken to redress the situation. And so it was that every ship the Navy had available in the South Atlantic and Pacific was put under the Command of Vice Admiral Doveton Sturdee on the battle cruiser HMS *Invincible*, and sent on the trail of the Kaiser's cruisers.

Von Spee turned his victorious convoy and headed south towards the Atlantic by way of Cape Horn. As his ship left the battle scene, he returned below to the quiet of his cabin. The seas were calm, the night fine and the enemy vanquished. He should have been most satisfied with his day's work. He paused a few minutes, contemplating the sea through the porthole, then summoned his two sons, both sailing with him as junior officers on the *Scharnost*. Soon, there was a knock at the cabin door and the two boys entered. Still in their watch uniform they stood stiffly to attention. "You called for us, Sir?"

"I did boys. You have seen action today and, like all our crew, you have done well. None of us knew how it would turn out, but it turned out well for us, very well. But there will soon be another action, and another, and eventually perhaps it will not turn out quite so well. Whichever way it should turn out, we know what we must do, don't we?"

The older boy took a pace forward, "Our duty, Sir."

"Yes, exactly, our duty, and who have we learned that from?"

"You, Sir."

Von Spee stood up and walked around from his desk. "Not

entirely boys, we have all learned from the traditions of the British Navy, so when you engage them never forget that. Never think you will have another victory quite so easily."

"No, Sir."

He stood in front of them as they remained at attention. Then, first one and then the other, he cupped their faces in his hands and kissed them lightly on the forehead. "You may go now, and God be with us all."

It took less than six weeks for the British ships to find their opportunity for revenge. Von Spee, after rounding Cape Horn, stopped for three days at Picton Island at the eastern end of the Beagle Channel. Confident after having suffered only two casualties and some minor damage, and encouraged by the performance of his officers and men at Coronel, he decided to rub salt in the considerable wounds he had inflicted on the British by attacking the Falkland Islands.

The Falklands are one of the most strategically located island groups in the world's oceans. They sit off the Argentine coast, perfectly positioned to control the trade route south around Cape Horn into the Pacific or the return trip home. The commanders of the *Dresden, Leipzig* and *Gneisnau* tried to dissuade von Spee, believing that his intelligence about the Falklands being undefended might be faulty. But the normally cautious von Spee had convinced himself that he would be able to win the unprotected islands, put a force ashore and capture Port Stanley. It would be another humiliating blow to the British so early in the war.

HMS *Canopus*, in reality an old pre-war Dreadnought, built in 1897 and fatally left behind by Cradock as too slow to keep up, had made its way to Port Stanley where it had been beached on the mudflats in good position to cover the harbour mouth. Her topmasts were removed so she could not be seen from the sea, and she was camouflaged. An observation post was established on high ground and connected to the ship by phone. On 7 December 1914 the British battleships arrived for coaling. *Canopus*'s function was to act as a guard ship both for the port and for the British ships while they took on coal.

As he approached the Falklands, von Spee would have been shocked to know that not only were *Invincible* and *Inflexible* there but so were the armed cruisers *Carnarvon*, *Kent* and *Cornwall* and the light cruisers *Bristol* and *Glasgow*, recovered from their experience at Coronel, and the AMC *Macedonia*; all in all, a formidable British fleet.

At first light the next morning, von Spee's fleet approached the port, unaware they were being watched from the observation post. At a range of 11,000 yards, *Canopus* opened fire seemingly from nowhere and a shot skidded off the water and hit *Gneisnau*. Badly surprised and spotting the superstructure of the British battleships, von Spee fired a few broadsides. He hesitated. Should he press on with his attack on the port or, now aware of the size of the opposition within, take the safer option? Unaware that the British battleships had not yet completed their coaling, he turned to escape. This exchange of fire gave Sturdee time to coolly finish his breakfast while his ships completed their coaling, then set off in pursuit.

It was no day for ships to run and hide. The sea was placid, with a gentle breeze from the northwest, a bright, sunny, clear day. No high seas and low cloud casting dull shadows on the water to provide cover. Sturdee well understood his superiority. He ordered "General Chase", the order made famous by Nelson at the Battle of the Nile, which allowed all ships to break ranks and pursue the enemy. *Invincible* and *Inflexible* were bigger and faster than *Gneisnau* and *Scharnorst* and, while the light and the weather held, the result was inevitable. Travelling at full speed,

Invincible and *Inflexible* opened up with their 12-inch guns beyond the range of the German guns. *Gneisnau* and *Scharnorst* turned to face their pursuers but they were both soon ablaze. As the British ships approached, the two German cruisers settled low in the water and the British sailors watched in silence as their hulls reared up above the water, like two stricken whales, in a last convulsion before they were gone.

As the battle developed, the Intelligence Officer on the German cruiser *Dresden* wedged himself into the corner of the bridge, trying to steady his binoculars. He stared intently at the horizon off the starboard bow, and hardly even heard two explosions as shells from the pursuing British cruisers landed in the sea off their stern. Below decks, the stokers stripped off their shirts as they strove to keep up the supply of coal to the boilers. Sweat poured off them and their arms ached from the constant shovelling. The *Dresden* was at full speed, a plume of black smoke behind her as she tried to use it to provide some cover. The Intelligence Officer screwed up his eyes. He was almost certain he could see a thin, pencil-grey line of low cloud and mist on the horizon. "I think we have fog to starboard captain. We should run towards it. It is our only chance." The *Dresden* started to turn.

"Please God you're right," muttered the captain.

The remaining German cruisers in turn had their own battle but the British ships had 6-inch guns against the German 4.1-inch armaments. Better gunnery skills would not save the Germans and *Nurnberg* and *Leipzig* were sunk with almost all hands. Altogether the Germans lost six ships and 2200 men. Only the *Dresden* escaped.

It would have been understandable if Sturdee had been suffused with pride over so comprehensive a victory but in fact he was deeply saddened. Prior to the war the German and British navies exercised together and grown to know each other's officers and men and respect each other's professionalism. The last remnants of a knightly chivalry persisted between them, but it was to be extinguished by the brutality of the battles to come on sea and land. After Coronel, a German Consul who proposed a toast to von Spee and his men to 'the damnation of the British Navy' found himself frozen by the disdain of his naval guests. Von Spee responded icily. "I drink," he said "to the memory of a gallant and honourable foe."

Back in London no such doubts were entertained in Whitehall or the Admiralty. Fisher's phone rang again.

"Did we get them all Jacky? I want no survivors."

"All but one, Winston. The *Gneisnau* and *Scharnorst* were sunk by *Invincible* and *Inflexible*. Von Spee and his two young sons all went down on the *Scharnhorst*. In fact, there were almost no survivors. Then our cruisers finished off their smaller ships."

"All but one?"

"All but one. A light cruiser, the *Dresden,* has escaped behind smoke and a sea mist. We're on her tail. I've already told Sturdee his career depends on it. I want the *Dresden* sunk"

"Jacky, you need to find the *Dresden*. I want no unfinished business."

Before Fisher could respond he heard the receiver crash back into place. The First Sea Lord lay back with his hands clasped behind his head. He swivelled his chair around to survey his new office. His gaze brushed over the cartoon 'Spy' had done of him in *Vanity Fair* in 1902, in which he looked almost light-hearted, and stopped at the portrait of himself painted by von Hekkoner in 1911. It showed him in full Admiral's uniform, one hand in his jacket pocket, the other holding his cap and telescope. He wore the expression of a man not on any account to be trifled with.

Indeed he was not. With a grunt, he rose from his desk. Sturdee would need to be contacted again.

It hardly improved the mood of either Churchill or Fisher when weeks later Sturdee had to report that the *Dresden* could not be found. The Germans had tied up considerable British naval forces, vitally needed for the North Sea, for months. Every lead turned out to be false, every report the Navy received incorrect and all sightings led nowhere. To Churchill and Fisher's fury the *Dresden* had vanished.

CHAPTER 2

Harry stood firm, legs splayed against the heaving of the ship's stern, gripping the rail with frozen hands. The *Corinthic*, a near-new Shaw Savill Albion steamer, which plied its trade carrying passengers and the new refrigerated cargoes of frozen meat between Wellington, New Zealand and London, lurched sideways in the swell. Harry braced one foot and then the other. As far as his eye could see, a bridal veil of white spume was streaming from the tops of anthracite-coloured waves. A flock of gulls followed the ship, flapping frantically into the teeth of the gale. One by one they gave up the struggle and peeled off, to be flicked contemptuously out of sight in the ship's wake. Pulling his sheepskin jacket closer around him, Harry peered up at the glimpses of jagged mountains slipping in and out of view through the wisps of grey cloud. How on earth, he wondered, could Magellan ever have navigated this treacherous passage in the 1520s, recovering as he was from a mutiny and the loss of some of his ships? He could have had no idea what was before him, above or below the waters. His ships, tiny caravelles, would have been almost helpless in the face of the great storm that Harry was now experiencing. Still, to be in the Magellan Straits and see the southern tip of the Andes was a unique experience, whatever the weather. Harry reflected that it was a small compensation for the outbreak of war with Germany. On the advice of The Admiralty in London, the shipping company had rerouted him across the remote southern waters of the Pacific rather than the usual route across the Indian Ocean and around the Cape of Good Hope or through the Suez Canal. In any event, in a few hours they would arrive in the little port of Punta Arenas in Chile and he would go ashore and no doubt find a cheerful bar with a wood fire, warm drink and a floor that was still beneath his feet.

Harry wondered again why he was returning to England. After completing his degree in German at Cambridge University, he had returned to New Zealand. But now here he was, just after the war with Germany had begun, on his way back to Europe. He had come to know Germany and the Germans pretty well during his studies. He liked their directness and also their friendliness, which in some ways he felt made them more like New Zealanders than the English. He couldn't understand how two such civilised countries as England and Germany, which in many ways had so much in common, could have descended into war. As things stood, he could choose whether he would participate. He knew his mother and father had very different views on that subject and he was still sifting his choices in his mind. Clearly he was a member of the British Empire with all the obligations and privileges that that entailed. He felt British. But if he volunteered or if conscription was introduced, could he really shoot a German in cold or even hot blood? At least for the moment, he felt strongly that he did not want to be put in the position where he would very likely be confronted with such a choice.

Suddenly, through the mist, a lone peak appeared as if unattached to the earth. It loomed high above the ship and its tip glowed pink in a shaft of late sunlight whilst lower down its slopes out of the sun it darkened into steel-blue. Harry watched how quickly the mist, blown by the gale, raced up the side of the mountain and again concealed it from view.

Back at "Earnslaw", the homestead on the family property in South Canterbury, Harry's parents, Victoria and David, sat at the dining room table with Harry's younger brother Jack. Jack and his father had been half-heartedly discussing the poor state of some of the sheep in the high paddocks at the back of the farm.

"They're looking quite mangy, need drenching. I think we'll move them down a bit tomorrow," David decided. Victoria sat quietly, hardly listening. Finally, she put down her knife and fork and voiced what was really troubling her.

"I'm worried, David. I see there's been a naval battle in the South Atlantic. As I calculate it, that's where Harry's ship should be about now. It seems as if quite a few ships have been sunk by the Germans. It's unnerving not being able to find out anything."

David looked up. "They're mainly German ships that have been sunk from what I have read; some of their cruisers. A good result for Britain I would say. Stop worrying. I'm sure he's okay, Victoria. In any case, you can't do anything."

Jack intervened. "He'll be okay Mum, he always is."

Victoria looked unconvinced by these unsubstantiated expressions of confidence. "The fact is I don't know why this war is happening and what on earth it has to do with New Zealand. No-one seems to be making any attempt to stop it. Aren't all the Royal families related? Why on earth can't King George talk to the Kaiser, agree to suspend fighting and sit down and sort out whatever it is about Serbia that seems to be so important?"

David paused, "The Kaiser started it all and whatever the Empire does, we must support it. If the Empire is at war, *we* are. It's unthinkable for us not to support Britain and the King."

"It's not unthinkable. Many women are thinking it, I can tell you."

"Victoria, it's not women's business. Since you were given the vote you've all become tiresomely voluble. War is not your business."

"It is women's business. Every boy who dies is women's business. Every time a boy dies, a mother dies too. You think we went through the pain and the joy of childbirth for our boys to be sacrificed for nothing? It's not the same for men and never will be. If we were allowed to have women in Parliament, as we should be, we would be making more of a fuss, I can tell you."

"After watching some of your colleagues behaviour since you were given the vote, I must say I hope that never happens. Why can't you be content with voting? All this fuss about wanting your own Members of Parliament is unseemly."

"Unseemly? Have you looked at some of our Members of Parliament? They're stupider than Fergie the bull. That's what's unseemly."

"It won't be happening while Bill Massey's in charge. That I can promise you."

"That bull-headed Irishman. He's a good example but we will not give up, David, I can assure you."

"Victoria, enough of this. He is the Prime Minister and we must support him especially in the time of war. Anything else is disloyal to our Government and King. Harry will be all right, he can look after himself."

There was silence before Victoria stood up. "Excuse me,"

and she put down her table napkin and made her way to the kitchen.

Silence fell. David looked at Jack. "Her cousin George volunteered with a group of New Zealanders for the Boer War. They all thought it would be a fine adventure, apparently. In 1902 he was killed. It wasn't even in combat. He was one of 16 New Zealanders who died in a train crash at a place called Machavic, in the Transvaal. It was only a few months before the war ended. Your mother saw her Aunt Joan grieve. Joan never recovered from losing her only son and Victoria has never forgotten it. Now, we need to move the sheep tomorrow, Jack. We'll go early and move the sheep from the top paddocks first."

Victoria and David had married in Dunedin in 1890. Victoria's father, Malcolm, a local doctor of strict Presbyterian faith, had been rather shocked when David had asked to marry Victoria. After all, although David's father was a highly successful businessman revered in Dunedin for his philanthropy having been heavily involved in the setting up of Otago University, New Zealand's first, of which Victoria's father strongly approved, he was Jewish. On the other hand, David never mentioned the Jewish religion and he had all the characteristics Malcolm would have expected from someone born and educated in Otago. More to the point, his wife approved of David, whatever religion he might or might not belong to, and Malcolm had learned not on any account to contradict his wife. The final point that Malcolm would never admit to having even considered was that David's family owned the beautiful Earnslaw Station. Victoria would be living in the homestead, which Malcolm saw as a wonderful place to rear children in surroundings as remote as possible from sinfulness.

Earnslaw Station was a rambling old timber house with an

expansive ground floor and large attic rooms with bay windows overlooking the paddocks and the mountains to the west. Downstairs the house was surrounded by wooden verandas onto the garden. Here Victoria placed her rocking chair so that she could sit with a cup of tea and her book of the moment to watch the sun go slowly down behind the mountains. The front door had stained-glass insets, particularly admired in the district, and led into a broad entrance hall, which in turn opened to a vaulted living room with a fireplace surrounded by a Chippendale mantelpiece and topped by an Adams mirror. On the wall hung an oil painting depicting the Southern Alps, the distant peaks of which rose vertically in front of the house, its constantly changing moods an integral part of life on Earnslaw station. The gardens contained many species of roses, as well as beds of azaleas and rhododendrons which thrived in the cold winter and warm spring and summer. Beyond the lawn grew the fruit trees – apples, apricots, plums, peaches and figs and behind the house a thriving kitchen garden produced fine crops of vegetables. All in all, David and Victoria could congratulate themselves that, if necessary, they could sit out the frequent winter days when access from town was impossible due to snow. They were secure with their plentiful supplies of summer fruit, vegetables and meat in the larder.

Walking back from moving the sheep the next morning, Jack asked his father, "Why did we fight in the Boer War anyway, Dad?"

David hesitated, "It was the first time we had a chance to stand up for the Empire and show we could play our part. Everyone here was so proud of our contribution. When the first troops left Wellington, bands played and people sang and cheered their heads off and the women cried. The Commander,

Colonel Robin, became quite a hero. He had actually been born in Australia but he'd lived here since he was a child. Of course, as soon as the Kiwis reached South Africa they teamed up with the Aussies; they felt at home with each other. From what some of the local boys said, they didn't like the English officers much; too much parade ground and no commonsense. Anyway it was a coming of age in a way and confirmed our view of ourselves as an important part of the Empire and proud to be so."

Jack digested all that and then replied, "So what do you think Harry will do, Dad?"

David stopped, took his cap off and examined it for a few seconds. "I think your brother will do his duty son. But it may not make your mother happy."

Harry Douglas had always loved mountains, any mountains. He had been born on March 31, 1892 under the spine of New Zealand's Southern Alps where the two great tectonic plates in the South Pacific had crushed against each other with dramatic, mountain-building results.

As soon as they could leave the hospital in Christchurch, Harry's parents had taken their baby straight home to the family's South Canterbury station. They had almost five thousand acres of prime grazing country, with the mountains a towering backdrop. As they arrived home with newborn Harry, a sprinkling of snow lay across the drive and lawns surrounding the house. The mountains were as much a part of the family's daily life as the swift stream that carried the snow melt down, and the sheep and cattle that grazed there.

Harry grew up used to cold. When the winter southerlies blew up from the Antarctic, they swept across Stewart Island and the coast and finally exploded against the Alps, blasting the range with sleet and snow. South Canterbury could be a bleak environment. As he grew older, Harry would help when the sheep had to be rounded up and put in the home paddock and he would go out with his father and the two sheep dogs, Kaiser and Sultan. Sultan, a youngster, was Harry's dog and his dad would yell, "Sultan, get in behind, you stupid bugger. Harry, train that damn dog or he'll be dog tucker by Christmas." Sultan would hide under the hay cart until it was safe to come out, then he would run to Harry and leap joyfully all over him causing more expletives from Harry's father. As the light faded, Harry and his brother Jack would set off for the homestead. It could sometimes take a couple of hours to get home and the boys were glad to pull off their farm gear and stand with their backs to the log fire warming their backsides while their mother prepared the evening meal in the vast country kitchen.

Childhood days, although fondly remembered, were now in the past. Harry's journey from the Canterbury Plains to the Straits of Magellan was taking the young man from the close-knit South Island community to places that none of the surrounding families had ever visited. His parents had travelled and knew that South Canterbury was hardly the centre of the universe. What with letters from the family in England and books and newspapers with details of events in Europe, America and the Far East, Harry and his brother Jack were used to hearing about the wider world. His parents ordered *The Illustrated London News* from England and even though it arrived months after publication, the family pored over it, looking at the photographs and reading about the major issues of the day from around the world. Most of their contemporaries came from the farming community and had hardly considered the possibility of living anywhere but within sight of the Southern Alps. Harry and Jack grew up with an increasing awareness of the world beyond New Zealand; of the sporting combativeness of their nearest neighbours in Australia, of the looming presence of Russia and the growing power of the United States of America, a little about China and Japan, France, Germany and the other European states but, most of all, about the glory of the British Empire.

Not that Harry was always at home to listen to his parents' conversation or to peruse the books and magazines that lay about in every room in the house. Mostly he and Jack were off at boarding school in Christchurch, where Christ's College stood on the banks of the Avon River. A grand Gothic pile complete with spires and stained-glass windows, it could not have been a more English school had it been built in Kent.

Harry went to board there from the age of ten; Jack was a few years behind. They slept in airy dormitories of 30 iron-framed beds and wooden floors. Discipline was delivered by prefects, masters and, most terrifyingly, a ferocious matron who bellowed at them for minor breaches of behaviour. Lights went out at 8pm in the summer and 7.30pm in the winter. The morning bell rang at 6.30am and they were out for a quick shower, a walk around the school grounds followed by breakfast in the dining room – porridge winter and summer, baked beans or eggs, and toast with jam. Then off to chapel and so to class.

Harry, at ten, had developed an enthusiasm for reading almost anything he could get his hands on. He eagerly awaited a monthly comic book which he would take to an out-of-the-way place where he would devour every word. One day he was sitting on a bench at the far end of the rose garden, out of sight, when two of the older boys came along. "What are you doing Douglas? Here, give me that." The larger one grabbed it, tearing it in the process. Harry leapt up and tried to grab the comic back but he only did more damage and got a thump in the ribs for his trouble. He tried to swing a punch but it was easily parried and the return punch, delivered with all the venom his 16-year-old assailant could manage, hit him square on his left eye. He stumbled and then fell to the ground, receiving a good kick in the stomach to follow up. The smaller of his two assailants looked down at him: "You're nothing but a bloody Yid. My mother says Yids shouldn't be allowed at the school." They both aimed a few more kicks at Harry and then turned and stalked off, taking what was left of his comic with them. Harry lay there for a minute holding back tears. His eye had already closed and his nose was bleeding. He could feel the rage, the need for revenge, the unfairness of it all, knowing that he wanted to kill them both but knowing also that there nothing could be done.

Having collected himself, Harry stumbled back to the main school. Trying to avoid everyone, he rounded the corner of the music room and ran straight into Sister Grant, the formidable overseer of all things medical at the School. "Goodness me, Douglas, what on earth has happened to you? Come with me immediately and let's clean you up." Harry followed meekly, hoping to avoid the issue but it was no good. "Well then, Douglas, what happened?"

"Nothing, Sister Grant. I fell over."

"Fell over?"

"Yes, Sister."

"Rubbish Douglas, you have been in a fight and you can explain yourself to the headmaster. 'Nothing', really, what do you take me for?" And so it was that Harry found himself in the headmaster's study following morning chapel the next day.

"So, Douglas," said the headmaster, Mr Arthur Aloysius Thackeray MA, "you have been fighting and have the injuries to show for it. Now whom were you fighting and why?"

"No, I fell over sir, I wasn't fighting."

"Nonsense boy, what do you take me for, a numbskull? I have been headmaster of this school for 15 years and I know fighting when I see it. I will not tolerate fighting and I will not be treated like a numbskull. Do you hear me?"

"Yes, Sir."

"Over there and bend over boy, you shall have a taste of the stick to teach you not to fight and not to treat the headmaster as a numbskull. Is that clear boy?" Harry felt his stomach contract. The 'Big Stick'; every boy knew how much that hurt. It had never occurred to him that he would receive a caning on top of the injuries he had already endured. He had not even thought to protect himself with two pairs of underpants. The headmaster removed his jacket revealing a pair of scarlet braces holding his trousers up over an ample stomach, the reflection of his inability to say no to hearty school meals and puddings in particular. The headmaster favoured caning using the two-handed forehand method, aided by a precise step forward off the right foot coinciding with the forward momentum of the cane. Harry rolled on his toes and tensed his buttocks as each of the strokes from the two-metre bamboo cane landed with a thwack. The pain shot up to the top of his head. He tried to distract himself by reading the titles of the leather-bound books in the floor-to-ceiling shelves along two walls of the headmaster's study. Thwack, "*The Collected Works of William Shakespeare.*" Thwack, "*The Diaries of Samuel Pepys*". Thwack, "*Macaulay's History of England.*" Thwack, "*Great Expectations*". After four strokes there was a pause. "Now be gone, boy, and do not treat your Headmaster as a numbskull. Is that clear?"

Later that day, a small group of friends gathered around expectantly, following a time-honoured ritual whereby caned boys displayed the damage for comparison purposes. Harry lowered his trousers and then his underpants to display his bruises. Black and red welts were spreading rapidly upwards. There were whistles of approval. "Wow, what a cracker, you won't be sitting in a tub for a while," exclaimed Marshall minor, his friend and fellow rower. But next morning, as usual, Harry was back in the tub, the stubby wooden rowing scull that was used to introduce youngsters to rowing. The rowing coach chose to ignore the black eye and the way Harry kept shifting painfully on his seat after each stroke, but mercifully he ended the session on the river early.

Harry waited until the holidays before he took the opportunity to ask his mother what a Yid was. She looked at him hard for a few moments before replying. "It's an offensive term for a Jew. Why?"

"Am I a Yid?"

"Certainly not, and why are you asking?"

"I heard it at school. It's nothing."

His Mother tried to question him further but Harry sensed this conversation needed to end so he simply refused to continue. His mother persisted. 'Who called you a Yid?"

Harry again refused to answer but his mother persisted until finally Harry turned on her. "No-one did. Forget it. I wish I hadn't asked." He dashed away out to where the dogs were dozing in the kennels and even his father's enquiries could get no more out of him.

But really Harry had no trouble with school. The study was easily within his capacity and he loved rugby – the country's religion – and especially rowing. He was stroke of the school eight. His brother Jack used to tease him. "My God Harry, I swear you sleep with that oar. How do you stand all those 6am starts? The Avon's covered in chunks of ice."

The school followed tradition as far as it could: hearty food, badly cooked, chapel every morning and twice on Sunday. They sang hymns like "All Things Bright and Beautiful" and "Jerusalem" belted out with more enthusiasm than comprehension. The subjects they learned were the same as boys at school in England: English, Maths, French, Latin or German, and History. The history curriculum focused on the Kings and Queens of England and the glory that had become the British Empire, which they, as British Citizens and subjects of the King would be taught to revere. They had prefects to run the place, and fags to look after them. Shakespeare and Wordsworth were staples of the English department. Sports were mandatory as was the Cadet Corp, where they learned to drill and how to clean and fire a rifle, something Harry and Jack already knew from the farm. Corporal punishment was dished out for even the smallest misdemeanours.

School life had prepared Harry well for the next step in his education. His father counted himself fortunate to have attend Cambridge University. His headmaster at Christ's had been a Cambridge man and strongly advised David's father, Wolf, that if it could be arranged, David should also attend Cambridge. Letters were exchanged and David found himself on his way to England, to Cambridge and to the ancient College of Trinity Hall. David had always expected Harry to do likewise. After all, he would be second generation Hall, an adept sportsman who might help the College's rowing aspirations, and his languages were not bad, thanks to a natural facility and the endeavours of his teacher at Christ's College, an unforgiving German.

None of the boys knew how Herr Franz had arrived at the school, but in those days the South Island of New Zealand attracted many itinerant travellers seeking distance between themselves and some misdemeanour on the other side of the globe. In any event, the boys were far too scared of Herr Franz to ask. Herr Franz would stride up and down between the rows of wooden desks, turning suddenly to ask some disconcerting question. He kept a small leather riding crop and, for emphasis, would crack it on his desktop or against his long black leather boots. For all that, he never hit the boys and after a while they began to discern under the Teutonic severity a wintry sense of humour, which manifested itself in droll running commentary on the boys' stupidity. In the end, helped by his facility with German, Harry came to like Herr Franz.

So it was that at the end of his final term at Christ's, and after special coaching from the headmaster, Harry spent three long hours in the headmaster's study toiling over the entrance papers for Trinity Hall. Together with an effusive covering letter from the headmaster to the Senior Tutor at the Hall, they were then despatched to the College.

The senior tutor and vice master sat in two enormous Victorian armchairs in the tutor's sitting room. Sitting back in his armchair, the vice master looked anxiously at the sherry decanter on the sideboard. He hoped the decanter contained something more appealing than the college's own label, which he knew to be rather inferior. The senior tutor, noting the direction of his gaze, poured him a glass, passed it to him and awaited the verdict. The vice master sniffed apprehensively, examined the straw-coloured liquid, and took a small sip. The senior tutor raised his eyebrows quizzically. The vice master hesitated. "Hm, Manzanilla, excellent," he pronounced "it's my belief it's one of the best finos. I visited Sanlucar last year and thoroughly enjoyed the experience."

The tutor, trying to mask his annoyance at not being able to catch the master out, acknowledged that his assessment of the sherry had indeed been correct. Really, the vice master could be a colossal bore sometimes. Quickly he moved on to shuffling papers absent-mindedly until he eventually found what he was looking for. "We have this application from young Harry Douglas from New Zealand; he wants to read Modern Languages. German is his speciality. Rather surprising, don't you think?" The vice master pondered the matter, distracted by noticing that the other man had a large brown stain on the salmon-and-cucumber Garrick Club tie he was so fond of and which he appeared to feel went well with his maroon velvet waistcoat. Probably Windsor soup.

"His application indicated a rather agricultural approach, I thought," he eventually replied. There was a long silence, punctuated only by the hiss of the gas fire. "Father was here and did rather well by all reports. By the way he's obviously a jolly fine rower. We could do with that. We had a rather poor result in Bumps this year." There was another silence. "Strong recommendation from his Headmaster, who's an old Cambridge man. Anything else we know about him?"

"Not really, but being a New Zealander he will probably be frightfully good at Rugger."

The vice master considered this. "I'm not sure I entirely follow that last remark."

"New Zealanders are very good at Rugger. They thrashed England at Crystal Palace on their tour game. They're called 'All Blacks', you know."

There was a silence. A gust of rain rattled the windows, and the two looked out to see a group of undergraduates, black gowns flapping in a gust of wind, scuttling to their tutorial.

"Did they indeed?" The vice master paused: "The game's a-foot: Follow your spirit; and upon this charge cry 'God for Harry, England, and Saint George!'" The senior tutor greeted this sally in silence. "Well, why not give him a chance then? We have some room. A couple of our young chaps rather surprisingly appear to have received scholarships from Oxford. Besides, we always need a quota of colonials and I find the New Zealanders rather less, I don't know, rumbustious, than Australians." Another silence followed.

"'Pugnacious' I think is the word," corrected the senior tutor.

"Yes, indeed. Pugnacious is more correct. What can one expect from the descendants of whores and pickpockets?" The Senior Tutor considered this opinion for a minute.

"I put it down to the Irish. All those hideous boat loads of Catholic convicts; really, as you say, what can one expect? Still, we have had some very bright ones; surprising really." The vice master nodded, reflectively polishing his glasses.

"Well," said the senior tutor, "that's that then. We'll send him a note. I'll inform the master. He'll be pleased about the rowing." He stood and replenished the glasses, then drew the curtains as the light faded over the Fellows' garden, and they moved on to discuss other matters closer to home. Had he been asked, Harry could of course easily have supplied, in the finest detail, the story of England's 'thrashing' by the All Blacks. How 75,000 people had turned out at Crystal Palace to see the unbeaten All Blacks play the home side. How they scrambled up trees and hung off fences to glimpse the game. How they marvelled at the skill of Deans or Carbine Wallace, the leadership of Gallaher, the four tries scored by Dunk. How *The Times* had reported, "They played like eight men with one eye, and that an all-seeing eye." They had returned to New Zealand heroes and every young New Zealander knew their names, their stories and how they had beaten England but then lost to Wales after Deans scored but was dragged back into the field of play before the try was awarded, thus creating a legend that was never allowed to die.

And so it was that some months later Harry received a letter addressed to "Dear Douglas", and pointing out that thanks to some of the College's ordinary undergraduates accepting scholarships from Oxford, there would in fact be a place for him at Trinity Hall. The letter required him to present himself at the beginning of October at The Hall for the commencement of Michaelmas term.

CHAPTER 3

Harry had arrived in England on his first visit in April 1910, after six weeks on a Shaw Savill liner from Wellington, across the Indian Ocean, around the Cape and finally to Southampton. There he had received a warm welcome on the dockside from his father's brother, Nicholas. Uncle Nicholas, ten years younger than his brother David, had been born after Wolf and Elizabeth had moved to England. David and Nicholas had met only twice; once when David and Victoria had travelled to England after their wedding and on a reciprocal trip Nicholas had taken to New Zealand a few years later. The brothers got along well enough but in truth it was obvious to both of them that, with their different upbringings, they had little in common beyond the family relationship, which luckily they each believed was paramount. In keeping with their parents' views about allowing children to become fully integrated members of their community, Nicholas had attended a small prep school in Kent and then, for reasons never entirely clear, gone on to Shrewsbury, a public school south of Liverpool near the Welsh border. Nicholas was not much more aware of Wolf's Jewish heritage than David was and it never seemed to be mentioned in their day-to-day life.

Nicholas was more artistic than anyone else in the family and, as he hadn't attended University, Wolf brought him in to run the family importing business while they collectively worked out what he should do next. Years later Nicholas was still there running the business from an office in Berkeley Square, surreptitiously doing sketches of his staff with the door to his office closed, and watched with a hawk's eye by Wolf who, in spite of his age, usually managed to call in daily.

Uncle Nicholas's day consisted of dealing with the affairs of the business in the morning and then disappearing for lunch at his club. He had become a member of the Reform Club at an early age following in the footsteps of his father, a committed Liberal, even though, much to Wolf's disgust, Nicholas was actually a Tory, which Wolf blamed on that damn public school. The Reform Club, designed by Sir Charles Berry and built in Pall Mall in 1841, was one of the most splendid Victorian buildings in London, and Uncle Nicholas loved its Italianate flourishes and richly flamboyant interior. He had no intention of leaving, whatever the Club's politics. The Tory Carlton Club, to which most of his contemporaries belonged, was directly across the Mall and he could simply cross the road whenever he wanted a more politically agreeable conversation.

Harry and Uncle Nicholas travelled together on the train back to London's Victoria Station. Then it was a taxi to Uncle's house in Sloane Square where they arrived in time for afternoon tea with Aunt Lucille. Harry's aunt, a sparrow-like lady, at first seemed quite taken aback by his size. She was strikingly dressed in a long pleated skirt and a black lace jacket over a dark blouse buttoned up to her neck, with ruffles on the sleeves. Around her neck she wore an unusual triple string necklace on a gold chain with a series of different stones culminating in an oval emerald.

Her hair was carefully brushed up on top of her head and held in place with a pair of long pins. She sat very upright in her armchair and peered up at him as she diligently enquired after his family, whilst afternoon tea was laid out on a side table. Having exhausted the subject of family health and wellbeing, Harry's sea journey to Southhampton, and the dangers of the southern oceans, Harry was just wondering how to strike up some further conversation when she fixed him with a steely gaze and asked, "Now, tell me how it is New Zealand has managed to give women the vote when we cannot? I understand the world has not come to an end in New Zealand because of women's emancipation?". It turned out Aunt Lucille, whilst tiny, was not at all nervous and was heavily involved with Emmeline Pankhurst and the movement for women's rights. She had actually been arrested but let go with a cup of tea and a stern warning, but now things where becoming more antagonistic and women were in gaol and hunger strikes were in place. Aunt Lucille put down her tea cup. "The police are behaving abominably, but if they think they will intimidate us they are very much mistaken. They are trying to force feed the women on hunger strike. Holding their mouths open and inserting a tube. It is utterly barbaric."

Luckily Harry knew all about the women's movement in New Zealand from his mother and, having grown up with women having the vote, couldn't really understand why so many men were violently opposed to it. His Uncle Nick raised his eyebrows and quietly slipped outside to smoke a cigar whilst the conversation continued. Aunt Lucille suggested Harry might like to come along to the protests, a suggestion that Harry, as a brand new arrival in London, was not so keen on but couldn't for now find a way to wriggle out. A dose of flu might need to be employed.

Uncle Nick peered around the door and discerning that the

conversation on emancipation had ceased re-entered the room. "Our first job in the morning," pronounced Uncle Nicholas, "is to get over to see your grandparents. They are terribly excited to meet you, as you can well imagine; the grandson they have never seen. You should get a good night's sleep and prepare yourself for another equally penetrating interrogation. I have to go to the office early, then we'll have a quick lunch at my Club before we have tea with them."

Whilst his uncle was at the office Harry took the opportunity to do a little exploring. The bright red B Type London bus had only just been introduced to London and Harry found his way to the open top deck the better to see the sights. Although he had seen photographs of London and heard people in New Zealand talk about it he was quite taken aback by the sheer scale of this grand city. There were vehicles of all descriptions blocking the streets and people everywhere, walking, rushing to and fro, pouring in and out of buildings, riding in cabs, selling all manner of goods. Before boarding, Harry bought a muffin from a muffin man carrying muffins in a tray on his head. The bus took him from Piccadilly Circus to Trafalgar Square and then down the Mall to Buckingham Palace and Marble Arch. The size of everything astonished him. The buildings seemed huge, a display of grandeur he had never anticipated. He felt a sense of awe to be surrounded everywhere he looked by the physical representation of the world's most powerful Empire; but, bus ride complete, it was now time to meet his grandparents.

Harry's Grandfather Wolf had actually been born Wolf Schaglieg in Cracow in 1840, the son of a prominent Rabbi. It was the time of revolution throughout Europe and his parents concluded that, hard though it would be to part with him, he should be given the chance for a better life, free from persecution. Aged barely fifteen, he departed by sea for a land of opportunity.

The gold rush in California was over and the new frontier was the Victorian goldfields in Australia.

Although Harry had never met his grandfather, who had left New Zealand for England before he was born, he knew his story from his own father and had visited the company that his grandfather had formed at its head office in Dunedin. As far as he could piece the story together, his grandfather had not taken long in the frontier atmosphere of the Victorian goldfields to conclude that he had arrived too late to participate in the diggings, even had he been able, without money, to tolerate the poverty, drunkenness and brutality of the more than 20,000 prospectors who had besieged the little Victorian town of Ballarat. The town was a sea of rumours about gold prospects and when he learned about gold discoveries in the South Island of New Zealand, he decided to see if he could do any better there. When he reached the barely formed shanty town of Arrowtown, near Lake Wakatipu, he again found that he was too late. The Chinese in particular had already arrived and the best prospects were taken. Surveying the scene, he had quickly concluded that meeting the miners' requirements for their daily lives might yield a better result than mining itself. His first venture nearly ruined him after a ship carrying goods he had bought in Australia for sale in the goldfields was wrecked in a Tasman storm. Not dissuaded, he somehow managed to scrape together enough money for another attempt and this time he succeeded. By 1858, basing himself in Dunedin, he had set up the trading company that now spread its tentacles to England and had allowed him to enjoy the best of London life.

Grandfather's business, which had been left in the hands of loyal managers and staff in New Zealand when he decided to move to London, had done remarkably well and, on his arrival there, he had purchased a handsomely proportioned house in Queensgate, South Kensington, with a ballroom, dining room and two sitting rooms. "He likes entertaining. You'll be asked to a ball in due course." his uncle advised him. They arrived at Queensgate to an effusive welcome from his grandparents and their two ancient retainers, Hannah, the cook, and Geisler, a wizened old German who Harry immediately won over with a few words of German. Tea was served with a suitable degree of ceremony. Grandmother carefully poured the tea, the colour of Canterbury peat, through a sterling silver tea strainer, controlling the pour rate so that the tea bubbled through the holes in the tea strainer, aerating like wine, and into the Wedgewood china cups. Tiny cucumber sandwiches were served and Harry marvelled at the exactness of the slicing of the cucumber, like wagon wheels, each slice a replica of the other.

Harry was conscious that grandfather was watching him closely, the slightest trace of a smile visible behind the full beard. Wolf was indeed watching this large young man and wondering what sort of person contemporary New Zealand had produced. He remembered New Zealand with affection. Behind what appeared an almost uncritical worship of their English heritage, New Zealanders, he thought, were developing something unique, an unselfconscious feeling for their fellow citizens, a concern for each other which had produced an egalitarian streak. This was no conscious intellectual tilt at Marxism. There were no serfs and no 'dark satanic mills' in New Zealand. New Zealanders understood the rights of property, the need to be self-supporting and to develop the country. But they were also, like their noisy Australian cousins, beginning to assert their rights to treat and be treated as equals as they conducted their daily affairs. There are no aristocrats in the woolshed. Wolf strongly approved of this streak of nationalistic pride and self-sufficiency, of refusal to bend the knee to any man. He wanted to see how all this would manifest itself in this young man, about to be exposed to the deadly intricacies of English social etiquette in the cloisters of Cambridge University, a perfect microcosm of all that it meant to be English.

Grandfather had met his wife, Elizabeth, in Auckland. She was the daughter of an English sea captain. Her mother had died giving birth to her and, after she had completed her education, her father took her to sea with him to "see the world and meet a suitably well-born officer" as he optimistically put it. But Elizabeth had a strong will. She had met Wolf at a reception at Government House in Auckland and he was completely different from so many of the young men she had previously met. They were almost uniformly Anglo-Saxon and often military and she quickly tired of their company. Wolf was different. Good looking, interested in all sorts of curious subjects of which she knew little and slowly, in spite of herself, she was charmed. Despite expecting a strong negative reaction from her father, she told him about Wolf and her father eventually agreed to meet him. Gradually he began to see that this was perhaps a rather exceptional individual, and that his daughter loved him, so he gave his blessing to their marriage.

The wedding duly took place in Auckland in 1864, but the couple had agreed to make their home in Dunedin. Settled by the Free Church of Scotland in 1848, Dunedin's name is the Gaelic for Edinburgh, on which the city was modelled. Unsurprisingly it reflected the same fine architecture and pious ways but the latter had been undermined by the influx of immigrants drawn by the discovery of gold. Briefly Dunedin had become New Zealand's most prosperous city and it had been a natural place for Wolf to set up in business. When their first child was born Elizabeth had not had much trouble persuading Wolf, who was Jewish more by race than he was by religion, that the child would need to be given the best possible chance of prospering in an Anglo-Saxon, not to say Scottish Presbyterian, world. He should have a suitably English name and attend a Church of England boarding school not too far from home. The baby was christened David. Wolf thought with wry amusement that very few New Zealanders would be aware that David had been the greatest of the Kings of Israel, the slayer of Goliath, a Jewish hero. David means "beloved" in Hebrew and truly this infant was beloved. They both agreed, whatever the family history might suggest, David and any subsequent child should be brought up as New Zealanders first and foremost. They could choose for themselves which religion, if any, they might wish to follow. On the issue of education, Wolf agreed with Elizabeth that children should have the best available.

He had no opposition to her selection of Christ's College, recently formed in Christchurch a few hundred miles north of Dunedin, with a commitment to what was described without irony as the best in British education.

At boarding school from the time he was eleven, it was hardly surprising that David very quickly became a quintessential New Zealander. He spent much of his holidays on friends' farms in South Canterbury or Otago and with his physical strength and quick mind, soon absorbed the principles of farm life. Not only that, he loved the outdoors, the beauty of the surroundings and interaction with the animals. Wolf watched all this with some amusement but never tried to deflect David's attention away from farming towards the business. He would be what he would be and Wolf and Elizabeth would accept the outcome with grace. But it was with an eye to David's possible future that Wolf, to the surprise of his friends in Dunedin, bought Earnslaw Station. Earnslaw had suddenly come on the market, the result of a family's scandal and their need for a quick sale. Wolf knew a bargain when he saw one. He had little knowledge of farming but he was quite content to install a manager. It was soon clear that Wolf's lack of farming knowledge did not preclude him from having an excellent memory about what he was told, plus a disconcerting ability to add up.

Harry and Jack, a generation on, had very little awareness of their European heritage. Their paternal grandparents lived in England and Elizabeth's father was up in Auckland, itself quite a journey and one they undertook only infrequently. When they did see him, he regaled them with tales of the British navy and the glory of the Empire. They never considered they were anything but true New Zealanders and sons of the Empire, steeped in the majesty of the Crown, the dignity of the King and the authority of the Mother of Parliaments. They were used to people referring to England as 'home' and took it for granted that England would be the first place any New Zealander who wanted to feel truly educated would wish to visit.

For Harry, the first few weeks in London were an enjoyable combination of sight-seeing and social engagements, which appeared to be the principal activity of the upper class. Then came the death of King Edward on 6 May 1910. This seminal event overwhelmed all else and, despite the heat of an exceptional summer, the citizens of England turned out in their thousands to mourn the much-loved monarch. Uncle Nicholas arranged for the family to view the funeral procession from his great friend Bertie West-Watson's Club in Piccadilly. Well before the due time, the family stationed themselves, squeezed against other Club members on the balcony overlooking Piccadilly. The procession was to move along Whitehall, the Mall, Piccadilly and the Park to Paddington Station where a train would carry the body to Windsor for burial. Harry first heard it before he saw it. Above the murmur of the crowd came the muffled chimes of Big Ben signalling 9am and the procession's start, soon followed by the strains of "The Dead March" from Handel's

'Saul', played by the band of the Royal Horse Guards. Then the most impressive collection of the royal heads of Europe ever assembled in one place came into sight. Nine kings rode behind the coffin, accompanied by five heirs apparent, 40 more Imperial or Royal Highnesses, seven queens and an assembly of special ambassadors. The coffin appeared, wrapped in the Royal Standard and carried on a gun carriage draped in red, white and purple. Alongside the gun carriage, which was drawn by the Royal Horse Artillery, walked the late king's 63 aides-de-camp, all colonels or naval captains and all peers. England's three Field Marshalls, Lord Kitchener, Lord Roberts and Sir Evelyn Woods, rode together, followed by six Admirals of the fleet, including Edward's great friend Sir John 'Jacky' Fisher. In the centre of the front row rode the new king, George V, flanked on his left by the Duke of Connaught, the late king's only surviving brother. On his right, William II, Emperor of Germany, soon to be known to all Englishmen as Kaiser Bill, resplendent in the scarlet uniform of a British Field Marshall. It was the Kaiser's fierce stare from behind his huge upturned moustache that drew Harry's eye. Somehow, mounted rigidly upright on a grey stallion, the Kaiser managed to convey an impression that he was now the most important person present at this gathering. *The Times* seemed to endorse this primacy by acknowledging that to him "belongs the first place among all the foreign mourners who, even when relations are most strained, has never lost his popularity amongst us."

All of England's famous regiments were represented. The Household Cavalry, Cavalry of the line, the Coldstream Guards, the Gordon Highlanders, the Royal Fusiliers, Hussars and Dragoons of the German, Austrian, Russian and other foreign cavalry units and, provocatively, Admirals of the German Navy. The passing parade was more magnificent than Harry could have imagined. Crimson sashes and jewelled orders contrasted with plumed helmets and gold braid.

The dead king's horse, with empty saddle and boots reversed in the stirrups, was led by two grooms and, trotting behind came his wire-haired terrier, Caesar.

Adding to the pageantry were representatives of the dearly held traditions of England. Pursuivants of Arms, in emblazoned medieval tabards, silver stick in waiting, White Staves, equerries, archers of Scotland, judges in their wigs and black robes and the Lord Chief Justice in scarlet, bishops in ecclesiastical purple. Yeoman of the Guard in black velvet hats and frilled Victorian collars, an escort of trumpeters and the Kings, followed by a glass coach bearing the widowed Queen Alexandra and her sister, the Dowager Empress of Russia, and 12 other coaches of queens, ladies and oriental potentates.

In response to Harry's whispered questions, Uncle Nicholas tried to explain the identity of all these splendid personages. Afterwards in the privacy of the Club, Harry listened with great attention to Uncle Nicholas debating with Bertie and his friends whether the Kaiser had been a mite too militaristic and whether this was a warning of more trouble between Germany and England. The Moroccan crisis of 1905 had not been forgotten and many Englishmen were becoming uncomfortably aware of Germany's naval aspirations. There was a rising level of concern in Britain at the Kaiser's provocative plans to substantially increase the German fleet. More particularly, the Navy was concerned at rumours that Germany was intending to turn Agadir, located uncomfortably close to the British Navy base in Gibraltar, into a home for a German Mediterranean fleet. It was as if the funeral signalled the end of an era of relative peace and prosperity and that the passing of Edward, the peacemaker, would give way to more troubled times.

Uncle Nicholas did his best to introduce Harry to life in London, a lifestyle reflecting the prosperity that allowed the upper class, for the most part, to live in idle enjoyment. Dressed in a morning suit, and clutching a top hat which he tried his best not to actually wear, Harry accompanied his uncle to the enclosure at Ascot. He thanked God that none of his school friends could see him. He wandered rather aimlessly amongst the immaculately attired guests. Every now and then a question would be addressed to him about New Zealand. Were there lots of kangaroos? Were the natives still practising cannibalism? Were New Zealanders concerned about the revolution in Mexico? One gentleman with a trim goatee beard and gleaming white teeth raised the issue of the women's vote and it was his strong opinion that if these odious suffragettes should succeed in England it would herald the downfall of the greatest Empire the world had ever seen.

Later, with his clothes strictly selected by his aunt, he attended the Eton-Harrow cricket match at Lords, and thereafter a number of social engagements at which he tried his best to enjoy himself. In truth Harry felt most uncomfortable both in his mostly ill-fitting clothing and in the unfamiliar social context, in which he sensed he was not getting it quite 'right'. Not only that, he found he could not really sustain a conversation once it went beyond chit chat or the very limited knowledge of affairs of the world he had acquired in New Zealand. He felt gauche and as if he was regarded as a mildly amusing piece of passing exotica.

He was more comfortable attending the Henley regatta and, while eating strawberries and cream, viewing the rowing with a critical eye. Here was something he could talk about but he soon came to realise that most of his companions were more interested in activities off the water than on. Was he perhaps a rowing bore? 'Bore' seemed to be a particularly egregious insult in contemporary England. He was not given to feeling sorry for himself but every now and then he did wish he was back under the Southern Alps.

CHAPTER 4

In early September 1910, Harry caught a train up to Cambridge and then, on a day of dazzling autumn sunshine, a taxi to the Hall. He was shown to his room on 'R' staircase and introduced to his Gyp, whose name was Don Mace and who quickly ran through the rudiments of life on the staircase. He explained that Harry's Bedder, a woman named Ruby, would look after his room and that he should put his shoes outside for cleaning, calmly disregarding Harry's protest that he cleaned his own shoes. He also patiently explained that he should be referred to as Mace, not Mr Mace, and that Harry should just get used to him addressing Harry as 'Sir' notwithstanding the considerable age difference. "I understand you Australians," he said, enigmatically. Harry was quite uncomfortable with the whole concept. He had been a fag at school, doing jobs for school prefects and then having a fag when he himself became a prefect. But that was just school and you did your year and moved on. Having someone spend their life doing jobs for someone else who could do the job quite easily themselves seemed completely perverse. Then of course there was tipping, which most New Zealanders never did, regarding it as an insult implying inferior status. When then should one tip, how much, what if the service was poor, or you didn't have any money? Should he tip the bus driver or the shop assistant? Why not avoid the issue in the first place by just adding the tip to the price?

That evening Harry attended his first supper in the dining room. Not knowing anyone, he looked about and seeing a space, settled on one of the long tables at which the undergraduates were seated. A group of immaculately dressed young men were chattering loudly to his left and at first ignored him so he turned to his neighbour on the other side, who also seemed to be alone. The neighbour introduced himself as Fred Williams and explained that he was from Leeds and was up to study maths. Harry could hardly avoid noticing his threadbare suit, peppered liberally on the collar with dandruff and his extraordinary hair which seemed to sprout in all directions defying whatever minimal attempt had been made to brush it. Conversation was amiable enough but not helped by Fred's thick northern accent. Finally, Harry's companion on the other side, forced to acknowledge him by the necessity of requesting the salt, introduced himself as Roderick Willesden-Monroe. On discovering Douglas was from New Zealand, he guffawed loudly but paused to introduce "our colonial colleague" to the his companions. But he studiously avoided extending the introduction to Fred. Fortunately, Willesden-Monroe was rather curious about New Zealand, going so far as to ask Harry whether or not he rode to hounds and whether they had any trout in the rivers. Harry explained that he didn't ride to hounds but that he was more than happy to mount any horse, given the opportunity. He added for good measure that one of his favourite pastimes was fishing for trout. They chatted for a while about Willesden-

Monroe's family salmon run in Scotland, so the evening passed well enough for Harry but he was conscious of Fred's isolation in an environment for which he seemed supremely ill-prepared.

On enquiry, Fred explained that he came from a poor home on the outskirts of Leeds where his father worked in the textile mills. Fred had never been away from home but it transpired that he was a child prodigy at maths. It was through his school maths master, who knew someone who was a member of the Guild of Clothworkers, that Fred had obtained a scholarship. Dessert, which Fred referred to as 'pudding' was a huge dish of strawberries and cream which Fred had never eaten before. He was much impressed to learn that Harry's family grew strawberries at home and explained that his mother grew some very fine onions, beans and turnips on an allotment they shared near their home. Harry and Fred gradually became friends and Harry even developed a degree of bonhomie with the boisterous crowd of what turned out to be Etonians, arising, he felt sure, from his sporting accomplishments and also their discovery that his family owned 5,000 acres, a respectable plot even for an Etonian. However, he never saw them address a single word to Fred.

It was a few weeks later as he and Fred shared a pint at the Royal George that Fred raised the subject of women's suffrage. "I wanted to ask you about it. Do you think it's a good thing? I know New Zealand introduced women's suffrage in 1893, the first in the world to do it, my mother said. My mother joined the suffrage movement at home and my father gets angry about it. Says women should stick to women's business, and men to men's."

Harry laughed. "He wouldn't want to say that to my mother. Now they have suffrage, they're trying to make the next change to allow women members of parliament but it will be a long time until the men agree. It's funny, I'm used to women having the vote so it seems absurd that they shouldn't. My mother and her friends are a darn sight more capable than half the men I know."

Fred thought about it. "I wish my mother could talk to her. They get a bit downhearted and it would do the women a power of good to talk to other women who actually can vote. You haven't been in England long enough to know how furious many men get on the subject. I don't understand it myself."

"Why don't you ask them to write to my mother's group?" said Harry, "I'm quite sure they would be happy to hear from them and I've got no doubt they would encourage them not to back down under any circumstances." Fred was delighted with that idea and promised to talk to his mother the next time he was home.

Harry had talked with his father about life in Cambridge so he felt he had a good idea of what to expect but one thing had been forgotten: the weather. Cambridge is in the Fens, low lying marsh lands, near sea level and damp. In the mornings, a grey mist would drift across the Cam. Walking to tutorials through the narrow passages that connected the colleges or, crossing the bridges over the Cam, he would pass hunched figures, heads down and covered by whatever warming head gear they could muster.

By November, the days had shortened and Harry was finding the endless freezing drizzle chilling in every sense of the word. His room had a tiny gas fire and he huddled in front of it in his down jacket while trying to do his assignments. Bed was not much warmer with an unpleasant feeling of damp when he first climbed in. He finally gave up and wore his rugby socks to sleep after first toasting them over the miserable splutter of the gas fire.

Christmas was approaching when Harry managed to wangle a ticket to a service of carols in the Kings College Chapel. Although it was an icy evening, he walked the short distance from Trinity Hall and edged his way onto the end of a packed pew some way from the altar. The chapel was dimly lit by candles and he gazed up into the vaulted ceiling towering above him into the darkness. He peered at the altar and the stained glass windows whose history of survival he had read about. As he did so, the choir entered in processional singing one of the carols he remembered from school days and from Christmas in the middle of summer, which seemed so normal to him in Christchurch. He thought of the Tudors whom he knew had conceived and built the Chapel and wondered at the enormity of envisaging such a project. Henry VIII, he presumed, must have seated himself somewhere not too far from where Harry now found himself. He had not really known what to expect of the evening and consequently became more entranced as the service continued; the whole performance a revelation to a young man from one of the remoter parts of rural New Zealand. For the first time it dawned on him what a rare opportunity he had been given and then, for a few minutes as he sat quietly absorbing the music, he reflected fearfully that perhaps he had been over confident in his own abilities and that he would find Cambridge beyond his capacity.

Harry soon found there were many other aspects of Cambridge life he had not considered. He was having a pint in the Buttery one evening when Roderick Willesden-Monroe found him. "I say, Douglas. Wonder if you might help me out next Sunday?"

"What did you have in mind?" replied Harry.

"It's like this, old chap. I'm the Master of the Cambridge Hunt. We have a Hunt coming up next Sunday."

"And you're inviting me to ride?"

Willesden-Monroe looked rather taken aback by this suggestion. "Not exactly, the thing is foxes are rather scarce just at the moment so we have to have something for the hounds to pursue. We dip an old rugger sock in a mixture of anisette and urine and then drag it over the paddocks. The hounds follow the scent, we follow the hounds, and there we are with a jolly good fox hunt. We need some sporting chaps to drag the sock and I thought you might help us out. We have that South African fellow, Christopher Van de Styl and a couple of northerners, Yorkshire or Lancashire, I can never tell the difference. What do you say?"

Harry found himself out beyond Grantham on a sparkling Sunday afternoon with a map in one hand and a rolled up rugby sock tied with string and soaked in a foul smelling concoction in the other. Off he went on the command, across the broad acre field, a stile, a gate, around a copse and along a tow path, a couple more fields, until he eventually found Neville Jones, the lad from Cheshire, lean and fit in neat white running shorts and singlet, leaning nonchalantly on a gate whilst waiting to take over. "Cunning sod, running first," observed Neville. "I'd better get going." Harry handed over his sock, and with the sounds of the Hunt in the distance, headed across the fields on a shortcut towards the finish, a colourful marquee which was surrounded by tables of champagne and food, and smartly dressed young people.

He had just been handed a crystal champagne flute of black velvet, a mixture of chilled Guiness and champagne, by a young lady in a vast flame-coloured hat when he spotted Van de Styl clambering over a gate into the home paddock. He was closely followed by the hounds. "I say," said his companion, "are those hounds going to catch up with your friend?" She pronounced "friend" as if the r was a w.

"It looks like they just might," replied Harry, hoping he might be about to witness the first South African torn to pieces by a pack of foxhounds. In fact, when they did catch up, the hounds looked nonplussed and milled about Van de Styl, leaping up to have their ears scratched or lick him enthusiastically.

The riders soon arrived at the marquee. Harry's companion, who introduced herself as "Percy, short for Persephone, you understand," happily explained the etiquette of the different coloured jackets. Willesden-Monroe wore a scarlet jacket with four brass buttons signifying his status as Master of the Hunt. Harry fortunately avoided embarrassing himself by already knowing scarlet was called 'pink', in hunting circles. The other riders were attired in 'pink', black or green jackets and one or two in tweed, signifying younger riders. Harry watched as a riderless horse trotted up. In the distance a skinny young man in a black coat was being assisted to his feet, his breeches covered in mud. Willesden-Monroe arrived on a fine-looking bay mare, his face matching his jacket colour. He was waving his hunting whip extravagantly in greeting as he rode over to Harry and Percy. He seemed more than pleased with the whole affair, pronouncing it "a jolly fine turnout."

University life suited Harry down to the ground. His sporting ability had soon seen him make new friends and it was not long before he found himself in the College first eight, competing in the May Bumps, and finally in the University eight, a role that gave him an identity at university and later, just as importantly, in the wider university fraternity in the halls of power in London. He was six foot plus of raw Canterbury farmer, so pulling an oar was no great challenge and neither was pulling his weight in the College rugger team. Six years of boarding school had taught him well how to cope with life away from home and of course university life was infinitely sociable after the meagre opportunity for extracurricular experiences at school. Although the college had been formed in 1345, it faced the "Backs" of the River Cam and in that respect its overall feel somehow reminded him of his old school in Christchurch.

Harry loved rowing. He could think of nothing better than an early morning on the river in a low mist, the cold chilling until a few strokes began to warm his blood. He loved the feeling of power a good eight generated as it sprinted from the start, using short strong strokes to build up speed as quickly as possible. He knew that only happened when every part of the boat acted in perfect harmony and that was the challenge. Harry considered rowing the only true team sport. There could be no heroes, no-one could kick the winning goal, score a try in the corner or launch a six into the grandstand to win the game. The crew won as a crew or lost as a crew.

The Cam was much like the Avon in Christchurch, narrow and winding, and he couldn't wait to get out in an eight. In his first year, he was invited to join the Trinity Hall first May Bumps crew. He enjoyed the ridiculous idea that each boat in a division would line up behind the other, a length and a half between them. The idea was to try to catch the boat in front of you and bump it before you were bumped from behind yourself. The event was held over four days and the mission was to achieve a bump each day and advance four places so that next year's crew began its quest for bumps four places higher on the river.

On the first day of the Bumps, they were stationed behind Lady Margaret Boat Club which in one of those mysteries that abound in Cambridge, is actually St John's College. Harry was the stroke. "Listen boys, we don't want to row the whole course. We're not fit enough so I'm going to take us out really fast, 36 or more. It will be kill or be killed. Either we catch Maggies or we're done. Anyone have a problem with that?"

They all agreed, rowing the whole course or worse. Being caught by Pembroke behind them was too painful to contemplate. The cannon fired and they were off. The adrenalin rushed as

Harry could see the boat chasing them but the crew relied on the cox and the coach, who was riding precariously along the towpath, to tell them how they were going against the boat in front. Bit by bit as the crowd on the banks cheered they began to bridge the gap; there was a roar as they passed the drinkers on the lawn at The Plough. As they reached Grantchester corner, the cox was yelling, "we have an overlap" but Maggies changed the angle in the corner and they missed her stern. "Go again lads," called the cox, "a set of ten". This time they were more successful, much more. The bow crashed into the back of the Maggies stern and with a leap, the Maggies' cox, fearful of being hit in the back, ejected himself over the side. The boats slewed to a halt as the Maggies' cox struck out for the bank. Cheers all round; one down, three to go. Back at the boat shed, the boatman looked ruefully at the damaged bow, which would have to be repaired overnight, and the captain of boats gave them a gentle lecture about taking more care. The crew knew the first day was the important one; now they should meet crews who had been bumped the previous day and were coming down from in front. Sure enough, they secured their next three bumps over the next three days, fortunately without doing any more damage to boats or their occupants. With the victory of securing four consecutive bumps came a much prized trophy; the delicately decorated oar with their college crest and their names and weights painted on its blade plus the names of each of the crews they had bumped. It wasn't too long before Harry's ability was noticed and in the following year he found himself with a place in the University VIII, a much more serious proposition. Harry loved the experience but had to admit it was not as much fun as the Bumps. Rowing 4.2 miles up the Thames against Oxford was definitely hard work.

Practically the first person Harry had met was a cheery

Australian called Peter Houston. Pete was nuggetty and tough
and had that 'in your face' approach that Australians employ to
find out how far they can push you and whether you are someone
worth bothering with. In his second year, Pete was all helpful
information and saw Harry as a natural ally against the Poms.
"The Poms are okay," he would say, as if Harry was bound to
think otherwise. "Of course there are the usual bunch of wowsers
but there are plenty who like a beer almost as much as we do.
Just stand your ground with them and you'll be fine." Harry
had actually never had any trouble standing his ground so this
was unnecessary advice but he appreciated the spirit in which it
was offered. And then there was Rupert Winterbotham, a droll
Englishman from London who enjoyed the theatre of calling
Pete a convict in a phoney Australian accent and watching the
reaction. He invited Harry and Pete for tea. "Tea and muffins in
front of the fire, that's the ticket." Pete thought the whole idea a
typical example of effete English habits which would lead to the
demise of the Empire, but he came anyway.

A few months later, when Rupert and Harry had spent some
time together on various jaunts to London, Harry was invited to
Sunday breakfast in Rupert's rooms. Breakfast started at 10.30am
and Rupert served boiled eggs. These he cut with extreme
precision using a Mappin and Webb sterling silver egg cutter that
had been a present from his Godfather. Harry watched transfixed
as Rupert placed his eggs upside down and then proceeded to
delicately remove their tops, or, to be more accurate, bottoms.

"Why on earth are you opening them upside down?"

"Because," replied Rupert, "that way you only lose the
white and what's more it prevents all the yoke dribbling over the
side and the cutter stops one ingesting egg shell which I always
think tends to ruin the taste." Harry tried it himself and could
only ponder aloud why he had never heard about such a device.

It was not many days later when Harry found a small delicately wrapped parcel in his mail box containing an egg cutter, a small present from Rupert.

Pete and Rupert were reading law, so from time to time would repair to London to eat their "dinners" at the Inner Temple, part of their indoctrination into the English legal system. Harry would come too and take in a show or play in the West End and join them for a bout of clubbing afterwards. Rupert invited them to various social functions, normally black tie affairs. Harry and Pete tried to keep up with the minutiae of English social conventions by which the English instantly recognise the social classification of whoever they meet. Rupert helped where he could but could hardly contain his mirth when Harry, at a particularly starchy dinner party, managed to commit the double solecism of helping himself to the claret instead of waiting for the butler and then managing to select the incorrect glass. A small frisson passed around the table but quickly subsided; after all, he was at Cambridge and he was apparently very good at rowing.

Between these distractions Harry worked hard at his German. He didn't want to embarrass himself or family or appear a colonial dullard amongst his peers. He found that as long as he attended the lectures and kept up with his studies he could manage tolerably well. During the long vacations, in which three months of summer weather stretched out before him, he visited friends, stayed with his uncle or took trips to Germany where it was arranged that he would stay with German families. The practical necessity of making himself understood soon had him conversing remarkably well with his hosts and their friends. He enjoyed the German people he met and the beauty of the towns and cities as well as the richness of the countryside but he was also becoming aware of the social ferment around him.

The end of Harry's university life came after the May final

exams in 1913, after which he celebrated by again participating in the Bumps. Although he was still rowing in the University eight, for the May Bumps he was back in the College crew. The whole crew attended a May Ball at Trinity at which they were entertained most memorably by the first performance of the tango any of them had seen. They had read mainly scandalised reports in the press of this "invitation to licentiousness," as *The Times* had described it, so anticipation was keen. As champagne glasses were refilled an 'orquesta tipica' from Argentina entranced the guests and two professional dancers showed the undergraduates how the dance was done. Harry was partnered by a young Girton undergraduate he had been dating in a half-hearted way. They enjoyed themselves immensely crashing about as they tried to emulate the seductive skills of the professionals.

Before he left London to see his family and brother and before deciding what to do next, Harry's uncle approached him about joining the family business. Uncle Nicholas was a gentle character and Harry suspected that the combative aspects of trade held little appeal for him so it was no real surprise to hear him say, "You know Harry, the business really needs some fresh young blood and family is always the best blood to have. Besides which, your grandfather would be very keen and your German would be very helpful in discussions with our European suppliers. We really struggle with language misunderstandings; it can be most frustrating. Do have a good think about it. Visit the Dunedin office while you're home and let me know."

Harry had thought about it and while he liked the idea of returning to England and being able to utilise his language skills, he wasn't sure that life in an office was what he really wanted. Half of him couldn't think of a better life than running Earnslaw Station. But then, what was his education all about and what about brother Jack? He was almost sure that Jack's heart would be set on taking over Earnslaw whenever the time arose.

In any event, before he set out for home he had the opportunity for one more visit to Germany. Through the University it had been arranged that a Professor in Heidelberg would give him lodging and food for six weeks provided Harry undertook to spend an hour a day helping his students with their English. So for a time Harry put aside any further consideration of his options and concentrated on his visit to the continent.

Professor Solomon and his wife Sarah made him more than welcome. They patiently helped him with his German, refusing to let him speak English, even though the Professor was quite proficient in English. Sarah, much younger than the Professor and pregnant with their first child, sometimes preferred to stay at home so Harry accompanied the Professor to various cultural events and by the end of six weeks he felt he had really made progress with the language. Harry also became quite friendly with some of the students he was teaching and they agreed there could not be a better venue for practising English than their favourite beer halls. The talk sometimes turned to the possibility of war and Harry found himself caught between German militarists on one side and ardent pacifists on the other, some of whom it soon became clear were Bolsheviks. Everyone could see that the relationship between Germany and England was deteriorating but there was a feeling that they could do nothing about it. And surely the heads of state could sit down and resolve the 'strategic interests' issues that so concerned them? After all, they were cousins and families might squabble but should be able to live together.

A few days before Harry was due to leave Germany, one of his more outre friends from Cambridge contacted him. Stefan Redl, who was reading history at Clare, needed someone to join him whose German was better than his own. "You just have to see the Exhibition," he insisted. "There has been nothing like it in boring old England. There's no distance between Heidelberg and Berlin. I'll meet you there." Harry was reluctant. The mood in Germany was becoming more confronting with talk of war in every bar and night club. In June the Reichstag had passed a military bill at the third reading which approved the increase of peacetime troops by 117,267 men to 661,478. It seemed to Harry that the Kaiser was itching to use them.

But Harry confessed to himself he knew little about art and this seemed an opportunity to see Berlin and learn something about these bizarre artistic developments which had been gradually intruding on his consciousness. Besides when would he next see Germany? The exhibition was described as the 'First German Autumn Salon' in Berlin. It was held in a spectacularly transformed villa in the Tiergartenstrasse, and anyone who wished to be thought of as avant-garde was there. It turned out to be a sensation. In an aesthetic alliance for the future of 'new art', the art world from all over Europe and England descended on Berlin. Works by dozens of ambitious young artists including Delauny, Leger, Marc, Munter, Klee, Chagall, Kandinsky and young painters like Lyonel Feininger and Max Ernst turned out to be sensations. Paul Klee arrived from Paris and there were lectures on cubism and the Italian Futurists.

Harry tried his best to comprehend what he was seeing. He stood for long minutes in front of paintings he found incomprehensible, not helped by his friend Stefan's rambling explanations. Many were sexually explicit in a way that no-one he had heard of had ever dared to try before. Their meaning was abundantly clear. It was no wonder there was a running battle between German civic authorities and bohemians over what could or could not be displayed in public.

One painting particularly disturbed him. Franz Marc's

painting 'Wolves (Balkan War)'. It depicted a pack of wolves in sombre blacks and browns, in geometric form, but with the centre piece one blood red wolf. The wolves had sightless eyes. The painting reeked of violence. It seemed to Harry an ominous reflection of what had already occurred in the Balkans and, more troubling, what might be about to occur.

The public reaction varied between outraged and furious. The newspapers published insulting critiques, patronising the artists. Generally, the citizens of Berlin tried to ignore this subversive explosion disturbing their lives. As a result, the exhibition was a financial failure, but Harry spent many hours wondering about what he had seen and whether he was missing out on a whole world that he would never penetrate. It would definitely not do in New Zealand, he concluded, but then again maybe New Zealand needed some outrageous behaviour. Perhaps it was "the most bourgeois place on earth", as one of his friends who had visited averred. This tumult of ideas was actually disturbing him. He felt aroused to defend the things he had learned at school and university, and some of the questions being raised were not easy to dismiss. Then again, the feeling of being challenged, threatened even, by this contemptuous view of the world, was incredibly invigorating. Was it indeed possible there might be another way, another path to follow?

As they were about to leave, a young friend of Stefan's rushed up brandishing a book. "You must read this, it's sensational," he insisted, thrusting the book into Stefan's hands. Stefan examined it cautiously. It was called *The Tunnel* by Bernhard Kellerman and was the biggest best seller of the year, far outselling Thomas Mann's *Death in Venice*. It was the story of a tunnel constructed under the Atlantic between New York and Europe, an extraordinary proposition in 1913. Stefan passed it to Harry, saying, "My German's not up to this challenge. You read it and then tell me about it".'

Besides the avant-garde cultural turmoil in Europe, there was something else in the air in Austria and Germany in this seminal year of the twentieth century. Harry had a feeling of foreboding he couldn't shake off. He would never know of course, but in the Schonbrun in Vienna two strangers are strolling in the afternoon sunshine. One is Adolf Hitler and the other is Josef Djugashvili (Stalin). Do they respond to despised convention and doff their hats to each other? Then Josef Broz, Tito, also visits Vienna. Later Stalin meets Trotsky in Vienna too and the man whom Stalin will later order to assassinate Trotsky is born in Barcelona. Freud and Jung begin a furious dispute. Kaiser Wilhelm celebrates the 25th anniversary of his reign. He insists on being referred to as 'The Emperor of Peace'. Kaiser Franz Joseph writes a letter to a friend complaining of bunions. In Germany, jus sanguinis, right of blood, becomes the basis for citizenship. Everywhere the bohemians gleefully subvert the insufferably stuffy bourgeoisie.

If blessed are the peacemakers, in Europe in 1913 not many would be blessed.

Harry soon returned to England and a week later embarked for his return to New Zealand, his family, Earnslaw, and the mountains he had missed so much. On the ship he had plenty of time to read *The Tunnel*. Although sometimes he struggled with the German, it turned out to be a gripping tale. Dozens of ant-like workers are busy tunnelling from each end to meet somewhere in mid Atlantic. It was a crazy tale. The tunnel apocalyptically collapses, creating mayhem below the Atlantic and above. It is restarted, and finished 24 years later when the first train runs below the ocean taking a full day to complete the journey. But nobody wants to travel on it. Aeroplanes have arrived and besides who would risk another collapse? It is a tale of triumphant technology, progress, capitalism, dreams and all finally comes to nothing.

Arriving at long last in New Zealand, Harry had simply assumed he would be faced with a barrage of eager questions from curious friends and acquaintances. He found instead most of his friends treated him as if he hadn't been away; it was as if they assumed, since nothing in their world had changed, nothing in his had either. They showed little curiosity over what he might have done, what he had seen and where he might have been. He had so much to tell and no-one except his own family to tell it to. He was gone, now he was back.

He ran into the boss of the local shearing gang, one Robbie Tawhai, at the local pub. He bought him a beer and Robbie clapped Harry on the shoulder. "Good to see you back, boy. You've been away a while. Bet you're pleased to be home then. There's nowhere like home, as Mum likes to put it." Whilst he was clapping Harry on the back, Robbie's dog, One Too Many, a black and white mongrel of dubious parentage, had sneaked under the bar and they both looked down in time to see him lifting his leg on Robbie's bar stool. Robbie was outraged. Encouraged by general cheers from the other patrons he kicked One Too Many out the door, following him out with a string of curses and threats to castrate him. Harry knew he was back.

On his return Harry had given a short interview to the local paper, recalling his experience in Europe and in particular the spectacle that attended the funeral of Edward VII. He had thought nothing about it but soon afterwards he had called back into the pub. It chanced Greg Briody, a local odd job man, was propping up the end of the bar, squatting on a bar stool in his grimy overalls and work boots. He looked as if he hadn't shaved for weeks. Greg was no friend of Harry's family. Harry's father had once caught him lifting loads of gravel off Earnslaw when he was supposed to be helping with the harvest. He had thrown him off the property and told him not to come back.

Greg gave Harry a dirty look. "Saw your interview in the paper Harry. Our privilege to have you back eh. Back home to rule." Harry tried to ignore him but Greg stood up blocking his way. "Sounds like you enjoyed hob knobbing with the gentry. Your sorts were they?" Things were about to get a lot worse when the friend Harry had arranged to meet came over to see what the fuss was about. He grabbed Harry's arm. "Come on Harry, your beer'll go flat." He dragged Harry towards the other end of the bar. Greg downed his beer, put his hat on and slouched out. At the door he turned to Harry. "Piss off back to England. We don't need your high and mighty ways back here." Harry's friend was Rolf Randell, a riding companion who had covered many a mile on horseback with Harry. Rolf laughed, "You probably shouldn't have worn the club tie and blazer. Greg would've thought that was a personal attempt to upset him."

This brief interlude left Harry with a bad taste in his mouth. He wondered if the locals really thought he had become some sort of toff, but he quickly shrugged it off. Nothing was going to prevent him having a happy reunion with the family and from taking pleasure in a return to country life as he had left it. He thoroughly enjoyed helping on the farm, trout fishing in the river and lakes and playing the odd game of bush rugby with the local club team but he quickly realised that as much as he had not wanted to change, he had. Life had become less straight forward. Now many things were multi-faceted, complex, not given to clear, quick decisions, simple judgements or the unwavering views he used to hold on what was right and what was not. The world would never again look to him the way it had as he boarded the ship to leave for Cambridge.

After a few weeks he headed into the mountains further south with Jack and some of the rugby team, who introduced him to skiing on the new field at Lake Ohau. Here they spent most of the day tramping up to high points only to slither down on their immense wooden skis in a strange combination of cross-country and downhill styles.

On these snowy slopes Harry remembered the winters of his boyhood when, as the cold deepened, the sheep would bunch together, protected by the fence of macracapas and fed with the hay the family had harvested over summer. The dogs sulked in their kennels and warily watched the rising waters of the stream that rushed through the home paddock on its way to the Waitaki River. The family would gather in their warm, comfortable homestead. Built of heart rimu, the house had a corrugated iron roof and two huge brick fireplaces where fires burned all day fed by a plentiful supply of dried-out timber. They looked forward to the spring with the up-swelling grass, the new lambs and the planting of the wheat crop. Spring also meant one of Harry's favourite rituals, the annual pilgrimage to Mackenzie's Hut. Every year as the snow melted his father would load up some packs and they would saddle up three horses and head for high country.

Harry always remembered his first trip to the mountains, when he turned twelve. Father, Harry and Jack set out across the big flat home paddocks to the far end of the farm, Dad on the big gelding and the boys on a couple of ponies. From there the horses picked their way across the river flats, avoiding the spikes of the matagouri bushes, which their dad called 'wild Irishman', into the neighbour's farm and over the rolling foothills of the Alps towards the high country. They could see the craggy top of Mt Cook away on the horizon, over 12,000 ft, the snow gleaming on its sides and its peak draped with a wisp of soft white cloud like a shawl. Father gazed up at the distant mountain ranges. "Blowing hard up high," he remarked "not a good day to be up on the glaciers." The country became sparse with less grass and more tussock and scattered boulders and patches of stunted manuka, the tiny flowers attracting small birds and native bees.

Harry sat contentedly in his saddle as his pony picked his route along the rutted track formed by hundreds of sheep making their way across the slopes. He had called his pony Cracker after his hero, the legendary Canterbury prop who, in the rugby provincial final last year, had flattened his Auckland opponent with one short left jab. Harry loved Cracker; his special smell of warm horse, oats, and the sheep fat that had been rubbed into the saddle to soften and protect it. He could feel the cold wind flicking his face then pausing to allow the sun to warm his back, followed by another chill gust, signalling its arrival by bending the tops of the manuka that grew nearby. He glanced at the mountains. Shadows of the high clouds chased themselves across the mountain face, darkening the patches of green, the grey scree and the remaining snow that clung in the gullies. Somehow he always felt content up here, with only his silent father, brother and the horses. He had begun to feel that people bothered him. They either ignored you or always seemed to want something. Teachers wanted something, schoolmates wanted something, people in the town wanted something even if it was only to pass the time of day. Harry didn't really want to pass the time of day. He felt the mountains, when they were ready, would teach him all he would ever need to know.

There were patches of green beech trees growing sturdily in the gullies and the ground became strewn with boulders, which the horses picked their way gingerly through. The first night was spent in the sleeping quarters of the neighbour's shearing shed. It was built near a stream and the water had spread across the surrounding low ground creating a boggy marsh marked with brown peat-stained pools and clumps of tussock grass and flax bushes. Above the door of the shearing shed were two huge bones, white in the afternoon sunlight. Harry asked his father about them. "Come over here boys," replied their father, and he led them over to the edge of the water to fill the billy. "We came up to help put up the shearing shed years ago," he told them. "We all lent a hand and agreed we could share the shed between all the local farmers. During the excavation, almost where we're standing, we came across these bones. They were huge, bigger than any cattle on the property. You know what they were? They were moa bones and that's what the two above the door are. People reckon that, way back, there were quite a few around here but the Maoris liked to eat them and eventually they killed them all off. They used the feathers for clothing and eggshells to carry water. So the moas died out. Over 15 feet tall the big ones were. Must have been a sight to see, roaming across the countryside. Mum showed you the drawings didn't she?"

"What happened to the rest of the bones Dad?" asked Jack.

"They're in the Museum in Christchurch. You can go and see them from school one day. They're well worth seeing. It's sad they've gone. I believe they were the biggest bird of all, like a giant ostrich."

The next day's ride took them ever higher and the path eventually found its way through a saddle in the low mountains and skirted a giant boulder, its shaded side covered with grey and green lichen flecked with flame-coloured patches. Spread below them they saw the still, black waters of a lake that ruffled as small wind gusts spread like the fingers of a hand disturbing the calm water. At the far end stood Mackenzie's hut. Built of wooden planks with a corrugated iron roof, it had a cast iron stove, wooden bunks and a table and chairs fashioned out of old logs split to provide a flat surface on one side. A mountain stream, swollen with early snow melt, tumbled excitedly over some boulders and into the lake. The horses picked their way down between clumps of waist-high snow grass. A pair of rock wrens chased each other through the fronds, stopping to snap at unseen insects and high above a falcon hovered, its wings motionless as it rode a current of air up the face of a mountain. The boys dismounted gingerly, their bottoms sore from the long days on horseback. Their father laughed at them. "All that soft living at boarding school, boys. Those nice dormitory beds." They lit a fire in the rock fireplace outside and boiled the billy for some strong black tea. Much to the amusement of Harry and their father, Jack liked to whirl the billy round his head as fast as he could to separate the tea leaves.

As soon as the tea was done, Dad unpacked the rods they had tucked away alongside the saddles and the boys tried their hands at tying flies. This was an art they watched keenly. Their father used feathers he had collected and kept in his fishing bag, mainly those of the tiny birds of the area but also some pukeko feathers, blue and shiny. Impatient to get at the trout, the boys could hear the 'plop' of fish rising to catch the small flies that hovered above the water in the shallows where the river met the lake. The thrill of his first trout was something Harry would never forget and each year he looked forward to seeing what the lake would reveal and hoping they would at least see the big ones that his father swore he and his mate Bill Watson had seen in the early days. "Ten pounds, and I'm probably underestimating. There are some beauties in here boys. But cunning crafty old fish. It'll take a cunning crafty old fisherman to catch them." The boys thought in their hearts that they would certainly be cunning and crafty enough to catch one but that day they had to be satisfied with a couple of nice three-pound rainbows. As the sun went down and the cold enveloped them, they would build up the fire and cook the trout on the hotplate with potatoes, the bread and butter brought in their packs. Then they had more tea, and a tot of whisky for their father. He splashed a little whisky in their tea, to "keep the cold at bay". Jack was already asleep when Harry dashed outside with his jacket around him and took a quick pee in the stream, as the Milky Way glistened amazingly bright above his head, the Southern Cross off in the distance. It was too cold to stand and look for long but Harry stayed there for as long as he could, craning his neck until he had to look down to ease the muscles. The great sweeping mass of sky was so crammed with stars that in parts it looked like there were more stars than sky to hold them. Harry gazed mesmerised as a shooting star, in a single flash, disappeared towards the horizon, fading to nothing. When the cold finally defeated him he retreated to the stove inside and warmed his frozen feet on the iron fireguard. "It's a great sight son," his father remarked. "Maybe it's the greatest sight of all. You'll have to tell me when you see one greater." Harry climbed into the wooden upper bunk. With the sheepskin under him and the smell of lanolin in his nostrils, he lay on his back, still, listening to the sound of the river tumbling over the rocks and beyond that the great silence of the mountains disturbed by nothing but the whisper of the wind.

In the morning he awoke with a start to the sound of something rolling down the iron roof. He dashed outside. The keas, strange parrots living only in New Zealand, had arrived looking for an early meal. They had decided it was time for some action and, perched on the roof gable they were rolling stones down the iron roof. Jack emerged and the two boys stood and laughed at their antics but the keas jumped down, totally unconcerned by the human invasion. They marched about, their bright olive green feathers gleaming in the early morning sun, pecking curiously at anything strange. No wonder their father had made them store all their gear and the saddles inside the hut. A kea could rip a saddle into strips with no trouble, and they seemed to have special liking for leather. The boys fed them the breakfast scraps and watched as two of them conducted a ferocious tug of war over a piece of bacon rind. They would spend two blissful days up at the lake before tidying the camp, replacing the firewood they had used and heading back down the mountain trail towards home. Harry sometimes wondered why anyone would want to leave Mackenzie Country, when there were days like this to be had and the homestead to return to when a bit of comfort was needed.

One weekend, as requested by his uncle, Harry travelled down to Dunedin to visit the family firm. He liked Dunedin. Based on Edinburgh it contained an inner ring of fine sturdy Victorian or Edwardian buildings and was laid out in an elegant pattern much like other English or Scottish cities of a similar era. Scots emigrating to the other side of the world had made sure they would feel at home including the challenging weather.

The general manager took him around the firm's stately Victorian building in the business centre of Dunedin and he was fascinated to see the array of Manchester, all sorts of clothing and footwear, textiles, kitchen appliances, watches, and array of items displayed on the shelves. A network of travelling salesmen roamed across the South and North Islands carrying samples of the goods and making sales to many of the small stores and trading establishments that had sprung up in the cities and towns. Almost all the goods came from the factories in the north of England but there were also goods from France, Italy and Germany. In the office two ancient gentlemen in wing collars carefully filled in the ledgers in immaculate script, rhythmically dipping their pens in large inkwells and meticulously blotting each line of text and numbers. He was respectfully introduced as Mr Douglas, the grandson of Mr Wolf, whom he quickly discerned was still correctly regarded – notwithstanding being on the other side of the planet – as the proprietor and the ultimate source of instructions on the conduct of the affairs of the business.

In the evening it had been arranged by his mother that he would dine with Dr Emily Seideberg and her husband and parents. Emily, although much older than his mother, had become a great friend. She was the first woman graduate of the Otago Medical School and New Zealand's first woman doctor, currently the Medical Superintendent of St Helen's Hospital. She was also a founding member and President of the NZ Society for the Protection of Women and Children of which his mother was an enthusiastic participant. His mother had had two reasons for wanting to introduce Harry to Emily, the first being simply the friendship between the two, the second being to allow Emily's father Hans, a German architect, to have some conversation in his native language and to hear some reasonably up-to-date news from his home country.

Harry enjoyed his evening and was left in no doubt that Dunedin was a powerful centre for the promotion of the rights of women, a matter that it would be extremely unwise to ignore.

Back on Earnslaw, much discussion at the dinner table took place around the plans of the two boys. It soon became apparent that, as Harry had surmised, Jack wanted to be a farmer and David could do with his help on the property. This much was settled. Harry, on the other hand, had received another letter from his Uncle Nick inviting him to come back and help manage the firm. He also missed Europe, despite the belligerence that seemed to be steadily increasing between the Germans and Austro-Hungarians on the one hand and the French, Russians and English on the other. From New Zealand, this only looked like the usual sabre rattling of European States and not much to be concerned about but Harry thought back to his recent visit to Austria and Germany and was not so sanguine.

More specifically, Harry was determined not to let his German language skills regress in any way and that would require his return to Europe. So a ticket was booked for him on the Shaw Savill liner *Corinthic* for a return to England early the next year – 1914.

CHAPTER 5

The trip from New Zealand to the tip of South America had been remarkably uneventful. It followed a route just north of the Antarctic circle close to latitude 60 degrees south, but for once seas were calm and the sun was shining. Now the ship had arrived in Punta Arenas as the weather was turning. The wind was up and the swell beginning to roll in, its long even waves building up from far out in the South Atlantic.

The ship pulled gingerly into the quay at Punta Arenas. With its single propeller, it was difficult to manoeuvre but the captain, using the wind skilfully together with the assistance of an accompanying tug, finally brought it securely to rest alongside the little harbour pier. Harry and the few other first-class passengers leaned over the rail. The small town of Punta Arenas clung to the water's edge as if aware that any minute it could be blown backwards into the steeply climbing mountains behind. All sorts of craft cluttered the shore line – small row boats, some with masts and tightly furled sails, heavily timbered fishing boats festooned with nets and a few freighters and schooners carrying cargo. The harbour was dominated by a darkly camouflaged grey cruiser with three tall funnels, provocatively flying a large German ensign and straining at her anchor out in the roads. The purser came up beside Harry and seeing him staring at the German ship, remarked: "The *Dresden*, if I'm not mistaken. Fresh from the battle of the Falklands so I hear. Every ship in the British navy after her. She'll be getting out of here soon if she wants to survive. She's infringing the neutrality laws. Hope she's not going our way."

"It's amazing," said Harry. "How can she sit there so blatantly?"

"The Chilean Government is trying to keep faith with both sides. But she can't stay much longer." Harry stretched his back. "Well, I'm off ashore as soon as possible. Where's the best bar in Punta Arenas, if there is one?"

"There are always bars in ports, sir, that's one thing for certain. The only place in town for you though is the bar at the Hotel Jose Noguera. I'll draw you a map and you'll be there in 15 minutes, but have a meal here first if I could suggest, our food's much better. Might as well take advantage of it now we're not moving all over the place. And by the way, take care. There's every nationality you can think of here and some of them have very unusual lifestyles."

"What are you getting at?"

"We're in a very strategic place here, sir. A lot of shipping goes through here, so there's quite a large itinerant population, especially Germans, and not a few spies amongst them watching who goes where and when. On top of that it used to be a brutal penal colony. So, as I say, take care."

After a meal that validated the purser's recommendation, Harry set out as rugged up as he could be, sheepskin tight around him and hood up. The infrequent street lights threw little illumination. The wind continued to howl through the streets and the few citizens of Punta Arenas who were out either staggered head down into it or leaned backwards like mime artists trying to slow down their steps as the wind buffeted them forwards. Punta Arenas, after Argentina's Ushuia, the southernmost city in the world, is sometimes referred to as the world's windiest town and visitors struggle to cope. Notwithstanding, Harry soon located the nineteenth-century façade of The Hotel Jose Noguera and pushed gratefully through the double doors into the calm and warmth of an elegant reception area, beautifully timbered in rich panelling that reminded him of the heart rimu of the family homestead. He saw a sign for the bar pointing down a corridor and followed it to a large room crowded with people sitting in comfortable chairs. A convivial hum filled the room. The windows were covered with rich burgundy drapes tied with gilt tassels. The walls were covered with sepia photographs of local scenes and of some of the ships that had plied the straits. Gas lamps sent a golden glow over the guests. At the far end of the room, a long bar with high bar stools dominated the scene. An enormous wood fire burned beneath a marble mantelpiece, on which drinkers were balancing their glasses. Harry spied an empty bar stool at one end of the bar and pushed his way through.

The barman asked him twice in stilted English to repeat his order for a rum and black currant. This was a winter favourite at home and a sure way to warm chilled limbs. His neighbour, a dapper little man in a black fisherman's jumper, sitting alone, heard him order. "A navy man's drink I think," he remarked.

"A farmer's drink," Harry replied. Harry settled on his bar stool. The stranger was holding a glass jar of beer.

"Here's cheers," he said in the precise accent of someone who could not possibly be English. "On a night like this I think you've made the right choice."

"Well, a beer looks good too, so I might sample the local brew when I've warmed the blood."

"That's funny, I was thinking of trying the rum and black myself. By the way, my name's Felix. Felix Zylko. I'm from Cracow in Poland. Here to try to buy wool now that this damn war has interfered with our wool supply from Australia and New Zealand." Harry gripped his hand.

"Amazing, my grandfather was born in Cracow and emigrated to New Zealand. He lives in London now. I'm going to see him in a few weeks. At least I hope I am if we can dodge our way to England. Harry Douglas, by the way."

"Douglas, did you say? That's not a very Polish name I think"

"No, you're right. My grandfather changed his name. He thought Schagleig wouldn't be helpful in New Zealand and since everyone in the area he lived in was Scottish, he selected a Scottish name to help him assimilate." The drinks arrived. The two men clinked glasses. "Cheers" said Harry to his companion's "prosit". Harry took a large swig and felt the rum immediately start to relax his frozen limbs.

"So," said Zylko," You're from New Zealand. You could perhaps have helped me with wool, maybe you still can."

"I certainly could normally," said Harry, "We have had a very good clip this year. Best Romney, but none of the farmers know what will happen now the war's started. They may have to go and fight."

"Well, I hope not. How about that beer? And I might try the rum and black. How was it?"

"Excellent. Thank you. I'm happy to accept!" The two chatted on amiably against the babble of voices in the background, in which a profusion of languages could be heard. They skirted gingerly around the subject of the war that now affected all their lives. It seemed too serious for bar talk, too close to the surface of everyone's thoughts, too likely to stir up ill will at a time when it was better to enjoy the moment in this strange place before venturing into the wild weather and the reality that they were all living with. As the evening progressed, Harry began to notice that at the table immediately next to them voices were being raised in a garbled mixture of English and German. The tone was increasingly belligerent. He looked around and saw four men at a table littered with glasses and an array of bottles. He had turned back to the bar and to his companion when he felt a violent push in his back. Lurching forward, he spilled most of the contents of his drink. Turning to remonstrate, he saw one of the men at the table, a slight red-faced Englishman, defending himself ineffectually against a flurry of blows from one of the other drinkers, a short pugnacious-looking man almost as broad across the shoulders as he was high. He had great shaggy eyebrows and was intent on dealing his companion a thumping. Harry, in a reflex action, reached out his right hand and gripped the assailant by the throat. Jumping to his feet, he extended his arm and lifted the German off the ground where he was prevented from inflicting any further damage until the barman and waiter arrived to untangle the affray. The Englishman muttered a few words of thanks and scurried from the bar, followed soon after by the three Germans, as they proved to be, who stumbled out to their own embarrassment and the amusement of the onlookers. The remainder of the bar returned to their drinks and soon the hubbub had subsided.

The barman returned behind the bar, and as Harry apologised to his companion for the spilled drink that had splashed across him, the barman thanked him for his intervention and offered each of them a replacement. Orders were taken, drinks replaced and Felix lifted his glass in a mock toast. "If you will permit me to say so, that was an impressive intervention. He was quite large to be held off the ground by his throat. It was definitely not the action of someone who lives behind a desk".

"You're right about that. I've spent the last few months helping my father. Heaving hay bales or animals around is good training for that sort of caper. I probably shouldn't have intervened."

"I'm afraid we will see more of this sort of thing wherever Englishmen and Germans run across each other. Such a pity, the two nations are so similar in many ways. Disciplined, proud, honourable, but neither takes kindly to what they perceive to be insults. Have the people of New Zealand decided whether to support England in this affair or enjoy the protection of their home so far from it all?"

"Oh, we're in all right," replied Harry. "The day after England declared war, our prime minister committed to a small expeditionary force, on its way to Europe as we speak. I believe we've also had a spectacular success against Germany by capturing Samoa from them."

"Samoa? Really, I never heard of such a place."

"It's in the Pacific. I think we sent a thousand men and I understand no-one was injured. The Germans surrendered without a fight."

"It's good to hear of a successful battle in which no-one was hurt. By the way, I wanted to ask you. Could that be a duelling scar beside you right eye?" Harry laughed. "Good God no. Why would you think that?"

"I'm sorry it's just that it looks like a sword scar."

"It was caused by a bull actually."

"A bull? Sir Galahad and the bull then? You New Zealanders are bull fighters?"

"No, not at all. My dog, Sultan, chased a bull. It turned on him and then me. We only just made it to the fence. He went under and I tried to go over. Caught the stray end of a wire. It's never quite healed I'm afraid. My mother likes it. She thinks it gives me a mysteriously romantic look. I think that's what she said."

"She's right. But you know it's very hard for me to understand why New Zealanders should be so keen to die in this war. Do they think it will be 'romantic' to use your mother's words? What's your opinion?"

Harry hesitated, "We New Zealanders love our country, venerate the British Empire and honour our king. So if we're asked for a significant national contribution yes, I'm sure we will answer the call. What about the Poles?"

"We Poles have a different view. We suffer from an accident of geography; a flat country, with Russians on one side, and Germans on the other. We must tread very carefully or, as so often in the past, we will just be run over. But then war is a great misfortune in spite of what the German Moltke thinks."

"What does he think?" Harry asked.

"Eternal peace is a dream and not even a pleasant one. War is an integral part of the way God has ordered the world."

"In the circumstances," Harry replied, "that's particularly chilling. Would you agree with him?"

"No, the opposite. The Germans and the English have so much in common, intelligence, honour, love of country, and even a common royal family. The Kaiser and King George are first cousins. One fears that this war will be bloody and uncompromising and yet it could be solved by some level heads. In the meantime, the British honour their king and the Germans their Kaiser so I suspect the conflict will be long and bloody."

"What insults are worth killing each other for?" replied Harry. "Surely they will be able to stop this before it gets even worse. For us, we have no knowledge of Serbia and the arguments they have with Austria or who is right or wrong but, if the King asks us, we will respond."

Felix looked into his glass reflectively. "Perhaps we can simply drink to adventure. There will certainly be plenty of opportunity for that." They lifted their glasses and lapsed into a companionable silence broken when Felix announced, "I've had my limit. Time for me to find my way to bed."

"I think I'll leave too," replied Harry, "It's been a long and dramatic day actually, so I'm ready for my cabin." The two headed out onto the pavement having rugged up against the weather, which had not shown any sign of improvement.

"I must say it has been a memorable evening," said Felix, "I shall not forget you, Harry Douglas and I shall hope one day to find you again and share a rum and black."

"Thank you for your company," replied Harry "and I also hope we meet again, provided we are not found frozen to the footpath tomorrow morning."

He headed across the street towards the wharf. Turning to wave, he saw his companion standing motionless, hands thrust deep into his greatcoat and cap on his head, watching him with a keen expression, as if to fix Harry's features forever in his mind.

CHAPTER 6

Captain Ludecke stood at the far end of the bridge of the *Dresden* as the anchor clattered back into its hawse pipe. He was profoundly grateful to have completed his desperately needed coaling and to be on his way. The ship turned hard to starboard and quickly gathered speed as it headed down the Magellan Straits from Punta Arenas. Satisfied that all was well, the captain handed over to the first officer before turning to another officer standing quietly beside him. "So, we are away and thankfully it will be dark in half an hour. But we have the British cruisers hot on our tail, so what do you have for me?"

He addressed his remarks to Lieutenant Canaris, the intelligence officer on the *Dresden*. Canaris hesitated: "I think we have a small window of opportunity. As you know, the Chilean Government was pressured by the British to force us to leave, but fortunately the small inducements we paid local officials ensured we never received such an instruction. But the British now know we have coaled and therefore will expect us to head for the open sea. We know our presence in Punta Arenas has been reported to the British cruisers and we also know there are at least three ships in pursuit.. Even if we are in Chilean waters they will fire. They will be in no mood for compromise after the trouble we have caused them."

The captain paused, "Either exit from the Straits of Magellan will be blocked by the time we can reach them and we can't stay here. If both exits are blocked, I hope you have a good suggestion."

"Luckily I managed to locate a German fisherman in Punta Arenas," Canaris explained. "He has been extremely helpful. His name is Albert Pagels and, if you will observe off our port bow, that's his motor launch *Elfrida*."

When not arranging the disappearance of the Chilean Government telegram, Canaris spent his time quietly amongst 'Los Alemanes Magallanicos', the Germans of the Magellan Strait, learning all he could and seeking whatever help might be available to save the damaged *Dresden*. As it happened, he had been fortunate to quickly locate Albert Pagels, an ageless German seafarer who had found his way to Punta Arenas after the Boxer Rebellion and who was happy to put his small motor launch at *Dresden*'s disposal.

Canaris continued, "According to Pagels only a short distance from here is Hewett Bay. I have it here on the chart. The entrance is a narrow dog-leg and the bay is so remote that no-one lives there and fisherman do not often visit. With Pagels' guidance, we can slip in there and I believe we can hide while the British look elsewhere, a process which I will be able to assist by arranging some fortuitous sightings off the Argentinian coast and for certain wireless messages to be intercepted by the British which will suggest we are in the Atlantic. Pagels will know where we are and help supply us and be able, I hope, to tell us where the

British are looking. Fortunately, their security is quite poor. Once we are sure their cruisers are elsewhere we can slip out through whichever end of the Straits is unguarded."

The two men studied the chart carefully before the captain looked up. "It's a very narrow entrance but so much the better. We can follow *Elfrida* in and anchor up under the cliff face. If the chart is correct, we should then be invisible from the sea. We are in trouble if they find us but we have little alternative."

Later that night the *Dresden* edged slowly into the bay and, as *Elfrida* slipped back into the Straits, anchored as planned. *Dresden* was to stay there quietly for almost two weeks before, to the alarm of the captain and crew, a small boat emerged from the morning mist and headed straight for them. Rifles were trained on the sole occupant as he hunched over the tiller but the crew relaxed when a German ensign was spotted through binoculars. It was Pagels, who was soon welcomed on board. "You have to go. I had a visit last night. The British are on to you. Someone has betrayed you. You have only a few hours."

The captain wasted no time getting up steam whilst Canaris and Pagels discussed what to do next. "There is another bay not so far away. Look, I'll show you on the chart. It's called Christmas Bay. It's very remote, on the west side of Santa Ines Island. I think we can sneak out of here and along the Strait and in before the British arrive. Fortunately, the morning sea mist has not lifted and visibility is minimal in the Straits, but I saw one of their cruisers on my way here so we will have to remain as silent as possible. I hear they have orders to sink the *Dresden* no matter that you are in Chilean waters, so you must go now. I will escort you."

The captain and Canaris could see that there was little option, so again they found themselves moving into the open water of the straits. Slipping along as close to the shore as possible, the *Dresden*, engines barely turning over, enjoyed an uninterrupted few hours steaming before navigating its way into the waters of remote Christmas Bay. They anchored in the most protected corner they could find and thanked Pagels as he headed back to sea.

Out in the Straits, Admiral Sturdee was becoming increasingly frustrated. His mood was not improved by a series of angry signals from Admiral Jacky Fisher asking for an explanation as to how one ship, seen only a few weeks ago by every schoolboy in Punta Arenas, could have eluded Sturdee's ships, which were supposed to be blocking each end of the Straits. It was useless to protest that in the low cloud, sea fog and high seas, one grey German ship could be almost impossible to spot. Sturdee rued the day *Dresden* had escaped from the Falklands. The German ship's continued survival was an affront to his skill as a seaman and was tarnishing his triumph at the Falklands.

Glasgow, and her companion cruiser, the *Kent* continued to steam up and down at the western end of the straits but finally, on *Dresden*, Captain Ludeke realised he could delay no longer. Picking yet another day when there was a morning fog, *Dresden* crept out into the western Pacific where, unsure of her position, she stopped. As the fog dispersed, Captain Ludecke was horrified to see on the horizon a warship that could only be British. It was in fact the *Kent*. At full speed, *Dresden* managed to disappear over the horizon but in doing she burned most of her remaining coal supplies.

Sturdee, on *Glasgow* and with *Kent* in attendance, continued his search in increasing frustration until, a few days later, a message was received from one of the many British agents in Valparaiso. He reported that a paid agent he had at one of the ports had, in turn, heard from local fishermen that a German warship had been seen steaming north directly towards Cumberland Bay at Mas-a-Tierra Island. They had no name but it definitely had three funnels. "That's the *Dresden*," Sturdee remarked to Luce, *Glasgow*'s captain, "Unless of course it's another piece of damn misinformation like most of the other reports we've had from our so-called agents, but we can't afford to risk missing her." They set a course up the Chilean Coast. On the morning of 14 March 1915, they reached Cumberland Bay and there was *Dresden* at anchor, safely in neutral waters. But Sturdee had his orders from London and had given captain Luce his. As soon as they were within range they commenced firing and *Dresden* was soon hit.

Luce turned to Sturdee. "They've sent a signal. They're sending a negotiator, and they've run up a white flag."

One of the lookouts reported a launch on the way, also flying a white flag and with a German naval officer in the bow. Luce gave the order to cease fire and the German officer was allowed on board. He saluted and introduced himself as Lieutenant Canaris. Canaris had decided that attack might be the only defence available. "I must protest in the strongest possible terms. You have opened fire in neutral waters against all the rules of the sea and of international diplomacy." Luce, maintaining a chilly civility, replied that the Chileans had been informed and that his orders were to accept nothing less than unconditional surrender, otherwise he would resume firing. Canaris, knowing time was important, attempted to bluster on but there was little more to say. He was allowed to return to the *Dresden* to deliver the ultimatum. Captain Ludeke in the meantime had discussed the situation with his fellow officers and with Berlin. There were no good choices available to him, so he ordered the crew to be removed to land for internment and for charges to be laid about the ship. When all was in readiness, the remaining crew and officers, including Ludecke and Canaris, departed for the shore and internment by the Chileans. As they reached the shore and turned towards their ship, there was a violent explosion and quickly the *Dresden* settled in the waters and disappeared from view.

After the scuttling of the *Dresden*, Captain Ludecke was in a serious state of shock, barely able to comprehend the ignominious end to the *Dresden*'s adventures. Canaris took virtual command. The survivors were eventually evacuated on two Chilean warships and at first interned on a Norddeutscher Lloyd passenger ship. It was not long, however, before the British objected to the Chilean Foreign Minister and the crew members were then shifted to the small island of Quriquina, north of Coronel. The island would be home to most of them for the next four years and, aided by the German colonies on shore, their material needs were well provided for. The industrious Germans soon improved the facilities on the island, turning their hands to gardening, poultry farming and generally using their wide array of skills to improve their lives.

Canaris had absolutely no intention of whiling the war away in safety on the island, so set his mind to escaping. There were in fact many escape attempts but most resulted in the escapees being captured and returned quite quickly to Quriquina. However, Canaris had perfect Spanish without an accent, a critical advantage. He eventually obtained approval from Captain Ludecke to escape and, on 5 August 1915, for the sum of twenty pesos, had himself transported to the mainland by a local fisherman. He made contact with the Krause family who were of German background and who had entertained Canaris and other officers before British complaints tightened their terms of internment.

Senora Krause liked this polite German with such correct Spanish. She teased him, "You should have stayed on your island. I hear it is a quite beautiful place. The English call it Robinson Crusoe Island. Apparently an English book was written about it, about a man who was marooned there – like yourself really. You could have lived a pleasant life there until this war you are engaged in is over. You are lucky to be alive from what I have heard."

The Krause's friend, Pablo, was a local doctor, whose passion was the Andes. His study was full of books about the Andes and his walls covered by pictures and maps. Canaris studied the latter with great care. Pablo was aghast at what Canaris was going to try. In an attempt to dissuade him, he showered him with facts. "The Andes is the longest mountain chain on earth, more than 7000 kilometres, and the highest, some of the peaks run up to nearly 4000 metres and there are more than 50 volcanoes over 6000 metres and they are always covered with snow somewhere. And you have little money. You should stay here amongst friends until this lunacy is over. Even the local peasants can be locked in for months after a heavy snowfall. It will take you a year to cross, if you ever make it." Canaris suspected Pablo really wanted company to share his morning coffee, but nevertheless he heeded his warnings and prepared as well as he could.

The Krauses supplied him with some money and obtained a false passport from the local German community. He changed from his formal suit to the clothes of a pedlar with a low cap to cover his face and he exchanged his suitcase for a canvas bag. After some discussion about the best route, he set off south and aiming to cross through the high mountain passes of the Cordilleras, on horseback, headed for Neuquen – some 200 miles to cover in the dead of winter. Sometimes he wondered if Pablo had been right. Why was he was going to so much trouble to return to a war he could so easily avoid? In the mountain villages the locals were not in the least curious about this stranger who had arrived amongst them from nowhere. Canaris could easily have blended into the timeless monotony of a life determined only by the seasons and found himself work for the duration. When the snow stopped and the clouds parted, he could admire the grandeur of the Andes and pause to ask himself why he kept moving with such haste; but he was a German Naval Officer and his obligations were sacred. He pressed on. Resources were scarce so he carefully husbanded his food and he eventually arrived in Neuquen exhausted and weak. Fortunately, Neuquen was a railhead and he managed to cover the next 800 miles to Buenos Aires by a series of trains, arriving in early 1916, a journey that had taken him some eight months.

Notwithstanding powerful British commercial interests, Argentina, and Buenos Aires in particular, had a strong German community and Canaris soon located a cousin of the German Ambassador, von Bulow. They managed to convert the now recovered, sprightly German Naval Officer into a mournful Chilean widower, Reed Rosas, who wished to return to Europe to claim property left him in the Netherlands. He had a Chilean passport which showed him to have an English-born mother, all the better to ingratiate himself with his fellow English passengers on the *Frisia*, a Dutch Lloyd steamer heading for Rotterdam via Plymouth. Canaris entertained himself by playing bridge with the British passengers and agreed to help the Naval Officers in Plymouth interview passengers before they were allowed to continue on the journey. By the time he reached Holland and slipped across the border to Germany, Canaris was well versed in the customs and idiosyncrasies of the English.

CHAPTER 7

Oblivious to the dramas being played out nearby, the *Corinthic* had slipped out of Punta Arenas, turned to port up the Strait and was soon out into the Atlantic on her way to Southampton. Fortunately, it was an uneventful passage and Harry was soon back on shore in England.

On arriving in London, Harry stayed for a while with his uncle and aunt and helped as far as he could in the family business. It was boring work, the war having severely constrained international trade. Harry became increasingly restless and felt, more and more, that he must join the services. He liked the Germans and had no wish to fight them, but reports from the front hardly enhanced the German reputation for fair play and keeping to the rules. In any event, he was constantly confronted in his daily activities by a nation at war. Predictions of a short battle looked increasingly incorrect and Harry had decided that, whatever his feelings about individual friends in Germany, the country had forfeited any claims to having right on its side by its brutal and unprovoked attack on the Belgians.

He was contemplating what to do next when the news broke that the Cunard liner *Lusitania,* which had been on its way from New York to Liverpool, had been sunk off the Irish Coast by a German submarine. The *Lusitania* carried 1959 people and 1198 of them were drowned, including nearly 128 citizens of the United States. The sinking caused outrage on both sides of the Atlantic. The Germans had placed advertisements in newspapers in the US warning travellers of the risk they were taking but nothing was going to stem the outcry. Uncle Nicholas stormed home from the Reform Club. He had attended a lunch addressed by the retired Welsh MP David Alfred Thomas, who had somehow escaped drowning and had immediately returned to London to give his personal account of the ordeal. It didn't take long for Harry to pick up the phone to his old Trinity Hall friend Rupert Winterbotham, whom he had heard was doing something active in Military Intelligence. Harry explained his desire to join the cause, particularly since his German might be of use, and they agreed to meet for a drink at The Grenadier in Knightsbridge. Rupert turned up in a dark suit with regimental tie and after an exchange of enquiries about mutual friends, soon turned to the main purpose of his call. "Harry, as you discovered, I work for Military Intelligence, if that's not too bizarre an idea. We're very busy trying to help the lads at the front by finding out as much as possible about German intentions, their dispositions, their weapons capabilities, morale, leadership, anything and everything about them that could help the war effort. At the moment one of the things we're short of is good German-speakers to interrogate captured Germans. This is vitally important. A prisoner who's had the living daylights scared out of him is often ready to spout, especially if he thinks getting a bullet is the alternative. I know you didn't really want to go off shooting Germans, given the friends you made there, but we have to win this war and from what you said on the telephone, you're ready to lend a hand?"

Harry took a quick sip of his beer. "I was pretty sure you were up to something cloak and daggerish, Rupert. As a matter of fact, I've been feeling very guilty not to be pulling my weight and, after the *Lusitania,* pretty angry, so this couldn't have come at a better time. Besides which, I'm struggling to work up much enthusiasm for the world of textiles. I'm quite sure my uncle will understand."

Over the next few weeks Harry disentangled himself from the family business and began to learn the subtle intricacies of military intelligence. It turned out, to his surprise, that his induction was intense. He had expected bristling moustaches and parade ground rigidities, but he found himself with long documents on subjects such as agent recruitment, codes, secret inks, methods of communication by radio and ways of evaluating information and testing it for authenticity. He was given a critical primer on how the Service interrelated with various Government Departments, with politicians, and the tricky relationship with the various arms of the military. He was interviewed by all sorts of people, including his Cambridge peers. A group of them had been at King's and he remembered one in particular, Toby Naismith, not much more than five feet tall, hair slicked down and parted in the middle, and sporting a salmon cravat, who referred to him as a 'rugger bugger' following up with a high-pitched laugh. Finding that he had little in common with Harry in what he airily described as 'the Arts', he seemed to find it highly amusing that Harry was good at 'games', as he called them. Harry noticed his interrogator's hands. They were soft and pink with carefully tended nails. Harry imagined they had never been employed in anything more arduous than lifting a pen or a knife and fork. Harry carefully folded his hands in his lap to avoid falling prey to the temptation to punch him. Naithsmith sat back in his chair, folded his hands behind his head and stared at Harry with the faintest trace of a smile. "I have never had the opportunity to visit New Zealand but I hear it is very beautiful and has somewhat progressive social views. Do you hold such views yourself?" Harry confirmed that he did. "Hmm, perhaps you will be spreading seditious opinions in England then; votes for women etc." Harry hesitated. "My chief concern is to assist in defeating the Germans. Any issues of social change in England, irrespective of their merits, need to wait until that has been achieved, don't you think?" "Indeed, indeed." A further silence occurred before Harry was dismissed, wondering whether his talents might be better employed elsewhere in the war effort.

Harry had never suspected what a substantial organisation MI6 was and how many activities came within its purview. At least he would be able, he hoped, to lose himself within his particular area of expertise which was Rupert's bailiwick, and which was specifically about using a very wide range of persuasions to bully and cajole captured Germans into willingly, or more often unconsciously, revealing information that could help to turn a battle or even the war.

At first Harry interviewed only prisoners held in camps in England but in June 1915 he shipped across the channel and was picked up by a staff car driven by a taciturn Cornish sergeant whom he could barely understand. Harry had made only short visits to France before but they had been long enough for him to succumb to the seductive charms of the French villages and the plump fecundity of the surrounding countryside. His driver took him down narrow lanes between tall hedgerows flush with autumn colours and through villages where elderly locals, their sons presumably far away at the front, argued with the market-stall owners over the price of asparagus or artichokes. Ducks waddled across cobbled streets from the village pond and the morning mist burned away in the rising sun. It was hard to take the war seriously but gradually, as the miles passed by, the apparatus of war began to clutter the bucolic scenery. Troops began to appear, marching in columns or resting in small groups by the roadside. The road became cluttered with trucks, staff cars and other vehicles of all descriptions. Then a few ambulances or trucks passed by, bearing the wounded. Finally there were sentries checking papers before waving the car onwards.

Harry was headed for Epernay on the Marne, not much more than 100 miles east of Paris and close to the French Army Group Centre. It was closer still to the fortress of Verdun where Petain had been resisting the German assault with some of the toughest fighting of the war so far. Harry's final destination was a British military intelligence unit stationed near Epernay. But Rupert, who had preceded him, had arranged to catch up for lunch in Epernay both to share a glass of wine and brief him on what he had been able to discover during his few weeks close to the front line. When they met in a little café beside the main square, Harry noticed that Rupert had a different look. The boyishness had gone and there seemed to be a reticence about him. They exchanged a few memories and Harry was glad to see Rupert's face light up at the retelling of some of their more entertaining escapades. They tucked into a local boeuf bourguignon and Rupert ordered a bottle of burgundy that the sommelier opened with great ceremony and which Rupert sipped speculatively before pronouncing it superb.

"So," said Harry, "tell me, is it all going as swimmingly as the British press would have it, or are the rumours of frightful casualties and little progress true?"

Rupert paused for a moment. "I had a night out with a colleague from the French Intelligence a few days ago. The fact is it's not going well. German artillery is smashing our lines and we are taking terrible losses from machine guns. We're finding out about modern warfare the hard way."

"And Verdun?" pressed Harry.

"Ah, Verdun. Beyond belief. We're all using gas. The Germans are using flamethrowers; we don't even have them. Their howitzers are raining down shells each weighing over a ton, trying to obliterate the walls of the old fortress. The French have taken over 200,000 casualties already. We think the Germans are the same." He paused reflectively. "You know for some reason one of the most upsetting things is the horses. They're blown to pieces. In one day 7,000 were killed. My friend told me 97 were killed in one shell burst. There were tiny fragments of horse scattered in the mud and floating in the stagnant water lying in the shell holes." The two young men lapsed into a ruminative silence. "Enjoy the wine, here's to peace before we're all destroyed."

Finishing lunch in a more subdued atmosphere, Harry headed off for his final destination, which turned out to be a farmhouse of red and chalk bricks complete with dormer windows overlooking the cobbled courtyard. The farm animals nonchalantly shared the garden with the strange visitors, the Military Intelligence officers who were stationed there to try to piece together the jigsaw that made up the German offensive. Harry soon settled into a routine that consisted of interviewing captured Germans of all ranks. He either had them brought under guard to the house or, more often, he visited various camps or police cells dotted about behind the lines. Autumn turned to winter, the sunny afternoons to rain and finally to sleet and snow. Harry tramped around behind the lines. All about spread the detritus of war; damaged and rusting equipment poking out of the sides of shell holes filled with slimy green water, the smell of rotting mud, buildings pulverised into nothing but an insignificant heap of brick fragments and shapeless rubble. Worse by far were the corpses. Some stuck out of the side of shell holes, some lay twisted on the ground. There were shattered limbs with a hand sticking out from a severed sleeve. An empty boot lay upright, filled with water. The smell of gangrenous flesh was everywhere. But Harry found to his consternation he was getting used to it. It had become familiar, as if it were almost normal.

He took time out to try to catch up with his brother Jack who had joined the New Zealand Expeditionary Force. Jack had written him a rambling letter from some months back. In it he had said, "I've volunteered to join the NZEF. Mum's not happy but she and Dad know there is no alternative. We had to sign the register about whether we were willing to do military service. Of course I said "yes" but a lot of men said "no". They claim they're conscies but I reckon half of them are scared and the rest are shirkers. There's been trouble in the streets of Christchurch over it but I was on the farm so missed it. I might have belted a few heads if I had been there, so lucky I wasn't. I guess you would agree with my decision. All my mates who have been called up are pretty excited about getting to see the world but we got a bit of a shock a few days ago. Jim Buller from down near Gore was shipped home wounded and some of us who were in his class went to catch up with him at his Mum's place. Harry, he was pretty badly wounded. Bandages everywhere. Couldn't make it to the pub for a beer. He had been at Gallipoli with the Aussies. He didn't want to talk about it but from the little he did say it was a bloody disgrace. Did you know they landed in the wrong place – at the bottom of a cliff? There were dead and wounded everywhere and everyone had the trots. He reckoned it was colder than home in winter too. All he could say was he reckoned he was bloody lucky to be alive. Anyway I suppose the Generals have all learned from that and they won't be that stupid again. Mind you if they're like Wally from Cadets we've got no hope. Hope I'll see you in England soon. All the Best, Harry. Your Brother Jack."

By the time Harry received the letter, New Zealand had introduced conscription and Jack would have been called up anyway, so it was as well he had volunteered since the known conscies had a pretty hard time from the volunteers. Now Harry had heard from Jack again. He was in St Julien, facing the German lines that stretched across the little town of Passchendaele, and under the command Birdwood's ANZACs. Harry tried to engineer a chance to get over there and see him but he was still waiting for a leave opportunity. In the meantime, somewhere in the vicinity his friend Peter Houston from Cambridge days was leading a Company of Australian troops. These were troops that had originally come from the shores of Gallipoli only to find, having somehow survived that fiasco, they were now involved in another one. This time, however, they were directly under Monash whom they had at least learned to trust would not sacrifice them for nothing. Harry hoped to catch up with Peter too. His role gave him much more flexibility to move around behind the front lines than was ordinary troops, even officers. Harry finally managed to organise a driver who reckoned that if they left before dawn he could get him to St Julien for a brief catch-up with his brother. Harry could not get hold of Peter and, in any event, he had only half a day available so there would be time for only one meeting and Jack was his major concern.

As it turned out Jack was in a surprisingly cheerful mood. "We'll be in the pub at Methuen by Christmas," he confidently predicted. "What do you think Harry? You're the expert. We'll push these bastards back to Berlin and then we can go home."

Harry laughed. "If only, Jack, if only. But maybe we are seeing the turning point. But you just keep yourself safe. Don't go trying to be a hero. Mum told me to look after you. You know Mum and Dad will never get over it if one of us cops it, so how about you take a bit of care." Jack assured him he was not interested in becoming another cross on the soil of France and they went on to talk of home; of how the wheat crop would be, whether the new Romney–Leicester cross would go well in the winter and who would win the rugby competition now that so many of the best players were 'over here'.

Not long after getting back to HQ, Harry was called in by his commanding officer. "We have an interesting one. The Aussies have got their hands on a senior officer, God help him. We need you to get over there and interview him and bring him back here before they stick a bayonet in him. I've arranged an escort to show you the way. As soon as you can, please."

Harry quickly gathered his equipment and headed out with his two escorts. They followed a line of duckboards in and out of a constant patchwork of shell holes. The nearer they came to the front line, the worse it became. Sometimes there were shell holes inside shell holes. The duckboards were often smashed and they had to scramble up the side of a shell hole gripping any shredded tufts of foliage or broken machinery they could find to help them up. Their boots slipped in the mud and they slid back on hands and knees. Looking out, the whole terrain consisted of endless crater lips like breaking waves of mud with not a living thing in sight. Crossing a patch of water-logged bog, they paused to listen to a curious whistle followed by the 'plop' of shells landing nearby. The soldiers froze. "Gas" was all one of them said. Grabbing their masks, they forced them over their heads but not before they caught a deadly whiff as the cloud of gas spread towards them. They peered at each other through clouded glass and one of them gestured to Harry to cover up. It was mustard gas and any exposed skin would come up in fierce blisters. A little of the gas had seeped in and Harry could feel his throat rasping and eyes smarting. They rolled away for a few yards and Harry felt as if he was going to choke. He ripped the mask off and breathed in some fresh air. Coughing, he took a swig from his water bottle. One of the men offered him a small phial. Harry peered at it. "What's that?" he asked. "Ammonia. It'll help, they reckon. Don't know myself, but try it."

Harry took a sip and began to feel better. They set off again. After about an hour more of climbing in and out of shell holes they arrived at a line of trenches and he was conducted to a dugout. Outside, a skinny Australian soldier, dressed in a torn tunic with his bush hat pulled down and a smart pair of binoculars dangling around his neck, grinned at them. "Come to see our Hun have you? He's in there." He pointed at a small dugout built into the side of a trench with a sloping roof made of corrugated iron.

"You been 'ratting' the prisoner?" asked one of his escorts pointing at the binoculars. "Get anything good?"

The Aussie took a beautiful silver fob watch out of his tunic and swung it backwards and forwards in front of them. "Tick, tock," he said and winked at them. They pushed open the door of the dugout to find another Australian soldier sitting smoking. To their surprise beside him stood a caricature of a Prussian officer, a monocle, a pair of kid gloves in one hand and the top half of an immaculate blue uniform but without the trousers. He drew himself up and, having established that Harry spoke German, demanded his trousers back and to be treated as an officer. Harry turned to the Australian who shrugged. "We took them to make sure he didn't try to escape, Sir. They won't go far with no trousers. Too bloody stuck up." He waived his bayonet at the German's privates, but retrieved the trousers, which the German started to put on with as much dignity as he could muster. Just as he did so the whole room rocked to a colossal explosion that was quickly followed by further crashes of high explosive from close by. They all involuntarily ducked except the German who remained rigidly upright.

Months later, Harry was still trying to piece together what happened next. All he could remember was another blast and a shockwave knocking him sideways. A searing pain came from somewhere and he found himself totally buried in mud and debris. He must have blacked out. He next remembered opening his eyes to total darkness. He managed to establish he was buried. He tried to move his arms but only one arm seemed to respond. He flailed with it trying to scrape some earth away from his face so he could breathe, but then fell still, exhausted with the effort. A tiny sliver of light appeared from somewhere. He felt a great sense of relief. Thank God he hadn't been blinded. He must have blacked out again because he next remembered someone pulling on his legs and then a voice with an Australian accent saying. "Go easy mate. I think he's alive." They dug him out and sat him on what was left of the floor of the trench. He felt blood oozing down from his left shoulder and a terrible pain started to work its way through his consciousness. The Aussie put a water bottle to his lips and he took a deep swig and then spat out a mixture of mud laced with blood and saliva. His jaw felt as though it was broken but he began to notice the rest of his body as if it had been somewhere else and now decided to return to him. A soldier appeared from nowhere.

"You look a mess sir. Let's have a look," He peered at the mess that had been Harry's shoulder and then looked carefully at the rest of him. "That shoulder's bad, Sir. Looks like you've got some other damage to your leg and a few facial cuts but nothing serious. You OK for a minute?"

Harry wiped blood from his face. "I'll be OK. Deal with the serious stuff." The soldier propped him up and disappeared.

Harry sat there in a stupor as the pain surged through him in waves. It was bearable because he knew in his heart that however bad it was he would survive and that feeling that he had somehow cheated death overcame almost everything else.

He looked about wondering where the German and the guards were. After a while a stretcher-bearer appeared. "Let's get you out of here. Can you walk?" Harry nodded. "Good, we're out of stretchers anyway. The private here will give you a hand. We'll try to walk you to the dressing station."

Harry struggled to his feet. "What happened to the Hun and the two guards?"

"We pulled a dead Hun and one guard out, what was left of them. Don't know about the other one." Harry tried putting his weight on each foot but his left foot didn't seem to want to cooperate. He leaned on the private's shoulder and they shuffled out of what little was left of the shelter. As he stopped to take in the outside world, he noticed something shiny protruding from the bank of mud. He reached gingerly forward and grasped a tiny fragment of chain. A gentle tug unearthed the fob watch the Aussie soldier had been swinging so casually. The soldier looked at him. "Keep it," he said, "a good luck charm."

Slowly they worked their way over broken duckboards and more shell holes. For Harry, every step was accompanied by a stab of pain. At one stage they came across a larger than normal hole. Some soldiers sat silently in the bottom of it. One was white as the clay around them had once been. He was shaking with fear. His companion sat with his head in his hands his shoulders shaking and muttering incoherently. Two bodies lay beside them. One, its head almost decapitated, had been thrown across the other. They stopped for a minute. The private offered water but the soldiers only stared in incomprehension. "Shell shock," said the private, "worse than being wounded." They struggled on, stopping every now and then so that Harry could regain a little strength. Gradually they fell in with other parties of wounded all heading for the same dressing station. Some men were on stretchers, some managed to walk unaided and some were being helped to limp forward as best they could. They came to a track on which they were joined by a horse ambulance. Harry looked sadly at the worn out horse that was trying to pick its way across the terrain with its cargo of casualties. Finally, they came to what remained of a small village. Almost every house was damaged or destroyed. The dressing station was in the remains of the village church and an orderly found him somewhere to sit so he could prop himself up in a corner. "They'll be along to check you soon, Sir. I'd best go back and help. Good luck." Harry managed to muster the strength to thank him and then he was gone.

Harry sat in a pain-filled stupor. He lost track of time but could feel himself getting colder and colder but could not muster up the strength to move or find someone to help him. A few flakes of snow settled on his torn jacket. As the weak sun began to falter, an orderly bustled over to him. "Okay, let's get you inside and take a look at this." Harry had stiffened up and it was slow and painful progress into the dressing station. The orderly gingerly cut away the remains of his uniform from his shoulder and his left leg. Blood was still oozing out of the mangled mass of flesh that was his shoulder. He was given some morphine and a blanket. "We'll get you to a field hospital as soon as we can. We're overwhelmed at the moment but we'll get some heat in here and try to get you comfortable." Sometime later, he presumed the next morning as it was light, he bounced his way in a motorised ambulance to the field hospital. They put him on a slab and a doctor administered chloroform as they began to probe his wounds. The next thing he remembered was coming to on a stretcher covered in blankets. As he slowly twisted his head he could see all around, lying in all sorts of positions, the wounded and dying. Some muttered in pain, or cried out for some unhearing angel and some lay still, either dead or so close to it, it was not possible to tell the difference. A harassed-looking doctor came over to him and explained his injuries. "Shrapnel through the shoulder, plus a piece in the leg. The piece in your shoulder went through almost into your chest. You were bloody lucky. Another few inches and we wouldn't be talking. We managed to get both pieces out okay. You've got a couple of souvenirs. That shoulder is going to take a while to heal. You'll probably be shipped home but it's not up to me. Anyway we can't keep you here for long."

Harry was eventually shipped back to England on a rusting coastal cargo boat. They bucketed their way across the Channel rolling on a slight northerly swell and under low cloud that gradually broke up, allowing a weak sun to push through and provide a little warmth to those who, like Harry, had chosen to stay on deck. Harry sat sheltered by a lifeboat, his crutches beneath his bench, watching the upcoming cliffs of an England for which he now felt an affection that belied his brief time there. He had stayed on deck to stave off any sea sickness, fill his lungs with chill sea air and most of all avoid the stricken wounded crammed in rows on the lower deck. The more mobile sat or lay near him on deck. He kept his eyes on the horizon at least in part for some respite from the sight of pain and injury everywhere about him. Everywhere were men with limbs missing, with all parts of their bodies swathed in bloodstained or dirty bandages, with head dressings wound like turbans. Those who had been gassed sat with eyes covered, partly or totally blind.

He thought of the Kitchener poster with its picture of lantern-jawed hero, a Victorian Richard the Lionheart, eyes blazing as he pointed at the men of England with the words "Your

Country Needs YOU" written beneath. So many of these men had gone off in patriotism, a sense that the Boche needed to be taught a lesson, and with the jaunty confidence of a football team heading for a final they were bound to win. Harry wondered what they made of the war now. The death and destruction as vast armies pushed backwards and forwards to gain or lose a few hundred yards of churned mud and debris devoid of any living thing but rats revelling in the boundless supply of food that the mangled bodies of horses and men supplied. He had no sense that rebellion was growing in the ranks but there was no doubt that, as those who survived the trenches learned for themselves, character didn't cut it against machine guns and howitzers. Men were becoming less inclined to take orders from officers whose rank reflected their birth more than their brains. The same was not so true of the Germans Harry had lately been interrogating. Short of food, supplies and reinforcements the new, ever-younger German recruits were more inclined to surrender.

Here, there was almost a whisper of rebellion in the air. Could this be the beginning of a collapse in morale that would in the end see the exhaustion of their opponents? Was this what Commander Haig, Commander of the British Expeditionary Force, anticipated when he continued to order attack after attack whatever the consequences in blood and gore?

Harry was eventually moved to a small nursing home that had originally been a minor country house on the coast of Kent near the Cinque Port town of Sandwich. It stood at the end of a curved gravel driveway lined with chestnut trees. Manicured lawns surrounded the house on three sides, divided by garden beds full of thriving azaleas and rhododendrons. Assorted annuals and perennials thrust their way up between the shrubs.

As Harry lay in the sun he felt himself gradually relaxing and the pain from his wounds diminishing. He deliberately turned his mind back to an idyllic period of his life, and he began to recalibrate the trauma he had experienced by returning, to the best of his abilities, to these formative experiences.

CHAPTER 8

The Convalescent Home was full of mangled young officers mainly captains or lieutenants with the occasional major thrown in. Harry met with them over meals in the dining room and almost by force of habit listened to their stories, many of them remarkable for the ferocity of their experience. These men had been in the front line with the infantry and their rate of casualty had been appalling. Some had handled the experience remarkably well while others sat more or less silent, staring listlessly into whatever hideous memory was overwhelming them. Harry himself felt surprisingly sanguine about what had happened to him. He was more than grateful to have survived and supposed his insouciance derived from the fact that he had hardly been exposed to the sense-destroying experience of trenches and artillery barrages, where companions were killed or wounded day after day.

The first morning he had awakened very early with the sun barely above the fields and, not being one for lying in bed, had levered himself up and onto his crutches and quietly made his way to the garden. Finding a bench under the trees, he sat quietly watching the sunrise. He became aware of the total silence of the morning with only the chirps and whistles of the early morning birds. He watched a small thrush tugging enthusiastically on a worm in the garden bed. He could feel the tension, which he had hardly been aware of, seeping away in the warmth of the morning sun. It was good to be alive. Harry eventually wandered back to the breakfast room and found himself gravitating to a cheery Mancunian, a captain in the 46th North Midland. The man had lost his leg near Bellicourt, in one of the more heroic feats of the war when his brigade had crossed a deep fortified canal in the face of heavy resistance to achieve a small but significant British victory.

Ian Mellish joked with Harry about how on earth a British Territorial Division had acquitted itself so well in the canal where they had somehow managed to get themselves across under fire. In places the water was above their heads so that, encumbered with equipment and heavy clothing, they had struggled to help each other to the far bank from which they could attack. Most of them had hardly ever seen the sea, let alone experienced the fear that can envelop humans when first confronted by deep water. Ian and Harry told each other little snippets about their lives in the Midlands and the South Island of New Zealand. One afternoon they were sitting chatting when Ian had a message from an orderly. After reading it, he turned to Harry and said, "Come and meet my sister Kathleen". She's down from the Midlands for the weekend to see me. She looks after hundreds of orphaned children; little ones. She's a regular princess to the poor little things." They hobbled over to the foyer and Harry found himself looking at a tall, slim blonde girl with a face almost heart-shaped. She shook his hand rather tentatively, and looked speculatively at him through enormous brown eyes that Harry, in spite of himself, kept being drawn back to as they took tea in the sitting room. Ian and his sister chatted on as families do and Harry listened quietly until finally Kathleen turned to him and before he had realised what was happening he was burbling on about all sorts of trivia, a most unexpected reaction from someone more inclined to be taciturn. As Kathleen turned to go, Ian leaned over to Harry. "Kathleen's staying at the Blue Boar for the night. I'm taking her to dinner there. They have rather a good carvery. I'm sure Kathleen wouldn't mind if you joined us. She's probably tired of my company already and you can tell her all about New Zealand. What do you say?" Kathleen started to remonstrate with her brother about putting Harry in an embarrassing position.

"He's probably got all sorts of things on." She turned to Harry. "Please don't feel obliged to join us, but of course you would be most welcome if you genuinely are free." Harry quickly responded that he would be delighted to join them.

The Blue Boar was one of the oldest pubs in Kent, with low ceilings and crooked bay windows and a bar full of brass bits and pieces and a huge fireplace dominating one end of the lounge bar. Ian had been right, the food was excellent and Harry found some delicious lamb, small portions as expected under rationing, but which he had to admit was as good as their own Canterbury lamb. They chatted on amiably enough and again he found to his surprise that he was fielding questions about all sorts of issues connected with his life in the shadows of the Southern Alps. He apologised for talking too much about himself. Kathleen laughed. "Not at all, it's all such a different world, so," she searched for a word to fit, "so wild; and actually we do find your accent rather fascinating. You don't mind do you?"

Harry was momentarily taken aback but laughed himself. "Actually I find yours and Ian's a bit the same, especially those quaint northern sayings."

Ian and Harry chatted on for a while about sport, mostly cricket or rugby, until Harry ventured the view, which he secretly prided himself was well informed, that, even though professional football was currently suspended, he was amazed by the English obsession with soccer, and that he supposed Ian and Kathleen would have been brought up as lifelong supporters of the great Manchester United. He had picked up from the newspapers the names of a couple of United's star players and paraded them proudly as a credit to the game. The atmosphere seemed to chill a bit. After a pause, Ian cleared his throat: "Actually, we call it football and our family are lifelong supporters of Manchester City and the thing we hate most in the world, even more than Liverpool, even more than Blackburn, even more than Tottenham and Arsenal and those other toffee-nosed London Clubs, is bloody Manchester United." Harry tried a totally ineffectual back-peddle.

Kathleen gave him a smiled sweetly. "United are absolute rubbish. We'll let you off just this once, but only once." Harry soon found himself with plenty to occupy him. He was brought piles of captured German documents and before long being taken to various camps to continue the interrogation process. He soon dispensed with his crutches and hobbled about with increasing freedom. As he spoke to a wider and wider range of the German military, he noticed that a much greater proportion of them did not have any visual sign of injury. Questioning drew out from them the view that they had dispensed with the idea of fighting to the last man and were now more concerned about surviving, with the future of their families uppermost in their minds. There was also a whiff of Bolshevism clearly emerging. He began to feel that if pressure continued to be applied, especially with the entry of the Americans, the end could be in sight.

Rupert Winterbotham telephoned Harry one evening to say

that he needed to come down to the hospital. It was time they had a chat. Would tomorrow be too soon? It was agreed they would meet mid-afternoon. Rupert arrived and enquired where they might go that would provide some privacy. Harry thought for a minute and then suggested the rose arboretum, which was tucked away at the end of an expanse of lawn and offered the extra privacy of a small summer house. "So how are the wounds coming along?" enquired Rupert. "You took quite a belting, the doctor told me".

"I'm improving in leaps and bounds," replied Harry. "In fact I reckon it's time I got out of here. I could do anything I was doing in France, just a bit slower."

"I'm glad to hear that, it was precisely what I hoped you'd say. We need some really good up-to-the minute data from the front lines. To go back a little, you are well aware of what has happened in Russia. The Germans shipped Lenin back there from Switzerland in a sealed train. They knew what they were doing; it was a masterstroke. He has quickly gained control of the revolution and we believe the Russian army is no longer an effective fighting force. It is controlled by the Soviets and whether or not they continue is doubtful. But the interesting development is that Bolshevism is gaining strength in Germany as well. We believe the casualties they're suffering and our blockade is working. Ordinary Germans are starving, the meat ration has been slashed and people are starting to talk of revolution. We think it's affecting their front line troops and we're also worried it may be starting to poison the minds of the French. So far we think our own men are standing up to the fighting pretty well from a morale point of view. A looming problem is that if the Russians totally collapse then the Germans can turn their 50 divisions back onto the Western Front. Even with the Americans we're not sure we can resist that sort of onslaught. So there's a push on to try to finish the war before that happens. However, despite the new tanks, we don't know if we can make effective frontal attacks but we're getting the feeling that the morale of the new German troops is near collapse. One big push might finish them." He paused and lit his pipe.

Harry interjected. "It's funny, I've started to wonder the same thing. With the prisoners I've interviewed here I've had the feeling the fight has gone out of them. Even the officers have lost that irritating cockiness. What do you want me to do?"

"We want to get you back into France as close to the front line as possible. We need to know if they'll break and run if we rain a blitzkrieg like their own back on top of them. So how about it?"

"When do I go?" replied Harry. "I can be out of here tomorrow morning if you can fix the transport."

Rupert took a couple of puffs of his pipe. "We have a man coming out of Germany next week and we want him to brief us, and you, before you go. He's been back in the cities and his assessment of the atmosphere will help us all get this right. We're only going to get one crack at it. As soon as we know he's back, come up to London and we'll get the process going so you can leave when he's briefed us."

Harry was glad to be involved again and recounted to his friend Ian over dinner that he would probably be around for only another week or so and then expected to be returning to France. "I'm glad you're here for a few days. I was going to ask you. The family are putting together a dinner up north to celebrate my father's sixtieth birthday. It's quite a grand affair. I wondered if you would like to join me as my guest. My father would like to meet you. He's very curious about New Zealand for some reason. I'll understand if you don't feel like travelling that far. But the north's beautiful. Beautiful country, and beautiful people." Harry tried unsuccessfully to hide his elation at the chance of seeing Kathleen again and accepted graciously. "Good then. That's sorted. We can fix you up with a dinner suit if you haven't got one. Legs will need lengthening though," Harry said he had his own and, on his way up to Manchester, would visit his uncle and aunt and grandparents in London, and collect it.

Harry enjoyed his visit north and meeting Ian's family. He tried to disguise his anxiety over where he would be sitting at dinner but was immensely relieved to find he had Kathleen on his left. They chatted amicably about all manner of things. At one point she looked at him in silence for a minute and then said. "Now that you've been wounded I suppose you'll be invalided home, will you? Do you know when that will be?"

Harry laughed. "Not at all. They still need my skills at the front, so they say. I'm going back quite soon". And then, rather too quickly, "I'm not crippled you know. I'll be fully recovered in a few weeks. Oh, I'm sorry," he apologised, blushing.

"It's alright," she responded, "We have to get used to Ian's situation. I know you didn't mean anything. He's such a positive person, we are all positive too. We look around our friends in the north, in the Territorials, so many have lost a son, sometimes more than one. It's heart breaking to see. They put such a brave face on it but you can see the pain written in their faces. We know we're lucky to have Ian." She put a hand on his arm. "You should take care of yourself. The war's not over. Your family will be worried sick when they hear you're going back to France." "They never let me near the fighting" Harry replied, but Kathleen just looked at him. "Everyone in France is near the fighting. I'm not naïve in the slightest. Your family might believe that but I don't."

Back in home, the war totally dominated life throughout the land, city and country. New Zealand was making a huge contribution. Of a tiny country of one million inhabitants, nearly

20 per cent were recruited. Conscientious objectors were harshly dealt with; imprisoned and humiliated, Maori or white. Tales of death and injury abounded. New Zealanders did not need to be told. 'The angel of death had passed over the land and all had heard the beating of its wings.'

Back on Earnslaw, Harry's mother concentrated on her daily tasks and on seeing that David was well looked after. She was busy in the kitchen preparing the Sunday roast when she sensed his presence. Looking up, she realised he had been quietly leaning against the door post for some time, watching her. "I could tell you they'll be alright, Victoria, but I'd be lying," he finally said. "I know you never stop thinking about them but those two are pretty resolute. If anyone can get through this they can, and in any case Harry's involved in a lot of hush-hush stuff which he told me is mostly behind the lines. You should try not to worry. You can't do anything and I'm hearing that some of our politicians think the Germans are beginning to crumble." Victoria folded a towel and then turned it sideways and refolded it. "I know you're right, David, but there have been a lot of casualties lately. Poor Meg and Tony. They only had William and now he's gone. I guess the girls will get the farm but it seems like a game of chance. William was a great kid, just like our boys. I must get over and see Meg tomorrow. I'll take some of the early apples. She loves those. But you can't pull the wool over my eyes. I know you are losing just as much sleep as I am. So let's just hope the Germans collapse as fast as possible. In the meantime, say what you like, what else could possibly occupy our minds?"

Harry was back at the front within three weeks as promised. This time, there was a steady stream of German prisoners many of whom were without any injury. They were often demoralised boys who should have been at school but there were many officers and, noticeable among them, was an increasing theme of betrayal. Their conviction that they had not been defeated but were victims of Bolshevism or some Jewish conspiracy blinded them from the realities of their position once the United States had entered the war. The corrosive poison of revenge permeated their attitude and Harry found it hard not to react to their arrogance.

The Armistice finally came at 11am on 11 November 1918. Harry heard about it when one of the radio operators rushed into his room. They gathered in the mess and toasted anyone they could think of who had helped to bring about this momentous event. Harry had a great sense of release. He tried to get in touch with Jack but with no success, so it was eventually Jack who found him later that night. They figured out they were quite close and that they could meet in Harry's mess two days later. Harry was shocked at Jack's appearance and after they disentangled themselves from a huge hug, Harry pinched Jack's arms. "You're all skin and bones. Don't the boys feed you down there? I thought they had sent you secret supplies of Canterbury lamb. But, never mind, we survived. How did we do it? I got a message to Mum and Dad and Uncle Nick. There'll be beer flowing in the Canterbury pubs tonight." Jack laughed. "You don't know how lucky I am. Bloody Freyberg's a maniac. No wonder he got a VC. Christ, he thinks it's all a bloody game. When he found out the Armistice was coming he galloped the cavalry into this village and at five to eleven, he was still shooting any poor Boche he could find. Trouble was they were shooting back. My horse copped a bullet in the arse. Went berserk and threw me off. I was OK, just, but Freyberg thought it was a huge joke. He's a frigging brigadier general. You would have thought he was out on a fox hunt." The sheer madness of it, and the sheer relief, sent them both into hysterics.

It took over a year for the boys to make their way back to New Zealand, wangling their way onto the same ship for the leg home and finally arriving in Christchurch after a last night in which the mighty Southern Ocean threw everything it could at them as if determined to have one last say in their war. It blew from the south at over 60 knots and the swell, which felt as if it had been building up all the way from the Antarctic, rolled and pitched the ship so that eventually both the boys were sick. As a result, their parents found their sons white and sunken cheeked and not the robust war heroes they expected. It wasn't until they found themselves looking up at the Southern Alps and sharing a beer with their father while their mother cooked a roast in their honour that they felt the stress finally draining away.

After dinner, Harry went to help his mother with the washing up. Suddenly she dropped the plate she was washing back in the water and threw her arms around his chest. He could feel warm tears on his shirt. "It's OK Mum, it's OK." Jack came in to help and she released Harry and in turn enveloped Jack in a similar bear hug.

She dried her eyes with a tea towel. "I can't believe you've both survived. It seems like a miracle. I almost believe in God, but then I think of all the boys who didn't come back. I'm weeping tears of joy, but their mothers will never recover."

Harry patted her the top of her head. "I was never really in danger. Jack here is the lucky one."

Jack flicked him with his tea towel. "You venture up to the trenches and what happens? You nearly get yourself killed. You're not safe to be with, Harry." Their father had walked in to see what the fuss was about. He held *Illustrated London News* in his hand.

"Look at this." He held up the paper so they could all see the headline. In bold type it proclaimed the news of the forming of the "League of Nations" and expressed the hope that this would be the end of war. "It seems that even though it's President Woodrow Wilson's creation, his own country won't be joining. If the United States is not in, then I don't see how it will work." Victoria took the paper.

"Whatever happens, that's the last time you boys are going to be at risk and I hope the same applies to all New Zealanders."

A few days later Jack returned from a visit to Christchurch and announced that a ski weekend was being held up at the Ohau field, organised as an old school first-fifteen reunion. He had agreed that both he and Harry would go and they soon found themselves in one of the Club huts with some of the old team. After a day's skiing, they stoked the fire up and opened a beer. Outside light snow had turned to blizzard. Harry wondered if they would even be able to get out tomorrow. Talk soon turned to their triumph at the Quadrangular Rugby Tournament in Harry's last year at School. Jack gave him a poke in the ribs, "Hurry up and get us beer." He turned to Ehru, a thick-set Maori with a barrel chest who had played hooker for the first fifteen. "Remember how you chased Harry down and took a pass just has he was about to be flattened? You scored and Harry got flattened anyway. You were so slow, Harry, like an old porker." They clinked glasses. Ehru had fought with the Pioneer Battalion, which was called in Maori Te Hokowhitu a Tu or the army of Tumatauenga, the God of War.

"You guys copped it, Ehru. Lost a lot of mates I'm guessing," said Harry.

Ehru agreed. "We thought it was fun for a while. We liked the hand-to-hand stuff. We went after the Germans with bayonets. Scared the hell out of them. They thought we were cannibals and we didn't disillusion them. But then the shelling started. We hated that. That scared the hell out of us."

"So what now, Ehru?" Harry asked.

Ehru jiggled his beer. "Man, I'm going to do some Maori stuff. Our tribe and the Te Arawa boys and plenty more stood up for New Zealand. We nearly all volunteered. Jesus, you know my first cousin Maui was killed standing beside me. Now we want New Zealand to stand up for us. We want equality. We're not going to stand for any more bullshit."

Harry agreed. "I don't blame you, you've got my vote."

Ehru went on. "There's another thing though, Harry. The Treaty, Waitangi, we've been looking at it and we reckon it protects us. So we're going to want our land back. The Waikato and Taranaki tribes are right. Our land has been stolen. So what about you guys? Will you support that too?" There was a long silence before Harry answered.

"I tell you what, Ehru. I will, but my only reservation is Pakehas don't lose their homes and farms. There's plenty of land for everyone."

"Maybe," replied Ehru "you agree Jack?" Jack had been listening, frowning.

"Anyone tries to take Earnslaw and I'll be standing at the gate with the shotgun, but anything else is fine with me."

Ehru looked at him steadily, the firelight reflecting off his face. Harry could feel the power in the man, the conviction about what he wanted to do. Whatever happened, strife between Maori and Pakeha had to be avoided. Suddenly he could see Ehru relax. "Let's have another beer." He punched Harry on the shoulder and Harry winced. That wound was not completely healed.

For a while Harry and Jack mooched about helping their father and revisiting favourite places. They even took the rods up the mountain on a couple of horses. Eventually the subject of 'what next' needed to be faced. Their father had acquired a 750 acre adjoining block so now, as he put it, "I definitely need one of you boys to help, but not both of you. Harry, you have your degree and Jack, you have always seemed like you are a farmer at heart. So how about it? If you both agree, Jack stays with me and Harry, your mother and I know the future holds plenty of opportunity for you." The boys had not much trouble with these arrangements because in fact they reflected their interests. As it happened, Jack was a natural fix-it man. He could mend anything with some number eight fencing wire and a pair of pliers.

On the other hand, Harry was thinking of Europe again. The friends he had made and the opportunity to arrange his life around something that would use his German skills. He had the chance, since Uncle Nick had cornered him just before he left London. "Good to see you boys getting back to see David and Victoria. You will have a wonderful reunion after so long and after so much has happened. I know they never expected to see both of you again, whatever they said, but don't forget there's a job for you here in the firm. There are opportunities for us in Europe and your connections and knowledge would be of great help." Harry was almost too quick to agree that indeed he did want to return to England to pursue 'opportunities', as he put it.

He saw his mother watching him with a little smile. Later in the kitchen as they finished the washing up and whilst Jack and David were talking in the living room she looked him in the eye. "Opportunities is it now? Are you going to tell me about her or not?" Harry hesitated and she laughed and turned away. "Tell me when you're ready then."

Harry figured that a position in the family business would be enough to get him started in England and after that he could see what developed. Besides, as his Mother had divined, there was Kathleen. He could hardly believe how much he thought about her. They had had quite a few opportunities to meet since the dinner in the north. She had come down to London for a Ball at the Hyde Park Hotel and it had seemed like a magical night to him but then as she left on the train for home next day she had seemed quite withdrawn, even brusque.

He had decided to write to her before he left but couldn't decide how much to say. If he said too much, she might be offended or perhaps she only really saw him as a friend. So he had written an awkward and elliptical rambling epistle, which he was sure could only have completely confused her. But as the mail was picked up from their R.D.5 post box each day, he waited in slowly diminishing anticipation for some reply.

CHAPTER 9

It was September 1926 and Harry had returned from yet another visit to Germany and had called in to pay his respects to his aunt and uncle. He found his uncle pacing up and down in the drawing room muttering to himself. "Damn Bolshies. The cheek of them. Oh, hello Harry. You've heard all about it I suppose?" Harry hadn't heard about anything. "The damn Trade Union Congress has called a General Strike. They're trying to bring the whole country down. Call in the army, I say. Now look, Harry. Hope you don't mind. I've volunteered you as a Special Constable. Help keep a bit of law and order before we're all murdered in our beds. I'm too old, but I thought you would be just the chap."

Harry was not too sure what all this meant but seeing how agitated his uncle was, he deemed it best to agree until he could discover what was really involved. As it turned out, nearly two million workers across Britain had gone on strike led by the miners. 'Not a minute on the day, not a penny off the pay' was their slogan. Harry was given a uniform and bussed over to Bethnall Green to help keep an eye on a street march. It was one of those bitter damp London days when the cold seeped through you and the sky was the iron colour of one of His Majesty's ships. Hardly had he arrived than fog began to swirl up the street towards him. The visibility soon reduced to a few feet and the sky turned into a mist of olive-green vapour. People's shapes could hardly be discerned, fading in and out of vision, and the sounds of the city were hard to identify by source or direction. Harry soon felt disoriented and to avoid becoming completely lost in the unfamiliar part of the city, headed for a small tea room and ordered a pot of tea. While waiting, he picked up the only newspaper in sight, the *Workers' Weekly*. It was the mouthpiece for the British Communist Party. Circulation had soared since the strike, aided by the publicity over a nasty legal battle in defence of a libel suit. Copies were everywhere in Bethnall Green. Harry was just beginning to read the lead article when a scrawny young chap in overalls and a cloth cap pushed the door open and seeing the only remaining free chair was at Harry's table, sat himself down.

"Here's a state of affairs – a Special Constable reading the *Workers' Weekly*. Looking for evidence against us are you, or are you a communist spy?" Harry explained that he had nothing against the strikers but you had to keep law and order whatever the situation. "Is that right?" was the reply. "You wouldn't know, but them bloody mine owners have extended our working week – as if seven days wasn't enough already. I was told my wages were cut and then, when we objected, they locked us out. How would you like it, eh? We can't live on what we make now. I've got kids. Can't feed'm on fresh air." He jumped to his feet and, although Harry would have towered over him, grabbed the paper and thrust it back in Harry's face. "Take this to them buggers in

Parliament what sent you. Tell them to read it before they call us bloody Reds. Tell you what. We weren't before, but by God we are now." Before Harry could respond, he had disappeared out the door and was swallowed by the fog.

Events pottered along a little uncertainly for some time until the 1929 Wall Street crash. Life after that became progressively more difficult. Bills remained unpaid, stock piled up in warehouses and customers became bankrupt, unable to meet the demands of bankers or their own creditors. People read the papers and were confronted by the stories of financial hardship, suicides and the misery of the unemployed. The unemployed had no money to spend and those people who had money conserved it wherever they could. Governments generally made things worse by tightening purse strings. Economists and other experts sagely advised that "we must all learn to live within our means." The family firm struggled, and Uncle Nicholas muttered and complained, increasingly agitated by pressure from the firm's bank in New Zealand to address its deteriorating financial condition. Grandfather stood somewhat aloof but began to appear in the office without notice, to Uncle Nicholas' considerable discomfort. Harry was invited to tea by his grandfather who sat him down before telling him, "I am sure you understand the family business is not enjoying the best of times at the moment, a situation in which we are not at all alone. I am afraid your uncle has limited facility for business and I am finding my presence required more and more. This cannot continue. I am too old. You are an intelligent young chap and clearly you could take over if it was to be arranged tactfully. However, I am not able to estimate your level of enthusiasm for commerce. If you have other goals, then this opportunity is not for you and I will have to make other arrangements. Don't answer right now but lest you are concerned about receiving a poisoned chalice, I can assure you that I have sufficient resources to maintain the situation for the moment. Think about it and let me know your decision as quickly as possible."

Harry didn't take long to make up his mind. He enjoyed his role in the business and the opportunity it gave him to visit the continent but he could never see himself settling down to running the business as a full-time occupation and on no account did he wish to be the source of discomfort to his uncle. He turned the chance down as tactfully as he could but making it clear he was happy to continue in his present role. His grandfather took it well and refrained from mentioning it again. There was also concern from all of the family in England as to how Harry's family was managing in New Zealand.

The harsh impacts of the Depression were felt everywhere in the early 1930s and even remote corners of the world like New Zealand were badly affected. Harry received a long letter from his father. Following the usual family news, he went on to say how hard these times were for families. For Victoria, David and Jack, who had recently married, life was tolerable despite the fact the price for agricultural exports had fallen nearly 40 per cent. They could live off the property and were never short of food. The house could be kept warm and there was always enough for necessities. His father hated the Prime Minister George Forbes. He had met him when Forbes captained the Canterbury rugby team and thought it 'no training for a Prime Minister'.

"What a fool!" he wrote. "A young fellow in the Government reckons the only reason Forbes graduated from primary school was that the school burned down. He has cut our public works programmes, cut wages and lowered pensions. You will hardly believe that we had riots in both Auckland and Wellington. There has never been such a thing happen in New Zealand before, but all Forbes has done is call in the police to smash up the crowds.

I hope things are better where you are but I read that in fact this is not so. May it be that the family at least can keep their head above water."

It was shortly after this that Harry received a call from Peter Houston who was about to return to Australia. "Harry, how are you? Listen, I'm heading back home soon but the May Balls are on in Cambridge next month. Why don't we get Rupert and some popsies and go? God knows when we'll get another chance. What do you think?" Their last May Ball had been at the end of their university life and they remembered the tango fiasco. It was swiftly agreed they would get together a table and it didn't take Harry long to decide to invite Kathleen. The night was as memorable as they had expected. They found themselves a table for six. Rupert had invited his cousin, the daughter of a retired colonel, full of fun and anxious to enjoy some laughter in those gloomy days, and Peter an Australian girl, in the middle of the obligatory visit to relatives in 'the old country'. Peter had made an art form of disconcerting the 'Poms' as he insisted on calling them, by telling gruesome stories of the deadly Australian fauna. Taipans that could kill you in a minute, funnel web spiders, blue-ring octopus, small and deadly, great white sharks and so on. His Australian girlfriend tried to stop him but Kathleen was enthralled. "Barbarians from a barbarian land," was all Rupert would say, but Harry enjoyed seeing Kathleen's wide-eyed interest.

Later she said to him, "Of course it's not true, is it?" He confirmed that actually it was all, or mostly all, true. She wagged a finger at him. "I know that Australian is pulling my leg but don't you start."

The champagne flowed, Depression or not, and three bands kept them going until the sky started to lighten. Harry gazed at Kathleen, amazed that she should ever have agreed to be his guest. As the sun rose they grabbed a bottle of champagne and two glasses and found their way down to the Cam where Harry was pretty sure he knew there was a punt hidden. Sure enough, there it was under the foliage of a willow. Harry scrambled down the river bank, swept Kathleen up in his arms and deposited her in the back of the punt. He pushed off from the bank and they lay back and allowed themselves to drift out and away down the river turning slowly in the current.

Kathleen travelled back to London with him and he took the opportunity to introduce her to his aunt and uncle and then his grandparents. He took her to the station and helped her aboard the evening train to Manchester. "So, shall I see you again soon or are you buzzing off somewhere more mysterious than London?" she asked him as the train departed.

"If I could arrange it, it would be tomorrow," he replied.

She looked at him with an ironic smile. "Hmm" was all she added.

Not long after the ball was over, Peter called Harry in London to say his goodbyes. He was leaving from Southampton at the weekend. They chatted for a few minutes before Peter said, "By the way Harry, great popsy. Wouldn't let her out of my sight if she was mine. Don't mean to intrude but anyway, that's my opinion. Anyway, if you're heading home come through Sydney. I'll introduce you to the sharks at Bondi. You'll love it."

Harry knew what he wanted to do but couldn't quite pluck up the courage to do it until he received a letter from Kathleen saying how much she had enjoyed the ball and suggesting that she was missing him and hoped to see him soon. Harry unburdened himself to his aunt and received her blessing.

Harry and Kathleen were married six months later in the Church at Stockport, near Manchester. Harry chose Rupert as his best man and Peter sent effusive greetings from down under.

Harry's parents could not make the trip. It would have meant staying away from Earnslaw for too long in those difficult times, so Harry and Kathleen decided to make their honeymoon a trip to New Zealand, stopping of course in Sydney to see Peter on the way through.

Peter was as good as any host could be. They travelled on a boat on the harbour, visited the zoo so that they could see the deadly creatures Peter had described, plus of course the more common and less harmful marsupials, lunched at the Royal Sydney Yacht Squadron across the water from the city and even swam in the crystal waters of Fairy Bower at Manly, keeping close to the shore to avoid the sharks and peering down as they trod on the sand to ensure no blue-ring octopuses were lurking. Kathleen had never seen water like that in Fairy Bower, so clear she could stand with it up to her chin and see her pink toenails as if there was no water intervening. The sun too seemed to be different to the sun at home; it was burning hot and direct so that a broad-brimmed hat was necessary whenever she ventured out. She found the Australians she met an interesting mixture. Either they were a sort of ersatz form of the English at home, socially conscious and seemingly keen not to be thought of as ill bred, or they were direct with a sardonic sense of black humour and just a hint of belligerence about the Poms, even whilst straining to be polite. She found she liked the latter better and especially once she started to return serve.

They caught the steamer across the Tasman Sea and endured only some modest bad weather by the standards of the Tasman, one of the roughest stretches of water in the world, but they were more than happy when it was time to disembark. It was a slightly dishevelled pair eventually greeted by Harry's parents on the dockside in Wellington but they soon brightened up and even enjoyed the short ferry ride across Cook Strait to the South

Island and their journey down the east coast to Christchurch and on to Earnslaw. As Harry had hoped, his mother and Kathleen, although they had dissimilar upbringings, had the same practical uncomplicated approach to life and got on well. They tackled things head-on and were blissfully unaware of how bluntly they could state their position should they be asked. Kathleen was astounded by the beauty of the country and the sense of freedom and space the Canterbury Plains provided. She stood quietly with Harry and watched the sun go down behind the Alps and understood exactly why his heart belonged here.

After a week, Harry announced he was taking her off on a special trip. He wouldn't tell her more except that it would involve some serious hiking. Victoria helped Kathleen with her outfit, sensible and capable of protecting her against any weather and she found a suitable pair of boots for walking. They journeyed overnight to the western end of Lake Wakatipu where Harry had booked accommodation at the only inn available. Over dinner he explained to Kathleen that in the morning they would be joined by a mountain guide and ride as far as possible up to the head of the Dart River and then up to the lower reaches of the mountains. When they could go no further on horseback, the horses would be taken back and they would walk over a mountain track into Milford Sound – as Harry described it, one of the wonders of the earth. They would have to carry their own food and would be sleeping in bushmen's huts on bedding of tree fern. Kathleen was initially quite alarmed. "What if it's too much for me? I'm not sure how far I can walk. How can we get out if there is an accident?" Between them, the guide and Harry calmed her down and they set off with their guide, a taciturn local with a weathered face almost entirely obscured by a bushy ginger beard and a large hat which he tipped to her in a gesture of minimum recognition.

Harry had been as good as his word and, for the first few days the weather was fortunately kind. As they climbed and made their way further west, the bush became gradually thicker, up to the snow line, at which point it thinned out and the views became breathtaking. As they approached the highest pass on the track, the weather started to deteriorate fast. The wind rose and was accompanied by fierce bursts of rain. They struggled on, heads down, until they reached the head of the pass, marked by a cairn of local rocks. At this point, the full fury of the storm blew sleet horizontally in their faces and the temperature dropped to near freezing. Harry walked in front of Kathleen to shield her from the blast and offered to carry her backpack as well as his own. She could see he was enjoying all this and, refusing to concede any discomfort, insisted she could manage perfectly well.

An hour later the weather was worse if anything. Kathleen was cold and wet and starting to find it hard to put one foot in front of another. Then she slipped and landed hard on her bottom. "Bugger!" Harry looked around and burst out laughing. "Why did you bring me here? I hate it, I'm freezing and sore." Refusing help she rose unsteadily to her feet and took a few deep breaths and with a muttered thanks took the proffered walking stick that the guide had hastily fashioned. She readjusted her pack, brushed her damp hair out of her eyes and smiled wanly at Harry." You are such an old romantic. What more could a girl desire."

With the aid of another walking stick fashioned for Harry they descended nearly five hundred or so feet very rapidly, finding their way over boulders and through the streams that had suddenly appeared from nowhere. Eventually they reached their destination, a small hut, which fortunately had a large fireplace and a stock of dry wood. Kathleen felt the warmth gradually seeping through her wet clothes and after a hot meal, found herself falling asleep mid-sentence. Her back ached and her feet and bottom were sore but she knew it had been a great day.

Harry had to shake Kathleen awake the next morning but the sun was out and their guide explained that after a short climb over a saddle it would be down hill, through a long glacial valley, until in the late afternoon they would reach another hut. Kathleen, her bottom sore and bruised from her fall, struggled a little up the barely formed track to the saddle but on reaching the top they looked down on a deep valley. They wound down the path and then made their way along the river bank following a barely discernible track until eventually it was time for lunch. The guide boiled the billy for tea and Harry investigated the rock pools to see if he could spot any of the tiny native crayfish. Kathleen decided to make her way to a small patch of stunted trees to see what toilet facilities she could fashion. Having found a suitable branch to perch on, she was startled to hear a low scratching amongst the dry bracken. Peering anxiously into the undergrowth she was astonished to see, peering back at her like the Cheshire Cat, a whiskery face. Slowly it assembled itself into the strangest bird she had ever seen. Large and rotund, it had a short stubby beak surrounded by mutton chop whiskers and two beady eyes with which it contemplated her soulfully. Its plumage was bright iridescent green interspersed with streaks of brown so that it blended almost invisibly into its background of leaves and branches. It seemed not the least put out by her presence and advanced slowly towards her, waddling slightly on sturdy feet, stopping every so often to investigate the ground for food. She rearranged her clothes and stood feeling foolishly that perhaps she should introduce herself to this local resident so happy to welcome her.

When she returned to the lunch spot, the guide explained that she had bumped into a rare local resident, the kakapo or owl parrot. "This evening as the sun goes down, we'll stop and listen for their breeding call. It's a strange sound indeed. They used to be everywhere up here but predators and men have devastated their numbers. They're too trusting for their own good and the Maori like them for their meat and feathers. They're going the way of the moas, I shouldn't wonder." That evening as they sat watching the sun disappearing over the ridge line they did indeed hear in the distance the "boom, boom" of the bird calls like some ghostly drum reverberating out of the valley floor.

The next morning the sun was out again and all three woke enthusiastic about finishing the last stage down into Milford. Overnight, the rain had filled the streams so waterfalls cascaded everywhere, one of which they took the opportunity to stand under, enjoying the mountain water crashing down over them. Harry insisted on inspecting her bruise, now purple and blue. "That iced water will fix it." He wisely resisted the idea of giving it a pat.

Kathleen took a short stroll looking for a sunny patch to sit in for a few minutes. She emerged onto a small open platform which led to the edge of a precipice overlooking a valley floor, hundreds of feet below. In the foot of the valley, a river tumbled too far away to be heard. On the other side of the river, the cliffs climbed vertically up again and then flattened out into a series of rolling hills and peaks covered by a dense forest, or 'bush', as New Zealanders liked to call it. It seemed to stretch on into infinity and only the occasional bird call disturbed the calm. Her attention was caught by flashes of crimson from the native mistletoe flowering in the tops of trees. Kathleen sat enjoying the sun and wondered to herself if any human had ever been here before. She could see why Harry deeply loved this place but wondered what she would do if he decided he wanted to live back in country New Zealand. How would she cope with such a remote place and so very far from home, from family and everything familiar to her? She though it was unlikely; he was too entrenched in his German and in the excitement of what he clearly perceived to be the life and death struggle for ascendency currently being waged in Europe. But of course, she reflected, if he made that decision one day then she would be with him and part of her could see that it might actually be a great adventure.

It was early afternoon before they finally emerged besides the still waters of the Sound. Harry had been correct; with its mountains rising vertically out of the dark waters, cascading waterfalls and strands of ancient trees, Milford was a special place.

The one thing Harry had forgotten to mention was the local sandflies. Scenting fresh English blood, they attacked Kathleen at every opportunity. She covered up as best she could, shielding her face with a muslin cloth, but they still managed to get through and pretty soon she had the most irritating bites she had ever suffered. The guide tried to help with some soothing cream and Harry puffed on his pipe to dissuade them, but she was not altogether sorry when the steamer arrived to take them out of the Sound. The sight of the dolphins jumping around the boat was so much more enjoyable freed from the assault of the sandflies. They rolled about in the wake, turning this way and that, and looking back boldly at the passengers crowded on the stern rail. Over towards the shore, some penguins were swimming along placidly, diving for fish and then reappearing to swallow their catch. A few seals basked on a rock in the sun. The black waters of the Sound reflected the surrounding peaks, stretching straight up vertically from the water's edge, the reflection broken and then reconnecting as the ship made its way steadily out towards the sea.

They were back in England before Kathleen's sandfly bites

finally began to fade. They quickly found themselves a small flat in Beaufort Street in Chelsea where, if you leaned far enough over the veranda, you could glimpse the Thames. They both loved the flat and only minor bickering occurred over where to put Harry's cherished picture of the All Blacks' George Nepia, finally grudgingly settling on the corridor. Kathleen soon found a job working with children at Guys Hospital and Harry was within comfortable range of the company's office, which for now he had joined.

Harry found the job hardly tested his skills. He enjoyed the visits to the continent, Paris and Germany, to keep up the contacts with the suppliers. But in truth business was slow and the pay was hardly enough to allow them to make do without Kathleen's contribution, even though they were not extravagant spenders.. Harry was in fact quite bored by the day-to-day life of the firm and it was therefore only a matter of time before Harry and Rupert found themselves together again. Rupert enquired about his business activities. "I hear you are in Europe quite frequently, especially Germany. Your German skills must be immensely helpful. Can I ask you, do you have any time or inclination to perhaps do a little work for us? In truth we are very concerned about what is happening in Germany at the moment. There is constant social and political upheaval. They have had unemployment and inflation, which has nearly destroyed the middle class, and a near Bolshevik revolution so it is no surprise that most Germans are looking for some form of Messiah to lead them out of their troubles. However, we are very concerned that the Messiah they choose may be this chap Hitler and restoring Germany's military pride may be the way he chooses to achieve it. We would really appreciate it if you would be able to provide another set of eyes and ears."

Harry was delighted with the idea, which was of much more

interest to him than buying bits and pieces for the business, so he readily agreed and it was quickly arranged that he would receive a small stipend for his trouble and would report back to Rupert each time he returned from a trip.

CHAPTER 10

It was February 1933 and, having enjoyed a family Christmas and New Year in Manchester with Kathleen's family, Harry was now comfortably accommodated in Herr Professor Landau's house in Heidelberg. Kathleen had stayed behind with her family for a few days before her work called her back to London. In any case she was now a few months pregnant and didn't fancy Heidelberg in February. She was also conscious that Harry would not want to speak English if he could avoid it during his trip.

The Professor was an old friend going back to the days when Harry had been a student visiting Germany for his language studies. It was easy for him to accept the invitation from him and his wife, especially since the Professor's home was a snug haven away from the icy temperatures that had frozen the Neckar River. Harry rather enjoyed walking through the town rugged up against the cold. Stalactites of ice hung from the gutters, and the snow crunched beneath his boots. His breath misted in the air and the grey sky melded with the tops of the surrounding hills gleaming dully in the sunless sky. There was the added attraction of seeing the Professor's two daughters, Rebecca and Hannah, who had grown into young women since he had first known them as gawky teenagers, wearing their hair in ridiculous plaits. He was nearing the end of his week-long stay, and had already made most of his scheduled calls on suppliers, or potential suppliers of goods for the family firm. He had also been paying close heed to the intense political debate occupying the citizens of Germany at the time. Adolf Hitler had recently been appointed Chancellor by President Hindenberg and a feeling of Nazi triumphalism permeated the daily lives of ordinary Germans. It was a feeling of optimism tinged with fear. Herr Professor, as Harry always addressed his host, arrived home from the university and announced he would be hosting a small luncheon party in favour of an old and honoured family friend who would be visiting on Sunday. Harry accepted with good grace and thought no more about it. On the Sunday Harry dressed in his best dark suit and, knowing Professor Landau's attitude to punctuality went down to the dining room at 12pm sharp where he was introduced to the other guests. The table was set for ten and, so far, there were nine people assembled; Harry, the Professor and his wife and two daughters, a couple who were colleagues of the Professor at the university, and the neighbours from across the street who were fellow members of the local Jewish community and whom Harry had met briefly before. Drinks were served and the Professor was explaining that, unfortunately, it appeared that the guest of honour's arrival from Berlin had been somewhat delayed, when the doorbell rang and a new arrival was admitted. The dining room doors swung back and a small dapper figure in naval uniform strode in. The Professor and the new arrival greeted each other warmly, then suddenly his eye fell on Harry, who had been standing transfixed. The Professor looked back and forward as the two men continued to stare. "Surely you two recognise each other?" he asked. "Am I correct?"

The naval gentleman was the first to react. "My God, it's Harry Douglas is it not? My rum and black companion from Punta Arenas."

Harry stepped forward, "And I recognise Felix Zylko from Cracow if I'm not mistaken. You have joined the German navy, I see." The other guests watched fascinated as this unlikely tale unfolded.

"Well, not Zylko actually. I must apologise for that subterfuge. You see I was actually the intelligence officer from the cruiser *Dresden*, which you will remember was in the Punta Arenas harbour at the time. My real name is Lieutenant Canaris. It's a long story but I could hardly have introduced myself to you as German if I wanted to proceed about my business unremarked. I hope you will forgive me but it did nothing to dim my admiration for your response to the little fracas that occurred." Harry was overwhelmed by a mixture of emotions but quickly remembered how he had enjoyed the evening and, given his later activities in the war, he could well understand how Canaris had needed to disguise himself. The guests clamoured to know more of the circumstances of this unusual meeting and Canaris swiftly explained, giving what Harry felt was an exaggerated description of his part in defusing the fight.

The guests sat down and conversation soon returned to more general topics. There was much to discuss. The Reichstag fire had taken place only two weeks before and rumours were sweeping Germany about who was responsible. "It seems it was the communists," suggested the Professor, "some unemployed Dutchman trying to make a name for himself. But now the whole Communist Party has been blamed and their delegates will lose their seats. Conveniently, this will give the Nazis a majority in the Reichstag. Well at least the Jews are not being blamed and thankfully this Dutchman is not Jewish." Canaris nodded his general agreement to this view and when pressed by one of the guests, added that Germany would have to deal with this communist menace; there could be no compromise with such an ideology.

Harry politely asked the Professor for his broader views on the political situation, knowing all too well his likely reaction. The Professor frowned. "We are worried for Germany and we are worried for Jews. There are many signs of increasing pressure – even in our wonderful old university, such a bastion of freedom, we are being discriminated against. My old colleague in the Law Department has mysteriously lost his job and we cannot ask why. The unemployed are everywhere and increasingly we are blamed for the most ridiculous things. There is more and more violence against us and I worry when Rebecca or the girls go out that they will be insulted or worse. What does the navy think, Wilhelm?" Canaris hesitated.

"The navy is a professional military service Herr Professor. We do not engage in politics but it is safe to say I doubt there would be many Nazis in the navy."

Both Canaris and Harry were bursting to know what had befallen the other after their encounter. However, it was hardly possible to dominate the conversation on this topic, which was likely to be of marginal interest to the other guests. As they stood up to depart, Canaris came over to Harry. "I would really like to know what happened to you Harry. I have another day in Heidelberg. Would you be able to meet me for lunch; just the two of us? I am burning with curiosity as to what you finally did." Harry was equally curious. A million questions began to surface in his mind so they both agreed that Canaris would arrange a suitable meeting place through the Professor and they would indeed meet the following day at the same time.

By the next morning the Professor had arranged a venue at his Club and given Harry instructions on how to find it. "By the way," he added, "Herr Canaris has an important role in Naval Intelligence in Berlin. It would perhaps be wise to keep his friendship with the family to yourself. It would not help him if it were known that he was such a close friend to a family of Jews, or even perhaps that he is friendly with foreigners."

They met promptly at noon. A table had been arranged in a discreet corner of the dining room and Canaris took time to study the wine list with care before ordering a particularly rare Bordeaux from what was clearly an excellent cellar. Harry had had time to think overnight and realised he really knew nothing about Canaris but that, given his current major interests, he should tread carefully. Quickly he glossed over his own activities during and after the war emphasising his humdrum role with the family business. Canaris, looking at him with particular attention, asked many questions. Finally, he commented that Harry had done pretty well to become a Major and went on, at Harry's request, to tell his own story.

The wine arrived, suitably decanted. Canaris took his time to judge the aroma and to taste it carefully, giving the same concentration to the wine as he had given to Harry's story. Finally, and to the evident relief of the wine waiter he pronounced it excellent. He then waited for their glasses to be filled before beginning his tale.

"Of course the night I met you I had caught up with some of our many informers in Punta Arenas. We knew that under the neutrality rules we had to leave the next day and we knew the British cruisers were close on our tail. I had met with a German subject who was also the captain of a fishing boat. We were trying to work out whether we could escape east to the Atlantic or west to the Pacific. Either way we would be spotted in the Straits of Magellan and be caught and destroyed as we emerged."

Canaris went on to explain how the *Dresden* had hidden out in the bays around the Straits and had then tried to flee up the coast, how it had been found by the British cruisers, eventually scuttled and the crew interned. "We were first interned on a Norddeutscher Lloyd passenger liner in Valparaiso but after protests by the British we were brought to the small island of Quiriquina, north of Coronel. There was quite a substantial German community there and they looked after us well, so most of the crew were more than content with their lot. However, I determined to escape if I could. I had to gain permission from Captain Ludecke since my escape would affect the treatment of those who remained, but he eventually gave his blessing. Escape was easy. The Chilean fishermen would take you to the mainland for twenty pesos.

"So in August 1915, using a map torn from a school atlas and my Spanish language skills, which are better than my English, I found my way to a German family on the mainland. Here I changed my clothes and, dressed as a pedlar, my face partly covered by a cap and all my belongings in a canvas bag, I set off with the aim of reaching Buenos Aires. Partly walking and partly on horseback, I went first south almost 300 miles to Osorno and then another 300 over the Andes to Neuquen in Argentina, and finally 600 miles by train. After eight months, nearly starving and with my clothes in tatters, I finally reached Buenos Aires. The city, while dominated by the British, had plenty of German residents and I managed to locate a cousin of von Bulow, the German ambassador in Rome. They were more than willing to help and over a period we managed to bury Canaris and create a grieving Chilean widower, Reed Rosas, who was trying to return to Europe to inherit property in the Netherlands. I bought a ticket on the Dutch Lloyd steamer *Frisia* and enjoyed myself immensely ingratiating myself with the English passengers. I said many prayers of thanks to my English tutor from Cambridge who had taught me so well the English idiom. By the time we reached Falmouth, I was everyone's favourite widower and bridge partner. I helped the English naval officers interview the other passengers before we were allowed to leave for Rotterdam and from there, with a Chilean passport, it was not too difficult to return to Germany. I was soon back in the navy at Kiel and promoted to Kapitanlieutenant. Shall I go on? I don't wish to bore you."

"Do go on. What happened next?"

"I was transferred to naval intelligence and, with my Spanish, sent to Spain to set up a network to support our growing U-boat activities. I set up quite a network I can tell you, but in the end my presence became known to British and French Intelligence services and I had to get out. The borders were closed to me so in the end it was agreed I should rendezvous off the coast with one of our submarines. This proved extremely difficult. I laid low for a while in Cartegena and the first attempt to pick me up by submarine failed. In the end I, with some other Germans, enlisted the help of a Spanish sailing boat. It was arranged that we were to rendezvous with *U-35* on the night of 20 September off the lighthouse at Cape Tinoso. For two hours we made the morse recognition signal, with dimmed light to seaward, but with no result. As it turned out, *U-35* had come close under the lights of Tinoso and had managed to pick out our recognition signal from the many fishing boats. They stood off, repeating the morse K signal, but we failed to see it. Finally, I saw an enemy trawler stop and come towards us. We made course for Mazaron going slowly and hoping they would lose interest in us, but as it came closer and it was clear it was under French command we hid under the sand ballast inside the boat. The trawler stopped on our stern but saw only the Spanish crew and pulled away. We returned to our rendezvous and fortunately sighted the periscope off our stern so we showed our red recognition pennant. *U-35* surfaced and almost before the water had finished cascading from her decks, we were aboard and we made course for Cattaro (Kotor) at that time under Austrian administration. I was awarded an Iron Cross for my adventures. This was late in 1915. By the end of 1917 I had become a fully trained U-boat Commander and I was given command of *UC-27* and sent to lay mines in the Mediterranean. I have to say the boat was one of the most mechanically unreliable vessels I have ever been involved with. What a crate! Thank goodness that eventually, in 1918, I was given *U-34*, a much better boat. I am afraid to say I sank quite a few tons of British shipping in this period. In March 1918 I was ordered back to Kiel to work up *U-128* and had terrible problems off Norway. We were very lucky to make it back to the Mediterranean in one piece. The boat was under repair in Cattaro until all U-boats were ordered back to Kiel. I don't know how we survived the return trip. We were depth-charged and fired at trying to get through the Straits of Gibraltar and eventually I knew I had to surface where the patrol boats and searchlights were waiting to greet us. I heard the screws of a ship overhead and decided to surface behind it and by luck there was a destroyer so close it screened me from the patrol boats and searchlights. Eventually we slipped away into the Atlantic and, as you know, the Armistice was signed on 11 November 1918. We naval officers were bitter, I can tell you, and as we headed to Kiel we heard there had been a revolution by elements of the navy in Kiel. A revolution! It was unthinkable. We felt we had been betrayed by both the Kaiser and the communists. Many of us never thought we would see Germany recover from such a blow.

Eleven U-boats sailed into harbour flying the Imperial ensign and the home-coming pennant, and we swore that the red flag would never be hoisted on our boats. So, that's my story until the end of the Great War at least."

There was a long silence while Harry tried to digest all he had heard. He sat back in his chair. "Well, what can I say? That is truly an amazing story. I never suspected for a minute, way back in Punta Arenas, that you were not what you said you were. I should have thought about it, especially with the *Dresden* in port, but I was engaged in a great adventure and tended to just accept whatever was in front of me. In any event it is great to meet up with you again. It's funny. Although I served in the British forces on the Western front and was wounded I can't feel hatred for Germany. I think if I am honest both sides were to blame."

Canaris agreed. "You know in the German navy we had so much admiration for the traditions of the British Navy. We tried to emulate it. I once heard our Admiral admonish a German diplomat for showing insufficient respect for the deaths of so many British sailors at the Battle of Coronel. So now we have Hitler to revive Germany's crushed spirit and give us some certainties in a sea of troubles. What do you make of that?"

"I can understand how the Nazi Party has come to power but I have to say it deeply troubles me. I must say it is more than a little disturbing to see the unrest in Germany at the moment. I am rather worried for the Professor and his family. The treatment of Jews is unacceptable, if you don't mind a foreigner being so bold. But what is your opinion?"

"Some of my colleagues think that Hitler is a good thing. They think the communist threat is real, that Hitler will control them and we will control Hitler. Many of the communists are Jewish. They are not helping themselves but nevertheless I accept your rebuke. These acts of violence are not the acts of civilised people."

Harry hesitated. "And how do you think this will this develop, if I may ask?"

Canaris sat back in his chair. "Perhaps my colleagues are right and we will let these people do the hard work for us and then we will take back power. But they may have underestimated these Nazis. I sense they might be more ruthless than us. We are still gentlemen like the British. We share that British sense of duty and that includes honesty and fair play, but we are playing with a group that acknowledges no rules except power."

The two men fell silent for a minute, sipping the last of the wine. Canaris continued. "Germany needs to restore her pride. The Versailles Treaty humiliated us and, like you British, we are a proud people. We feel we were betrayed and the rumours that have spread about the Jewish role in the peace process do not help their cause. There are five million unemployed in Germany. Hitler is offering jobs and persuading them it is the fault of the Jews, not the Kaiser, that Germany lost the last war. Under the circumstances, a good strategy, wouldn't you say?"

Harry could only agree. He thanked Canaris for an excellent lunch and they to meet if they could whenever Harry was visiting Germany. Canaris's car and driver arrived and he offered Harry a lift back to the Professor's house but Harry decided he needed a walk, notwithstanding the hostile weather. He had much to think about.

Early the next morning, Harry left the house to walk a few hundred yards to a small tobacconist, which he knew had copies of *The Times*. As he rounded the corner he was confronted by the sight of the tobacconist, a tiny Jewish man in a rumpled cardigan, lying on the floor with his hands over his head. Two Brown Shirts were on top of him, one holding him while the other kicked him in the stomach. The contents of the shop were strewn everywhere and the front counter was tipped on its side. Harry shouted at the top of his voice for the assailants to let go. They looked at him in astonishment. Perhaps because he was large or a foreigner they let their victim go, stood up and, aiming one last kick, turned and left pausing only to stare at Harry and promising to return. Harry helped the proprietor unsteadily to his feet and sat him down on his chair. His wife appeared, even smaller and more bent than her husband. She fussed over him as together they thanked Harry for his intervention. He spent a few minutes helping them tidy up and to lift the counter back into place. He found a copy of *The Times,* which they refused to let him pay for, and he wished them good morning.

Harry reported the morning's events to the Professor. As the Professor listened, Harry was suddenly struck by how thin he had become. His jacket hung from his shoulders as if it were two sizes too big for him, with sleeves dangling below his wrists. His knotted tie left a large gap between his collar and neck and his baggy trousers were tightened around his hips by a belt pulled to its last buckle hole. "We will try to help them but it is getting increasingly dangerous. One of my colleagues has been expelled and other Jewish staff members have reported intimidation and violence. Many Jews, within the University or just in the town, have been murdered or have disappeared. Unfortunately, we are the focus of attention of one of our graduates now high in the Nazis Party, one Joseph Goebbels. He was never originally anti-Semitic, but now he is constantly on our backs. We don't know what will happen to Germany. The violence simply increases and it is hard to know what outcome there can be that is anything but bad for Jews and bad for the great traditions of academic freedom in our university."

Harry felt helpless to do more than utter a few words of meaningless sympathy and silently gave thanks that he would soon be leaving this oppressive atmosphere of threat for the still-open society of England.

As soon as Harry reached London, he called Rupert. They met beside the Serpentine and although it was cold, there was at least a wintry sun to warm their backs as they strolled along the path towards Knightsbridge. "So how was Germany this time? Must have been pretty dramatic I suspect." Harry filled Rupert in on all that had occurred in Berlin, including the Reichstag fire. "We think the Nazis organised the whole thing," replied Rupert. "It's perfect. Blame the communists, suspend their deputies and pass legislation restricting Democratic freedoms. It's a bad business. So, anything else of interest?" Harry hesitated. He knew he should mention his extraordinary meeting with Canaris, but then there was the Professor's request for discretion and this curious feeling of comradeship he felt for the man. He changed the subject and they strolled a little further while they chatted about some local turf wars going on in the office.

Finally, Harry made up his mind. "There was something."
"What?"
Harry cleared his throat. "I had lunch with Canaris."
Rupert turned to look at him. "You did what?"
Harry went on to explain the details of his original meeting with Canaris way back in 1914 in Punta Arenas and then the subsequent coincidence of the lunch together with all the events of Canaris's life up until then. Rupert listened without comment until the end. They were outside the Hyde Park Hotel before Harry had finished.

"Harry, we need to see Sir Stewart about this immediately. We both know how important this could be."

Harry found himself in Sir Stewart's office the next afternoon. He retold his story as to how this strange association had come about and, as Rupert had done, Sir Stewart listened in silence.

"Remarkable," was his immediate response. He took a cigarette out of a silver box on his desk. "Did he tell you how many British ships he had sunk when he was a submarine Commander?"

"He mentioned it rather regretfully, as if it was a necessary burden of war."

"Did he now? And did he mention how much trouble he is causing for us, and the French, in Spain? Or how many spies he is running in England at the moment? You know about the *Dresden* story but you won't know how close Jacky Fisher came to sacking Sturdee over the whole debacle. In any event, it is extremely important you maintain this friendship, Harry. Canaris is right in the middle of the web of relationships that holds power in Germany at the moment and obviously we need to know all we can about this."

There was a short pause whilst a few pleasantries were exchanged and tea and biscuits were served. Harry was surprised to see through the rather grimy window that the morning clouds had departed and the day had turned bright and sunny outside. Somehow the sight of sunshine lifted his mood notwithstanding his conviction that things in Europe were about to get a whole lot worse.

Some hours later Harry emerged, better informed about why Canaris was so important. He had some qualms about using a relationship he regarded as a friendship, but Sir Stewart quickly disabused him of any feeling of reluctance he harboured. "I can assure you Harry, Canaris is far too well-informed not to have realised that you are not in Germany just to buy bits and pieces for the family company. He will use you as much as you use him and you must remember that. He has direct access to Hitler and to all the senior Nazis but he plays his own game, does Wilhelm, very much his own game. I want to know every squeak you get out of him. Is that clear?"

For no particular reason, Harry wondered if the rumours that Sir Stewart's father was actually Edward VII were true, but quickly dismissed them as irrelevant.

"So does that make him friend or foe?" asked Harry.

"Ah, if only things were that simple, but they are not in the least bit simple. We know he hates the communists after his experience with the revolt in Kiel. We know he was somehow involved in organising the murder of two high profile communists in South Germany in 1919. Karl Liebknicht and Rosa Luxemburg were leaders of the Spartacists, a communist collection who at one stage were actually manning the barricades with machine guns. They were in the custody of the military when they were mysteriously shot down and Rosa's body thrown into the Landwehr Canal. Canaris sat on the subsequent enquiry and the accused got off with ridiculously light sentences. Subsequently Canaris has even been accused of organising the whole thing. He also has been accused of complicity in murders following the Kiel uprising. Nothing has ever been proved. So we know what he doesn't like but what does he make of Hitler? We must make sure we know the answer."

CHAPTER 11

When Harry returned to the office, there was a message asking him to call in on his grandfather as soon as possible. He found him seated in his favourite chair studying his book on chess strategies. Although the day was warm, he had a rug draped over his knees. He greeted Harry warmly. "So you've just returned from Germany for the firm? It seems only a few months since the previous visit." Harry replied that there were some opportunities in the area that he had needed to follow up. "How is the situation for the Jews there, Harry? I hear that it is not good at all. The Jewish community in London does what it can but we have limited resources and immigration is not straightforward."

"You are right, grandfather. It has deteriorated every time I visit. There are more bashings, arrests, violence of every kind. Whole families are being deported to camps and the rumours from those camps are chilling."

His grandfather was silent for a minute. "You know I am not so well at the moment Harry. The doctors are not exactly sure what's wrong at the moment but one must be prepared. In any case, I am lucky to have lived such a long and full life and I have no regrets, but would hate to leave your grandmother on her own. I know you will always keep watch on her but there is another thing. I would like to ask you to promise me you will always have a strong regard for the Jews. I know I am not in the least religious and that you and your family have had little contact with Jewish society. I should know that – I deliberately brought your father up like that and he did the same for you. It was to give you a proper opportunity in New Zealand and I am more than satisfied it was the right thing."

It did not trouble Harry to give such an assurance although he hardly thought his grandfather's death looked in any way imminent. His grandfather continued. "I know your mother has some reservations about the Jewish connections even though she is careful to keep them to herself. We are all victims of our education and parentage so it is hardly surprising. I am very fond of her as you know but we all need to remember our history. You would not be aware of the many kindnesses your grandmother and I received from the Jewish community, especially when we arrived in London knowing next to nobody. We originally lived in Bethnall Green, within the sound of the Bow Bells. There were as many Jews as Cockneys and both groups took us into their community as if we had been born there. I feel I need to have this conversation with you in case my medical situation deteriorates and knowing you as I do, I am comforted with your assurances, which I know are not given lightly. Anyway enough of all this, come and help me with this chess problem. It is far too multifaceted for me at the moment." Harry and his grandfather chatted on until his grandmother returned from her shopping expedition at which time he changed the subject.

"So what have you two been chatting about?" she asked.

Grandfather looked up, "Nothing special, a bit of history." There was a silence and she looked at Harry, hesitated, and then said "History creates context, not obligations from one generation to another Harry. It's interesting context, that's all."

Harry laughed. "It's certainly interesting when you know as little as I do."

As Harry went to leave, his grandfather went over to the bookshelf and took down a well-worn leather-covered book, its title indecipherable. He used his sleeve to brush a little dust off its spine.

"This is a history of the Jewish people, Harry. I would like you to have it, but please read it some time, not all at once but in small pieces. It is as fascinating and tragic a tale as there is to tell. It will help you understand the context of our lives, as your grandmother chose to put it, and even of yours."

He shook Harry by the hand with a grip that belied the frailty of his frame. A rare letter arrived for Harry from his brother Jack. It was full of family news, wool prices, rugby results and bits and pieces about old friends and school mates. At the end, Jack put in a plea for Harry to go to Berlin for the 1936 Olympics.

"You remember my old friend from Timaru, Jack Lovelock? I'm not sure you ever met him. Anyway he's representing New Zealand in the 1500 metres and out here we reckon he might win. He'll have to beat the American, Cunningham, but the locals are saying his form's good. Harry, he'll need some friendly faces. I can't get there, but with your connections you should go. It will be a great spectacle anyway and I bet you could wangle some tickets."

Harry didn't take long to think about it; if he could get tickets he would go. But where to get them at this late date? He would ring Canaris and ask for help. Canaris was very happy to help and rang back within 24 hours to say that a seat close to the finish line had been organised for the 1500 metre race and he would nominate somewhere for them to meet to deliver the ticket in person. Naturally he would be in Berlin for the Games and would attend a number of events himself.

Harry arrived in Berlin the night before the event, having managed to organise a room in a small hotel on the outskirts of the city. He had let Canaris know where he was staying and they agreed to meet at a nearby café for a quick breakfast. Canaris was clearly very busy, so breakfast was indeed brief and they confined most of their talk to the Games and a little to the Landau family in Heidelberg. They were both worried about them and Harry formed the strong impression that Canaris was quietly keeping an eye on their safety. Canaris was driving his own car and was dressed in nondescript civilian clothes. He turned to Harry. "We need to be careful, you and I, Harry. Life becomes more dangerous in Germany and I doubt these Games will make it any more relaxed. You must take care. Too many visits in the pursuit of trade opportunities will be noticed. I'm sure you understand me. In the envelope is a number to call if you want to talk to me. Please use only that number and no other. If it changes, I will make sure you know." Harry thanked Canaris, and promised one day to return the favour if a suitable opportunity arose.

Canaris, as Harry had requested, dropped him in the city, which was some way from the stadium, with plenty of time on his hands. Harry decided to wander through the streets that had become familiar to him on his previous visits. It was with a rising sense of alarm that he looked around him at what the Nazis had created. The new buildings and streets had been built to a new scale, unlike anything he had previously experienced. Everywhere huge Nazi banners had been draped over every conceivable location, or papered onto walls and fences. Most of the crowd seemed to be in uniform, even the children, and everywhere military units were marching or engaging in elaborate drills. If the intention was to overwhelm visitors with the might of the Reich, its purpose had succeeded. As he looked about, he could see that not a speck of rubbish disturbed the pristine surroundings. A wagon pulled by an elderly draft horse passed by and, as it did so, it deposited a large pile of horse droppings on the road. From nowhere a youth, face despoiled by chronic acne and not more than 15, wearing a uniform which seemed far too grand for its purpose, bustled out and swept up the pile before it could offend the tourists or the group of Hitler Youth that were striding down the sidewalk, elbowing other Germans and visitors alike out of their path.

Harry set out down a small side street. He had been there before and remembered enjoying a café owned by a young Jewish immigrant, which served good food at great prices. As soon as he turned the corner, the silence struck him. There was no-one about. He looked around. The little shops were boarded up, many with broken windows. He found his café but it, too, was shut and a wooden plank was nailed across the broken front door. Above the lintel, a large yellow star was stuck to the wall. As he progressed further down the street, he saw more stars attached to doors or windows. The owners, obviously Jewish, had apparently vanished.

At the end of the street, he found himself standing outside what appeared to be a small art gallery in the midst of closing down. It boasted the inevitable yellow Jewish star. Inside he could see boxes and packages but some pictures still remained hanging on the wall. Some instinct made him go inside where he was confronted by an elderly Jewish gentleman with an enormous grey beard. Harry apologised for intruding and asked if the gallery was still open. "Not officially," was the reply, "but look if you want to, I must be gone by tomorrow, out after over twenty years. There are still some paintings upstairs, so have a look whilst I continue packing." Harry clambered up the stairs and there at the top as he emerged from the staircase was a painting looking down at him that he immediately recognised. It was in bright primary colours, simple, in cubist style, and of blue horses. He recognised the style instantaneously. It must be by Franz Marc. He looked closer and found that indeed it was and had been painted in 1913 here in Berlin. He stood looking at it for some time. It had the same compelling qualities as the wolves so long ago and seemed to him incredibly cheap but even so a bit much for his rather modest means. He was about to retreat when the Jewish gentleman stuck his head above the top of the staircase and saw what Harry was looking at. "It's marvellous, one of my favourites. Perhaps you would be interested to buy it?" Harry quickly told him of his encounter with Marc in Berlin in 1913 but reluctantly decided he could not really afford such an extravagance. The gallery owner scratched his head. "I am not usually given to bargaining. For me prices are what they say they are but as you see these are special circumstances. You can have it for half price provided you immediately take it out of Germany and care for it well. By the way, you may know there will be no more paintings by Franz Marc. He was killed at Verdun in 1916."

Harry quickly calculated that at that price it was actually something he could afford. He reflected that of course it would never be allowed to be set above the mantelpiece at Earnslaw while his father was alive, but on the other hand, and more importantly, Kathleen would be likely to approve. She had recently dragged him to a cubist exhibition in London. He knew that she loved the modern art styles that were everywhere and she would surely love this Marc.

The sale was quickly concluded and arrangements made

for the painting to be sent to London. He stepped out into the side street with a lift in his gait and the feeling he had acquired something they would both treasure but, more, which would always give him powerful memories of everything he had experienced in Germany over the years. He felt almost dizzy with happiness at such an unexpected windfall.

He was grateful to leave the empty shops and cafes behind and to find himself back in the main street but he was soon brought back to earth. Feeling he needed a drink he found a small bar and was surprised and pleased to find a solitary New Zealander, identifiable by his black shirt with a New Zealand flag sewn onto the breast pocket. It turned out that his companion, Bruce McLaren, was also from the South Island, a farmer and sport fanatic from Invercargill. The conversation naturally fell to the subject of Jack Lovelock and his chances in the 1500 metres against the great American, Cunningham. McLaren had spent the previous evening with a few members of the small New Zealand team. It turned out they were worried. Lovelock had a persistent problem of inflammation in his right knee, aggravated by his habit of training at night running through the streets of London. It kept flaring up but Arthur Porritt, the team captain, who was a surgeon at St Mary's Hospital in London with Sir Alexander Fleming, had been giving Lovelock injections of some sort of new treatment neither Bruce nor Harry had ever heard of. Bruce thought it might be called penicillin or some other wonder drug that Lovelock's fellow medicos had come up with; either way the Olympic 1500 metres final was no time for a sore knee.

The two men made their way to the stadium in plenty of time for the race and Harry entered through a gate between two towers. Back in October 1933, when Hitler was newly appointed Chancellor, the self-styled Fuehrer had visited the stadium. It was first built for the aborted 1916 Olympics and was now being expanded for the 1936 Olympics by the original architect's son, Werner March. The 1933 visit was low-key by Nazi standards. The group drove the 20 kilometres from the centre of Berlin in two armour-plated Mercedes. Hitler, in beige overcoat without hat, was accompanied by the usual SS bodyguards and by Wilhelm Frick, the Reich Sports Minister and Werner March, who was anxious to gain Hitler's approval for the enlargement. Hitler looked about him in silence. He turned to March. "Demolish it" he ordered, "a new one must be built with seating for 100,000. It will be the task of the nation. If Germany is to stand host to the entire world, her preparations must be complete and magnificent." The stadium was to be the central Nazis showpiece for German nationalism. If the intention had been to shock and awe visitors to the new Germany, thought Harry, Hitler had succeeded in every way. It was indeed awesome.

The atmosphere was electric. There were men in uniform everywhere. All branches of the German services were represented and Harry was deeply uncomfortable when he found his seat to be surrounded by Germans in SS uniform and to see huge swastikas displayed in every corner. The crowd, which must have been close to 100,000, was working itself into a frenzy. The event before the 1500 metres had been won by a Frenchman and he had refused to give the Nazi salute when accepting his medal. The crowd had erupted. A few bars of 'La Marseillaise' had been played but when the third-placed German had stepped up to the podium, the full martial pomp of 'Deutschland Uber Alles' rang out and the crowd leapt to its feet, arms stretched out in homage to the Fuhrer deafening the visitors with an increasing crescendo of "Sieg heil, Sieg heil." There had already been uproar over the success of the great American, Jesse Owens. It was clear the Hitler was not impressed by the achievements of the black American, the more so as it was clear he would be the winner of multiple gold medals before the Games were over.

Harry's neighbour was an SS officer in an immaculate dress uniform. He looked at Harry in surprise as Harry unfurled the small New Zealand flag he had acquired for the event. "So you are from New Zealand?" he enquired in English, "Welcome to Berlin. This should be a good contest. I think your fellow countryman is one of the favourites." Harry was not keen to chat but could hardly afford not to answer when the German enquired how he had managed to acquire his seat, since this area was reserved for German military.

Harry decided it might be better to stick to English. "Luckily I have some contacts at the British Embassy," he replied.

His companion looked at him hard again. "How curious." He hesitated but Harry did not respond. "Well I hope your man Lovelock can win since our German entries are not likely to. By the way I am Captain Schaefer." He put out his hand and Harry took it, hesitated and then introduced himself.

"Harry, Harry McMahon. I hope you are right, but Cunningham and the Italian are both threats."

Just at that moment Harry was relieved to hear a great roar break out as the 1500 metre runners entered the stadium. Harry could see Lovelock in his distinctive All Blacks' running outfit. He jumped to his feet and frantically waved the New Zealand flag. The athletes trotted past on their warm-up circuit and Harry saw Lovelock glance up in surprise to see his country's flag amongst a blanket of black uniforms and waving swastikas.

The 12 contestants moved towards the starting lines with the cheers of the Americans for the race favourite Glenn Cunningham, the 'Iron Horse of Kansas,' drowned out by the cheering and seig-heiling of the Nazis for their two contestants and for the Fuhrer, as he entered the stadium, filled to its maximum for this feature event, just after 4pm. Apart from Cunningham and the two Germans, there was Lovelock, the Englishman Cornes, Beccali of Italy, Ny of Sweden and five others. The diminutive Lovelock was easy to spot in his All Blacks' shorts and top, decorated with a capital 'N' for New Zealand. The race started quickly with Cornes and Beccali going to the front but to the joy of the German crowd, their hero Boettcher soon took the lead. Lovelock was tucked away in seventh. Cornes quickly regained the lead but was then passed by a surging Cunningham, with Lovelock shadowing him, looking frail against the bigger men but also relaxed. Passing the halfway mark, the Swede Ny staked his claim and he and Cunningham were matched stride for stride. Lovelock, still in third place, was content to watch the two battle it out shoulder to shoulder. The bell sounded with Ny and Cunningham still in the lead but then Lovelock, still nearly a lap from the finish broke all the tactical rules that might have been expected of him by surging to the lead. He was not a fast finisher and as Harry leaped to his feet shouting his support in a corner of his mind he was thinking, "No, no, you've gone too soon, Cunningham will mow you down."

At the 1200 metre mark Lovelock was still striding in front. Ny could not match the pace but the huge form of Cunningham was after him. The crowd went wild as the two battled towards the tape with Cunningham closing the gap but, just as it seemed he would pass, Lovelock glanced to his right, sensed the danger and kicked again. He won by just over a metre in 3.47.8. He and Cunningham broke the world record and the next three finishers broke the Olympic record. As many had predicted it was the greatest 1500 metre race ever. Harry was almost delirious with excitement and found himself punching the air. It was a small extra satisfaction to see the two Germans trail in well behind, tenth and twelfth. Captain Schaefer was effusively complimentary and nothing was mentioned about Lovelock's lack of a Nazi salute at the medal ceremony. Notwithstanding, Harry felt uncomfortable in his position and took the opportunity to depart after the next event.

His new friend congratulated him again as he left and wished him a safe trip home "to New Zealand, is it?"

"Oh yes" he replied, "to New Zealand. Eventually."

Harry had booked a flight out of Templehoff early the next morning so he decided to seek out some friendlier company for the evening. Bruce had told him the New Zealanders and Australians were frequenting a beer hall near the city centre which they were using as an unofficial base. Harry found it easily enough and it wasn't long before he found some kindred spirits to celebrate a truly great victory with numerous rounds of beer. Finally, he began to relax. He admitted to himself that his German companion had unnerved him, especially after the warning Canaris had given him. The night became noisier and noisier. The Germans sang drinking songs, the Australians responded with 'Waltzing Matilda'. Then Bruce turned up, ecstatic over Lovelock's win. "How about the sprint that far from home? Who knew he could do that?" The Kiwis launched into a patched up haka. Harry found himself with a couple of Australians who, like himself, had come over from London to support the Australian team. They laughed at the remorseless lack of humour of their German hosts. "Christ, you should have seen the opening ceremony. They released 20,000 doves over the stadium, 20,000. Some genius then started firing cannons in a salute. The bloody pigeons shat themselves, all over the athletes. We pissed ourselves. Mick here yelled out 'Crap on the Krauts' and we were nearly in a fight with a bloody bunch of them standing next to us. Jesus, we can't wait to get out of here."

Toasts were drunk to Lovelock, to the All Blacks, to kangaroos, to Bondi Beach and to anything else they could think of until

Harry realised it was definitely time to leave. In spite of the beer he had drunk, he looked around with more than usual care before he located a cab to take him home and therefore noticed a black Mercedes with two men in it standing with its motor idling as he climbed into the back seat. It did not improve his night's sleep to see the Mercedes still behind his cab as he disembarked at the hotel.

It was completely out of the blue that Harry received a call from Peter, his Australian friend from Cambridge days. "Hi Harry, I'm back in London. How about a beer and see if you can get Rupert awake enough to come along?" They agreed to meet the Scarsdale in Holland Park, scene of many a rowdy night in days past. Harry bought the first round and they wedged themselves at a corner table with a low room divider separating them from the main room. Since he guessed the conversation might stray into some highly sensitive areas, Harry took care to manoeuvre Rupert into a corner where his back would be towards the other customers. Rupert was the second son of Sir Jervis Winterbotham Baronet. Sir Jervis had been named after Admiral Jervis to commemorate the fact that a member of the family had been with the Admiral at the battle of St Vincent in 1797. To Rupert's secret regret, as the second son he would not inherit the Baronetcy. Nevertheless, he had the ringing tones of the English upper class. While he was extremely discreet with respect to matters of security, his precisely enunciated vowels and tone of authority, could normally be heard in the four corners of any room. He had been raised to command the respect which the English upper class took for granted. Without even considering the matter, Rupert expected to be heard when he spoke and expected to be obeyed. None of this bothered Harry or Peter since Rupert clearly regarded them as some sort of 'non' class, an antipodean subculture, annoyingly insubordinate although perversely to be admired and, since they could not be intimidated, to be treated as equals. But Rupert's accent did make him very easy to overhear. Rupert liked to tease Peter about his Aussie accent, and Peter liked to tease Harry about his New Zealand one. "How many balls in an over, old chap?" he would ask Harry in a mock English accent. Harry would sigh. "Sux, same as ever," taking care to exaggerate the flat vowels that distinguished strong New Zealand accents. Of course Harry had never thought he had an accent until he came to England. After all, Christ's College was a model English boarding School and the curriculum included teaching the boys to speak the King's English, so in fact his accent was remarkably muted.

Peter took a large swig from his pint and sighed. "Warm beer. I'll never get used to it." Rupert smiled. "You've made a very determined effort to overcome your misgivings over the years, though. You should get a reward from the British brewing industry."

Peter grunted. "So Harry, haven't seen you since the Olympics. Lovelock was sensational, what a fantastic run. What about it, Rupert?"

Rupert took a long draw of his cigarette, and expelled a cloud of smoke. A strand of lank blond hair strayed over his eye and he brushed it way with his hand, careful to keep his cigarette out of the way. "Indeed it was, fantastic is exactly the word Peter. 'The greatest race ever', Harold Abrahams called it on the BBC. The reporter for the *Manchester Guardian* was so carried away he called it 'a race magnificent beyond all description'. But Harry, tell Peter about Germany."

"Every time I go, it looks worse, Peter. Berlin was terrifying. Everywhere I looked I saw German triumphalism. They are all, including the very young and the very old, in uniform. There's aggression everywhere. It's a bit more violent each time and there are regular incidents in which people, mainly Jews, disappear or are beaten up. And I see more and more signs of the military and the Gestapo. Any German who has not joined in the fawning admiration of Hitler has been intimidated into silence. I think it's really bad."

"So what are the English doing about it? You're a spook Rupert. You should know. Are we making preparation or is the usual British dithering going on?"

Rupert looked about him. "You wouldn't believe what's happening. We're beside ourselves. The Chief of the Imperial General Staff was an old fool called Lord Cavan whose ideas on warfare have been described as about 800 years out of date. We finally got rid of him and now the new C.I.G.S is Field Marshall Montgomery-Massingberd, who, unbelievably, is nearly as stupid as Cavan. We have in this country one of the world experts on tank warfare called Fuller and they've pushed him out of the services. Now they've got rid of Liddell Hart, who has been described as 'the most important military thinker on the age of mechanisation in any country'. And what's worse, we know the German General Staff are all reading his book. To make matters worse still, the Kirke Report on the last war, which has just come out and is very politely critical of the conduct of our forces, has been banned for distribution by Massingberd. Why, you might ask? Because he was Chief of Staff at the Somme.

"The Somme," muttered Peter. They looked at each other in silence. They knew only too well what had happened. The soldiers had been ordered to walk towards the German lines which their officers were smugly confident had been destroyed by heavy artillery. The German machine guns did the rest. On the first day, there were 57,000 allied casualties. Rupert looked up from staring into his pint. "By the time it was over, total terrain gained, five miles, total casualties 420,000."

"My uncle was killed on the Somme," said Peter. "Of course the family blamed Haig and so did most Aussies. The popular view was he thought we were just a bunch of ill-disciplined yobs and expendable. There was plenty of bitterness, still is. What about the Kiwis, Harry?" Harry shrugged, "Most thought the British Officers were stupid poohbahs but we all knew there were good and bad officers in every army. You were just bloody lucky if you got a Monash."

Rupert looked up, "For Christ's sake fetch another round Peter, before I burst into tears." Peter obliged and Rupert resumed. "I'm very out of line on this so please don't repeat any of it. Hitler's just announced his 'peacetime army' will comprise 36 divisions so Massingberd in response has decided that the allowance for horse forage should increase from £44,000 to £400,000 and that all cavalry officers should be provided with two horses not one. He still thinks machine guns are for cads. So much for the lessons of the Somme."

Harry sat back. "Something I saw in Germany that also worried me was a sky full of some pretty sophisticated looking aircraft. The Luftwaffe has expanded from nowhere. Do our chaps realise the threat of aircraft to both the army and navy?"

"This is again supposed to be highly confidential, although of course half the world actually knows. The Navy decided to prove how ineffectual aircraft would be against well-defended ships. They invited the King and various luminaries to watch a demonstration in which they flew a Queen Bee drone in a straight line down a line of ships at 80 miles an hour to show how quickly they could shoot it down. They blazed away and not one of them could hit it. Eventually they deliberately crashed it into the sea. If you want to be further depressed, the army are even more dismissive of aircraft"

Peter sighed and turned to Harry. "I'm not sure anyone in charge is any more alert at our end of the world although in Australia we've been worrying about the Japs for years. They don't like us one bit. You know Billy Hughes, our PM and a tough little bugger, stood up to them at the Versailles conference. It was all about the 'White Australia' policy. Pretty shameful really and the Japs were mighty offended. They were supposed to be our allies. Well they're not now. I just have this feeling in my stomach we're going to go through the slaughter all over again."

"I always thought Hughes was an Aussie hero."

"He was at the time, and he still is for many, but Japan wanted to be recognised at the Peace Conference as a foundation member of the League of Nations. Australia had a veto and Hughes used it. It fuelled the militarists in Japan and now we're looking at a war involving all of us."

Harry responded, "War's not a topic anyone wants to contemplate here. Churchill keeps trying to warn people but no-one's listening. It's as if the people are still exhausted from 1914–18 and the Depression and war is too depressing a subject to speak about. Maybe I should take the family back to New Zealand and disappear in the high country but poor old Uncle Nick needs me."

Harry looked around the pub. There was a quiet contented buzz of conversation as young men chatted to girlfriends or clustered together arguing about sport or the political situation; perhaps there was even some talk of Germany. A few old regulars perched in their favourite corners. War hovered beyond the immediate consciousness of most people in London and it was hard to conceive that most of those enjoying the beer and smoke-filled atmosphere could find themselves in uniform before the year was over.

They agreed to have another catch-up when Peter returned to London from visiting family in Scotland but in spite of the pints consumed it was a sober group that left the pub at closing time.

It was some time later before the three of them found themselves back at the Scarsdale, summoned this time by Rupert. Even before the pints had appeared, Rupert was waving the newspaper. "Have you seen this? Chamberlain came back from Munich yesterday and made a speech when he landed at Heston all about what a jolly good agreement he and Herr Hitler have come to. Now he's stood outside Downing Street and revealed that he had had another chat with Herr Hitler and has announced peace with honour; 'Peace for our time' as he called it. He's recommended we all go home and sleep quietly in our beds."

Peter brought the pints over. "You don't believe any of it, do you?"

"Harry has been over there and we are monitoring our sources from all over Europe. No, we don't believe it. Hitler won't be able to believe he's got what he wanted without a peep from us. Now he'll take the next slice. Am I right, Harry?"

Harry agreed. "All the signs are he's only just started. I managed to attend one of his rallies. It was spine-tingling. I've never in my life seen anyone arouse an audience like he has. They are just waiting for the orders. He's effectively militarised the whole of Germany and Austria." Peter stared at them. "You're going to tell me the Army has got off its arse and is prepared, aren't you?"

"I wish I could but it's terrifying. Of all the stupid things, they've removed Hore–Belisha from his position as Secretary of State for War. He is the only person who has seen what's coming and tried to boot the bloody Generals into the real world. Would you believe the Army doesn't trust him because he's Jewish?"

CHAPTER 12

Harry was sitting in the small boardroom at the family firm when his uncle's secretary entered. She excused herself for interrupting before addressing Harry. "There's a gentleman on the phone for you, Mr Douglas. I told him you were in a meeting but he's very insistent." Harry's uncle waved him out with a smile. Harry picked up the phone.

"Harry Douglas here. Who is it?"

"It's Rupert, Harry. Sorry to interrupt but we need to meet. Urgently. Could you make it six? My club might be best." Harry agreed to meet him and on the dot of six presented himself at the Oxford and Cambridge Club to find Rupert waiting for him in a tiny ante-room off the main bar. They exchanged the usual pleasantries while their drinks were brought. "What's so urgent, Rupert? It takes a lot for you to use that word."

"It's like this, Harry. This relationship you have with Admiral Canaris. We've had a message from sources in Germany. We've double-checked it and we're sure it's genuine. Canaris wants to talk to us but says he wants a personal meeting and he wants it with you. He says you're the only Englishman he knows whose German is as good as his English and he wants to make sure that what he has to say is conveyed accurately. He trusts you and he doesn't want anything written down. He suggests that if you agree, we fly you to a remote airfield on the German border and he'll have you picked up there. You meet, he'll have you back in twenty four hours and we'll fly you out. I've discussed it with 'C'. We think you should go if you'll agree."

Harry sipped his drink. "Any idea what it's about?"

"We don't know for sure but there's some tension under the surface between the Wermacht and the Nazis and our fundamental analysis suggests that if we and the French don't play the right cards there's definitely going to be a war. We don't know what Canaris wants but we believe the risks of finding out are manageable. They might just want to kill you, but we doubt it."

"I see. Of course I'll go. When?"

"Tomorrow. Have a small bag packed and we'll pick you up at 11am to drive to Northolt airfield. This is of course top secret. And by the way, your code name's Aardvark."

"Aardvark!? Where the hell did that come from?"

"First name on our list."

"Really?"

"Not exactly. We get them from someone called the ISSB. The names are supposed to be completely innocuous. Rare animals are probably as neutral as anything else. They rotate them, so they're probably back at the beginning of one of their lists. Winston wants frivolous names but we're not having that. The stupid Germans try to be smart and it's not hard to figure them out. They call America "Samland" and us "Golfplatz". Uncle Sam and golf course. I ask you."

Harry went back to his flat and sat for almost an hour in the gathering darkness thinking about this mission. Then he picked up the phone to Rupert. "Rupert, there's a request I'd like to make. It's not a condition. It's my job to go anyway but I'd like you to accommodate me if you can." Rupert listened attentively and replied that he would see what he could do and would tell Harry when he picked him up.

Harry was putting a few things in his holdall when Kathleen arrived home. He explained what he was up to and that he should be away only a day. She arched her eyebrows.

"So, not dangerous then I suppose?"

"Not a bit, just something that needs to be done face to face. I'll be back before you know I've gone." Seeing the unconvinced look on her face, he quickly kissed her cheek and changed the subject.

Rupert arrived in his own car, without a driver, to pick Harry up.

"So what's the verdict?" Harry asked him.

"The answer's 'no' Harry. I'm sorry but we can't risk your mission being compromised. You could get yourself arrested. That would be a total disaster for everyone." Harry tried to argue but could see he would get nowhere since Rupert was himself reacting to orders. For the rest of the drive, Rupert briefed Harry on the most recent state of intelligence over the situation in Germany and some of the underlying tensions within the Government in Britain as to how to go forward. Everyone now knew that Chamberlain's 'Peace in our time' speech had been sadly mistaken and, with the Germans in Czechoslovakia, furious debate was in progress over how to react.

The plane was a small four-seat de Havilland and to Harry's amazement he found he knew the pilot, Peter Sutherland, who had played rugby with him at the Harlequins. He was small, nuggetty and had played fly-half. He and Harry had shared many a pint at Twickenham and were soon engaged in swapping memories of great tries scored, tackles made, pints quaffed and girls pursued. They chatted happily on as they flew low over the channel and Harry looked down at the myriad ships crisscrossing the white-capped water. They flew on over the beaches of Normandy and the French countryside alternately basking in the autumn sunshine or shadowed by the high cloud that drifted above them. They landed at what seemed like no more than a deserted field with a long and bumpy grass runway scattered with animal droppings. What appeared to be a barn with a small wooden veranda was the only building. Peter gave him a slap on the back. "See you tomorrow night. It's a 6pm take-off and don't on any account be late."

"Don't worry I won't. By the way, the two extra seats. Will anyone else be joining us?"

"Not unless something happens in the next 24 hours. You have something in mind?"

"I do actually. If I bring a passenger will you carry her?"

"Jesus, Harry you after skirt again? You Kiwis never stop."

"It's important Peter, life and death I guess." Peter looked at him for a minute.

"That's what friends are for, but how are we going to deal with it when we land?"

"Once she's in England it's too bad. They can't send her back. In any case it may not happen."

"OK but we'll probably both end up in irons."

"Thanks Peter, I wouldn't ask if it wasn't important. By the way, it's two girls. So there's one for you." Harry laughed and quickly walked away towards the barn before Peter could think of another objection.

At first no one came out to meet Harry but then a soldier

dressed in a sergeant's uniform emerged from a side door of the barn. "Aardvark, I presume?" he enquired of Harry and receiving an affirmative answer in German, took Harry's holdall and escorted him around the barn to a Mercedes parked in the shade beneath the drooping branches of a large elm tree. They were soon on the road and Harry could elicit little except that the drive would take a couple of hours. He tried to estimate the destination by following road signs from time to time and reckoned they were heading east towards Freiburg in Germany but close to the French and Swiss borders. Harry dozed fitfully in the back reflecting on the quietness and comfort of the car, a piece of German engineering excellence which he knew was echoed in the quality of the new weapons that intelligence confirmed were pouring out of German factories, in defiance of all Germany's Treaty obligations. The driver finally turned left over a small bridge onto an unsealed road past a heavily grassed field. A herd of horses galloped along the fence line, for a while keeping pace with car before turning away. Harry watched them intently. He had always loved horses and reflected that, if there was to be war, he hoped these horses would not go the way of the thousands killed or maimed in the First War. He had never forgotten stumbling across a shell hole in which a dismembered horse's body lay bloated and putrefying, the top half of its torso still intact, what was left of the bottom covered by stinking water.

A little further along the car breached the top of a hill. There below them was an airfield and along its perimeter Harry counted ten rows of parked bombers, each row containing about 50 aircraft. Heinkel one-elevens, Harry thought, all brand new, their wings and cockpits reflecting in the weak sunlight.

The sun was setting low over a misty horizon before they drew up at a small schloss. Harry was escorted in and his bag taken to an expansive circular room in the castle's tower, with a view over the surrounding countryside. It was sparsely decorated except for a huge oil painting of a stag at bay, wounded by a spear and with dogs tearing at its sides and blood streaming from numerous wounds. Harry wondered at the symbolism and decided he would have preferred more congenial company for the night. The porter invited him to come downstairs as soon as he was ready where he would find a drink awaiting him. After a quick wash and tidy up he found his way back downstairs, opened the door to a vast sitting room and was greeted by the outraged barking of two tiny dogs, Canaris's long-haired dachshunds. Harry was well used to dogs and was hardly likely to be scared by these tiny animals. He quickly had them jumping up and down at knee level as he bent down to scratch their ears. Canaris scooped them and tucked one under each arm.

"Welcome Harry, as staunch a friend as my dachshunds I do believe. May I introduce you to Kaspar and Sabine." He put the dogs down gently and watched as they scampered around jumping up at his knees for attention. "I'm glad you accepted my invitation. I could wish it was in less troublesome times. There is good riding and hunting in this area and we could have enjoyed a few days in the forest. I thought we might have a drink and then talk over dinner. But how are you? You certainly look as robust as ever." He put the dogs down beside him on a vast sofa where one laid its head on its paws and regarded Harry intently for a few minutes before drifting off to sleep. The other jumped down and scuttled out in a search for food.

Harry replied that he was indeed well and observed that Canaris, too, seemed to be handling the pressures of his role as head of the Abwher without any apparent signs of stress. Harry was unaware that although Canaris was comfortable with the culture of the Abwher, the Military's Intelligence Agency, he was becoming increasingly concerned about the rivalry from his long-time friend Heydrich, who was running the Nazis' own intelligence agency, the Gestapo, with utter ruthlessness and pushing hard into Abwher territory.

Heydrich reported to Himmler at SS Headquarters in the Prinz Albrechtstrasse. Canaris regarded Himmler as a demented civil servant, drunk with power, cruel and treacherous, but also stupid and cowardly. Himmler was easy to outwit, but Heydrich was a clever and barbarous fanatic.

Canaris began to talk generally about the situation in Germany. Harry listened politely and when he saw an opportunity, interrupted.

"Wilhelm, we are both good friends of the Professor in Heidelberg as you know. I do feel concerned about him. What do you make of his situation in these times?"

Canaris paused. "Did you know he lost his job and also that he was beaten up? He was probably too proud to tell you but he should leave Germany now if he still can, but he won't. He's too stubborn and it may cost him and all his family their lives. I could help him but only with extreme care."

"As it happens, I spoke to him a few days ago and he told me about the job. I know he won't budge but I convinced him the girls are at great risk and he must do all he can to get them out of Germany now. The future hardly looks rosy for them given the current treatment of Jews in Germany. So, I want to ask you a favour, which I am not sure you will be able to grant. There will be two spare seats on the plane out tomorrow. I want to take the girls with me and I would like you to arrange it. Before you say anything, I know this will pose some dangers for you but I also know that neither you nor I want these girls to suffer if we can prevent it."

Canaris hesitated. "You are right about the risk to me and to you as well. Who else knows about this request?"

"No-one. I have had to tell the pilot of course but it turns out we are old mates. My superiors have forbidden it since they think it endangers the whole mission."

"So the pilot knows nothing more than that the two girls might join the flight?"

"Exactly."

"Give me a few minutes." He walked out of the room, closing the door behind him. It was a good half hour before he reappeared and when he did his expression indicated nothing. "Well, Harry. We have some arrangements in train but I don't know yet how this will unfold. You'll have to wait until you're due to leave but I will do my best. But if this does happen it must not be known how it has happened to anyone except you and me. Not the pilot and not anyone in London. You know perfectly well why." They shook hands.

"I know we have to trust each other Wilhelm. Somewhere along the line we live or die on trust." Canaris looked at him with the piercing stare Harry remembered from all those years ago.

"You're here because I trust you. Now, let's go and eat dinner."

The dining room was oak panelled and the candlelit table set for two. Large paintings, in the same baroque style as the one in his room, decorated the room interspersed with two stag heads, both eight pointers, and a huge boar's head. Canaris shut the doors and used a bell to summon the waiter whenever assistance was required. The candles were barely enough to light the cavernous space and the roof disappeared into a vault above them.

"Harry, you know the situation to date as well as I. We are occupying Czechoslovakia and have liberated the Sudeten Germans. Britain and France are threatening war but I have to tell you, Germany will not withdraw. I have been briefed by the highest levels in the army and the Nazi party and it is clear Germany has no quarrel with either France or, especially, England. Our actions are driven by a need to regain our people to the east, to provide us with living room to expand, and also to rid Europe of the scourge of Bolshevism. We know your government is as concerned by the threat of communist ideology as we are. We believe it could undermine the whole German State but it could also undermine the whole of your Empire. The enemy that protects and nourishes it is Russia. They are a nation of peasants and they will undo us, and you. The proposal we have for England is a simple one. Give us a free hand in the east and we will not trouble you. You know very well that Hitler is actually an admirer of Britain. Many things we do have been learned from you, not least the organisation and aims of our navy. You should also know that we are aware that your military forces are not in good shape. Your governments since the war, no doubt for good reason, have totally neglected your army and air force and land battles in Europe cannot be won by the navy. Harry, you are not in good shape to fight even should you choose to."

"I passed rows of your new bombers in the car, Wilhelm, no doubt a deliberate sightseeing tour for me, I imagine." Canaris simply smiled. Harry remained silent for a minute. "Much of what you say is true but the British public don't like what they see of Hitler. I don't think you are realistic if you think our politicians will trust him after Munich. Why should they?"

"The army in Germany and most of the middle class agree with your view of Hitler but they see that he has brought back prosperity and jobs after the devastation of the slump and the inflation that followed. The Army believes he should be allowed to finish the job and then he will be dealt with. Our Generals don't like taking orders from corporals. We will deal with it in our own way."

Canaris rang the bell and the waiter entered and tidied away the dishes, reappearing with a bottle of ancient brandy. Canaris tried it and pronounced it a privilege to drink. The waiter gravely nodded his agreement and retreated, closing the doors behind him. After a minute Canaris stood up and walked to the doors, looking out to see if there was anyone outside. Satisfied, he retreated with his glass to the mantelpiece above the huge fireplace.

"There is another matter," continued Harry. "In England more and more people are concerned about the Nazis' treatment of the Jews. The news of their persecution is alarming. They are being beaten up, their shops trashed and many have disappeared. And then there was Kristallnacht. It was all over every British paper and was the subject of universal condemnation. Hitler and the Nazis were quite rightly blamed. You know us well enough to know that the British have this public-schoolboy addiction to fair play. It comes from cricket I suppose. If this persecution of the Jews stopped, it would be much easier to see a way forward. You know how influential the Jews are in Britain, from the Rothschilds down."

Canaris was silent for a minute and then resumed his seat. "Do you know Vienna, Harry?"

"Indeed."

"In the 1920s, even before the depression, times were very tough. The country was in turmoil. The ordinary man in the street could hardly help contrasting his own lot with the magnificence of the buildings along the Ringstrasse, a construction that the Emperor Franz Joseph had started in the 1860s and which took twenty years to build. Each building was the product of the architect Hansen, whose Graeco-Roman fantasies were given free range to signal to the world the grandeur of the Austro-Hungarian Empire. It is by far the grandest street in Vienna and

I believe it would stand up to comparison with anything in any other city in the world. Amongst all this grandeur reposes the Palais Ephrussi. It had been built as some sort of monument or a signal to the world of permanence or just because he could, by Baron Ignace von Ephrussi. At the time he was perhaps the richest banker in Europe or at least in Vienna. Have you seen it?"

"Actually I have. I took a stroll down the Ringstrasse the last time I visited. You could hardly visit the Ring and miss it."

"I hope you rounded the corner to the Schottengasse. It is twice as big on that side." Harry agreed that he had walked along the side. In fact, he had been so surprised he had counted the windows, a row of nearly 20, repeated on five floors. "Then you will know it is huge, magnificent, a palace fit for any king, any emperor, any dictator; but for the people of Vienna it is different from the other buildings because it is owned by a Jewish family. But then, look further at the houses in the street. These palaces are owned by the Liebens, the Todescos, the Epsteins, the Schey von Koromlas, the Konigswarters, the Wertheims, the Gutmans and so on and so on. In the 1880s, Franz Joseph welcomed the Jews, their money and their industry. So by the 1920s Vienna had grown to have one of the largest Jewish populations in Europe, almost all of who had arrived in the previous five decades. The poor of course did not think to blame their bad luck and lowly station on themselves; their boorishness, their lack of education, their own Government's policies. They looked around for someone else to blame and here are these arriviste Jews, rich beyond Croesus. The Viennese who spent their days in winter freezing in the snow, with no jobs, no food and no place to sleep, chose to ignore the fact that the city's slums were also filled with enclaves of Jewish immigrants even poorer than they were.

"They saw the carriages full of rich Jews coming and going while they, themselves, saw what little wealth they had destroyed by inflation. In 1923 it took 1 million marks to buy one US dollar. People's savings could not buy a postage stamp. It was so bad employees had to be paid three times a day because by the end of the day the money they had received in the morning would be worthless. How did it happen? The poor asked themselves how the Jews came to be so rich, came to be in Vienna and to dominate so many areas – the banks of course, but also the law, medicine, the Arts, the media and so on. They concluded that it was not by hard work, astute investment and a passion for education but by some bewitching alchemy. The Jews have no army, no constituency except money. They were then, and still are, the perfect scapegoat for the tribulations of the Viennese and then of a nation, of Germany. What was so easily seen in Vienna was also seen in the rest of Austria and then in the rest of Germany. For Hitler, the Jews were the perfect target. A group bereft of defences to be blamed for all that had happened. Perfect."

"Whatever the provocation it cannot excuse their murder by the state."

"Of course not. I am not trying to excuse. I cannot. But I am trying to explain. It is necessary to understand before there is any chance of a solution."

"A solution? A solution is to immediately stop the violence against them."

Canaris sighed and stood to fetch the brandy bottle and refill first Harry's glass and then his own. "You know my personal admiration for the Jews but perversely there is another equally dangerous problem stemming from the opposite end of the social and economic scale. They are seen by many in the middle and upper classes in Germany to be the promoters of Bolshevism. From Marx down through Trotsky, the Jews are behind much of the Bolshevik agitation. They were behind the Spartacus uprising; Rosa Luxemburg and Karl Liebknecht were out to bring down

Germany. It's no wonder they were murdered. Many Germans see the Jews as traitors, responsible for the loss of the last war and enemies of the State. In both the United States and England we know there are many influential people who share the view that the Jews have too much power and we must ask ourselves – are these Jews Germans or are they Zionists? They are not helping themselves. For the poor they are too rich and for the rich they are too poor. Maybe they are just too clever for their own good.

"As you well know, I am not speaking for myself but you must understand the background to what is happening in Germany. However, if Hitler goes, then the Jewish problem will go with him but before any of this can happen we need to make sure that war between us does not break out. Once it has, then passions will be so inflamed it will be impossible to reverse the process. Once again the best of British and German lives will be lost, and I expect the best of young New Zealanders. We must try to prevent this happening. At all costs. Peace must be the goal of our two nations."

Harry hesitated. "You should know I have Jewish blood, Wilhelm. I'm not Jewish by religion but I feel for them and I cannot stand by while they are murdered, but I will carry your message as objectively as I can."

Canaris looked at Harry as if he was seeing him for the first time. "How can you be Jewish? Douglas. You're a Scottish farmer."

"I'm not Jewish as you put it but my grandfather was Jewish. When he left Poland and made his way to New Zealand he decided his life would be easier in the South Island of New Zealand if he changed his name. He looked at the Membership of the Dunedin Club and all he saw were Scottish names so he picked one and it happened to be Douglas. He was a rationalist. He cared about the welfare of his people but for him religion was just a method of controlling people no matter what religion it was. So he was quite happy for his family to go to Anglican schools and he believed to realise a full life in New Zealand we had to be New Zealanders and not Jews or anything else. The Jewish connection was hardly ever mentioned in our house. My mother's family were good Scottish Presbyterians so she was hardly likely to embrace the idea. At my school I attended chapel every morning and twice on Sunday. I have been baptised and confirmed in the Church of England. I can recite The Lord's Prayer, the catechism and endless hymns. I know nothing about Jewry except what I have recently learned from a book my grandfather gave me. None of the religious stuff makes any sense to me but when you're at school you do what everyone else does. Like the navy I suppose. But what am I? A loyal son of New Zealand and the Empire, through and through."

Canaris sat silent for a while staring into his glass. "You know I think I can envisage what your home looks like at least a little. After all I have been in the Andes so I imagine your Southern Alps are a bit similar, but I have no idea how you live. I mean how many maids do you have, do you have peasant workers, as great land holders do you have great privileges or a special title? I have no idea."

Harry laughed. "No maids, no peasants, no privileges and definitely no titles." Canaris was taken aback. "Who makes the beds, cooks, brings in the hay then? Who makes the rules?"

"We do" replied Harry. "We do it ourselves or we hire labourers on the farm and when we're finished we all have a beer in our kitchen whilst we discuss the latest sports results or how the price of wheat is going." Canaris persisted. "But who are the aristocrats?"

"We never had them," replied Harry. "No Junkers. We all

come from immigrant stock, we all came freely to find a better life and mainly to get away from 'aristocrats'. The price we pay is to do things ourselves but we think it is no price at all."

After Harry had gone to bed, Canaris took his two dachshunds for their evening walk. He found it a respite to stroll quietly along the path across the neighbouring field under a carpet of stars whilst the dogs investigated everything around them. They scurried hither and thither, sniffing suspiciously, perhaps the scent of a badger or fox. They lifted their legs on fence posts, barked ferociously at nothing at all, and then ran behind his legs for protection. He bent down and scratched their ears and turned back for home.

They had agreed to meet for breakfast at 6.30. Harry slept well enough and was down in time to join Canaris. There was more talk and they fleshed out some of the previous night's discussion, particularly the position of Germany and Britain's respective Empires. They briefly referred to each country's roles and interests in the Near and Far East and in the Pacific. Mostly Harry took note of what Canaris wished to convey and offered little in response, both because he felt he had neither the knowledge nor the authority to respond and because it was evident that Canaris was already well-informed on the British point of view. It was clear that Canaris and his supporters believed that Germany's goals could be achieved without detriment to Britain's position, provided they were given a free hand to deal with the Russians. Finally, it was time to depart. They worked out ways to communicate the response and to keep the communication channel open. Harry's code name would stay as Aardvark but they needed a code name for Canaris. "How about 'Dresden'?" suggested Canaris.

Harry laughed. "You Germans can be very obvious sometimes.

"What about 'Rum and Black?'"

"Yes, 'Rum and Black', how could I forget that?" The car arrived and the driver took some time to talk to Canaris.

Canaris came over to Harry. "We think the airport is being watched. Tell your pilot to taxi to the very far end. It is a long runway. At the far end there is a road hidden by bushes close to the end of the grass. Tell him to turn with the door towards the road. The girls should be helped in in a few seconds. Then go. If they aren't there you must leave. You must not wait."

They shook hands as the two dachshunds leaped up and down at their knees, barking enthusiastically. Canaris reflectively scratched one of their heads as Jack picked the other one up in his arms. "You know what first made me start to doubt the sanity of the Nazis?" he asked, "It was when the Jews were told they would have to surrender all pets because dogs and cats and birds should live only in pure Aryan homes." Canaris walked with Harry to the car. His last words were a simple expression of good luck.

The return journey in the car was uneventful enough and when they arrived at the strip Peter was waiting beside the plane. Harry looked around but could see no sign of any company. He explained the plan to Peter and they checked their watches and looked to the far end of the runway but could see nothing. "6.05, Harry. Let's go" They taxied to the far end and Peter swung the plane around and Harry unlatched the door. They peered into the bushes but could see no sign of movement. Peter gunned the motor in impatience. "Jesus, Harry. I don't like this. We need to go. Where the hell are they?" As he spoke the bushes parted and a short stocky man in dungarees emerged followed by the two girls crouched down and running to the door, clutching small parcels. Without a word, Harry hauled them inside and slammed the door. Before they could even reach their seats Peter had turned the aircraft and was off, the engine at full revs, with the aircraft yawing sideways as he counteracted the wind and the bumps. As they lifted off, Peter had time to see what looked like a black German limousine pull up at the arrival shed alongside the landing strip. He looked back at the two girls and smiled. Each of them had tears running down their cheeks but they both smiled back at him and Rebecca, the elder, mouthed the words "thank you".

David had decided to drive a mob of sheep down to the saleyards at Ashburton about 50 miles south of Christchurch. It would take him a couple of days but the dogs and his horse would keep him company and be more than enough to keep the sheep in order. He enjoyed these visits to the yards; he had time to think. He worried about his boys, of course. Harry was doing something nefarious with military intelligence, he never could quite tell what, since he only heard by letters from Harry or the family, carefully censored, and Jack was likewise involved in an administrative role with the New Zealand expeditionary force which kept him out of the front line but close enough to be at serious risk. David worried about Victoria too. He thought she maintained her optimism mainly because she thought it would stop him worrying. In any event, it was a fine day on the Canterbury Plains, the sheep were on their best behaviour and prices were not too bad either.

He arrived on time for the auction and caught up with the chat from his mates, mostly about the war and how their boys were faring. One of his mates from a farm further north had just lost a son and another was anxiously awaiting the recovery of his 18-year-old, who had crashed a spitfire into the Channel but miraculously extracted himself in time to be rescued by a trawler. The sheep milled around beneath the horses, harassed by the dogs, and the men chatted, waiting for the sale to begin.

Suddenly they all went quiet. 'Red' Bolger had arrived at the yards with a few mangy looking sheep for sale. Everyone knew Red, and Red knew everyone. He was a pacifist, although he had had a few fights outside the pub at closing time and could pack a pretty fair wallop. No-one had minded his pacifism to begin with. They just thought it was a bit weird but pretty harmless. But Red's son had picked up his Father's bolshie ideas and, for his troubles, was now incarcerated for refusing the call-up. That had hardened attitudes. The locals largely thought you couldn't leave the fighting to your mates' sons, whatever you might profess to think. So everyone knew the situation and all the men went quiet. No-one moved. Just then Ted Williams, the boss of the yard stepped forward. "We don't sell Bolshie sheep in these yards, Red, get them out of here." Red looked around. Just for a minute it looked as if he was going to withdraw but then he went to open the gate to the yard, to let his sheep in.

One of the men standing close by spat lazily on the ground near his feet. "Conscie bastard." Red tried to push past, there was a blow and next minute the two men were wrestling on the ground, rolling in sheep shit with the sheep scattering everywhere. It was soon over with not much more than hurt feelings. David had a fleeting feeling of pity for Red and quietly whistled his dog to bring back the scattered sheep.

Red dabbed at his lip. "Nothing changes. You think fighting will solve things, you bloody fools." With a muttered thanks to David, he drove his sheep away.

"You should have left him David," said Ted "your boys are over there." David shrugged but he thought about it all the way home, wondering if he should have helped Red sell his sheep. When he eventually reached home he told Victoria of the events of the day. She listened carefully and for a while said nothing. Finally, she put down yet another pair of socks she was knitting for the war effort. She detested knitting and had to force herself to keep churning out articles for the men at the front, but what more practical support could she offer? At least this was an opportunity to think about something else.

"You were best to keep quiet. It wouldn't have done any good, but I wonder if all the deaths and injuries will really lead to a better world. It certainly didn't the last time. When I went to town recently someone gave me one of those conscientious objector papers. I was going to throw it away but for some reason I kept it and read it when I got home. Some of it made sense."

David looked up. "Just bloody propaganda. We need to win this damn war as quick as we can and worry about stopping the next one. Get rid of it. I don't want it in the house Victoria. It's just propaganda."

Victoria stood up and walked out on to the veranda. She stood looking across the fields at the mountains. She wondered for a brief moment whether, if the Germans actually won the war, it would really have any effect on New Zealand; but it was only for a moment. She knew for absolute certainty that it would.

CHAPTER 13

The journey back was without incident and they landed safely back at Northholt just as the sun disappeared behind the row of poplars that fringed the side of the airfield. Rupert was there to meet them. "Who the hell have you got there?" he demanded. "Have you disobeyed instructions and endangered the whole bloody exercise? What are you playing at?"

Harry had been expecting this sort of response and had his reply ready. "Canaris knows the girl's parents. He not only supported me bringing them out. He insisted. They're here, no harm was done and at this stage nobody knows. Why don't we just keep it like that?"

Rupert paused, "What exactly are you proposing to do with them, may I ask?"

"My aunt in London will consider it a privilege to look after them." Peter was returning to London that evening and expressed himself more than happy to drive two such 'good looking gals' as he described them. This would avoid having Rupert or Harry any more involved and leave them free to talk together on their own drive to London. Rupert had arranged to take Harry to meet with 'C' the following morning.

Sir Stewart greeted Harry warmly enough and Harry launched immediately into a detailed report of his conversations with Canaris. Sir Stewart listened intently and then left the room. He returned some minutes later and he and Rupert then took Harry back over his report, asking more questions about every point. As they finished, a secretary entered the room with a note for Sir Stewart. Looking up from the note, he announced that the three of them would be meeting that evening with Chamberlain, Halifax, Eden and Churchill.

Rupert looked up. "Not absolutely ideal bedfellows one would think."

Sir Stewart stared at him. "Under the circumstances outlined, they are the only people who can deal with this matter and whom, should they possibly manage to agree, have the power to follow through with any decision. You won't be surprised to know there is a lot of this sort of traffic coming in at the moment, some reliable, some not, but Admiral Canaris has to be taken seriously."

Harry was told that Rupert would again pick him up at 6pm to be at the House of Commons by 6.45 for a 7pm meeting. Sir Stewart would see them there. Harry was not normally given to nerves but the thought of the interrogation he would probably have to endure and the importance of getting his report accurate troubled him. He felt he could not afford to mislead in any way. He dressed carefully in his best suit, white shirt and Cambridge University Hawks Club tie. It had not taken Harry long to learn that in England the right club tie could cut through days of suspicion and create a level of acceptance that would be very hard for the ordinary colonial to achieve. He needed each of the four politicians to treat him with as much respect as possible and, given that New Zealanders were likely to be well out of their normal range of day-to-day contacts, without his Cambridge connection he would in all likelihood be disregarded as a quaint colonial. Kathleen looked him up and down as he was about to depart. "You're really quite dashing when you try. Very much the city gent," she remarked, giving his lapels a quick brush.

They arrived promptly at the Commons and were shown to a wood-panelled meeting room overlooking the Thames. Sir Stewart was already present and they were offered a drink by the butler. Sir Stewart quickly briefed Harry. "Don't forget, Harry, you will be confronting the Establishment in all its glory today. Halifax and Eden are both Eton and Oxford."

"As of course are you," Rupert interjected, "and Winston is Harrow and Sandhurst and, with his family background is one of them, whereas poor old Chamberlain is Rugby and 17 years of managing some company in the midlands. He has to deal with an Earl, a Lord and the grandson of a Duke. You will see where power lies in Britain tonight." Sir Stewart grunted his agreement and was helping himself to a whisky just as the door opened and Chamberlain, Eden and Halifax entered the room together. Introductions were made.

"Cambridge I see," commented Halifax, who was tall and lean, with grey hair to match his silver tie, the 'Grey Fox' they called him, reflecting his odd passion for fox hunting. "What did you get your Blue for?"

"Rowing," replied Harry "and I'm sorry to say we managed to beat Oxford by nearly three lengths." There was general amusement and further small talk while they took their seats.

"Where's Winston?" enquired Chamberlain, but as he did so, in strode Churchill. Nodding to the others he introduced himself to Harry and Rupert and before the others could say a word he turned to Sir Stewart.

"Canaris, eh? I still haven't forgiven him for The Falklands. He led us all over the ocean in that damn *Dresden*. We got them in the end but he's been causing trouble for us ever since. Wasn't he responsible for all those problems we've had in Spain? Damn near got them into the First War on Germany's side." Sir Stewart agreed that Canaris had indeed been responsible for a whole series of difficulties for Britain in Spain but went on to point out that he believed Canaris had had a direct role in preventing a German plan to enlist Spain's help to retake Gibraltar. "Hmph," responded Churchill, "he's still a damned nuisance."

Chamberlain hastily brought the meeting to order. "Before we even start, Sir Stewart, why should we trust Canaris and what are the possibilities that he can deliver on any proposal?"

Sir Stewart sat back in his chair. "Gentleman, without going into detail, can I say that we have a number of channels in Germany as you would expect and, further, we have had enough dealings with Canaris to believe that the proposals we have already outlined are certainly in keeping with his own views of the way the world should be ordered. We should remember that he was directly exposed to the naval revolt in Kiel at the end of the war, which was deliberately provoked by the Bolsheviks. Sailors turned their guns on their own officers. Most of the German officer class have never forgotten that and will never forgive the Bolsheviks. Canaris is a lifelong anti-communist, of that there is no doubt. Now, before we go further I would like to ask Major Douglas to give you a direct recap of the proposal he has received."

Harry did so as precisely as he could. They listened in silence.

Chamberlain spoke first. "It's a very simple proposition as I see it, gentlemen. Do we fight to liberate Poland as we and the French have pledged to do or do we leave Germany to deal with the Bolsheviks for us and see Poland as collateral damage?"

Eden ran his fingers through his hair. "The French were keen to take action if the Germans walked into Czechoslovakia. We refused to make our position clear and have paid the consequence. Now Hitler will not take us seriously, however unequivocal our commitment. He thinks he has us bluffed. If we are serious we must send troops to Europe now. We must actually do something".

"We can't do that," replied Chamberlain, "that would be, in effect, a declaration of war."

"We should have done it years ago," muttered Churchill.

Sir Stewart interrupted. "You should all know that we have information that suggests that Hitler may be very close to doing a deal with Stalin on Poland. He is playing both sides of course since he does not want a war on two fronts."

Churchill broke in. "How can we possibly accept this proposition? The Nazis must be opposed in every way, including force. We should find every ally we can, grit our teeth and immediately negotiate a treaty ourselves with Stalin." The others looked aghast at such a suggestion. Halifax coughed into his maroon silk kerchief. "How do you intend to 'save' Poland without the Russians?" continued Churchill.

Chamberlain intervened, changing the subject. "Where are we with the Americans at the moment?"

"Nothing more than windy oratory," replied Halifax." Every large company in America is busy investing in Germany. They like the union-free environment and may I remind you that the business of America is business."

"A nation of cads," replied Chamberlain. "However, returning to the immediate business, I note the proposition is silent on the French."

Churchill did not hesitate. "Hitler treated us with utter

contempt at Munich. He made a laughing stock of us. We cannot and should not trust him. If the German High Command can remove Hitler and his lackeys it is a different matter, but I doubt that will happen."

Halifax sat back in his chair. "I'm not so sure. We basically agree with the German view of the Bolsheviks. They are a European phenomenon and are primarily controlled by Russia. They foment trouble in every European country, and in the Empire, even in places like India and Australia. We are ill-prepared for war, thanks to the policies of some of our Labour colleagues and the miserly attitude of His Majesty's Treasury. The Germans have totally ignored the restrictions imposed by the Versailles Treaty and the Naval Treaty and our intelligence is quite clear that their armed forces are very impressive. If we fight now, many more of our young men will die before we have even recovered from the last bloodbath. And all this possibly without achieving anything. Poland is an awfully long way from the Channel."

Chamberlain sat up. "And our treaty obligations to France, and Poland? Do we tear them up?"

Churchill looked up. "The French. Just over a hundred years ago we fought the French to a standstill at Waterloo, and who were our allies who saved the day? The Prussians."

"Your point is?" asked Chamberlain.

"His point," replied Halifax, "is that we are friends with the French when it suits us, with the Germans when that suits us and with Russians when that suits us. But the real point to consider is that there is no permanence in history. Time changes all relationships between nations and time will take care of Hitler. He is a madman but he will be gone and in the meantime maybe we don't need to sacrifice thousands of our young men again. At the end of the war in 1918 we had suffered well over two million casualties. The flower of our youth, as it was so poetically expressed. What did we really achieve? The borders are much where they were and the Huns are back. If we fight this war now, and even if we win it, we may well suffer similar casualties and I have no doubt the economic cost will be crippling. We may win, but lose our Empire anyway."

Winston scowled. "It might be more economical if we just had Hitler assassinated." Halifax looked at Menzies. "Could we do that?"

"Oh yes," he replied, "the assassin might not survive but we could do it with a little planning."

Chamberlain was appalled. "Assassinate another head of state? Like some South American gangsters? It's out of the question. We don't do that."

"We do actually," muttered Menzies.

"Why wouldn't we do it?" asked Churchill. "Seems a damn good plan. We can pay some eyetie a bag full of gold and deny all knowledge afterwards. You've got a few chaps like that on the payroll haven't you Menzies?" The others stared at him in disdain.

"It's not the British way." said Eden

"So you would send the young men of England to die in what I can assure you will be a brutal and unforgiving slaughter because it's not our way?" replied Churchill. There was silence until Halifax responded by changing the subject. "The question was 'what about the French?' I'm sure you don't need reminding that we are here to protect British interests first and foremost. Circumstances change. Our friends at the Foreign Office will negotiate our way out of Treaty obligations, so-called. If we pause, at the very least we can better prepare ourselves so that if and when we have to fight we are ready to do so. And don't forget the Germans and the Russians are not natural allies. It may suit them to cooperate over Poland but the Germans regard the

Russians as communist scum and they have conflicting interests over oil and wheat in the East and in Turkey. The Russians may fight our war for us."

Eden laughed. "Real politic at its best. Canning would have been proud of you, but Halifax has a point. We're in bad shape and bad morale to fight right now."

Winston could hardly contain himself. "Canaris can't deliver and even if he could how will Britain's prestige look to the world if we cave in? First Munich and then Warsaw, not to mention Prague. It's an invitation to every country in the Empire to tweak the Lion's tail. We cannot do business with that man."

"You mean Hitler, I take it?"

"Of course I mean Hitler. He's murdering anyone that opposes him and we cannot turn a blind eye to what's happening to the Jews. This is genocide."

There was a long silence. Chamberlain looked at his hands reflectively. "As I see it, we agree we have an affinity with the German people but not the Nazis. If they removed Hitler and stopped this maniacal persecution of the Jews, then the objective of crushing Bolshevism would meet our broader goals? Even you would agree with that Winston, would you not?"

"I would sooner trust a cobra than these Nazis but I might support that strategy. But I warn you, once you have given the German military a free hand to gobble up Eastern Europe they may turn on us for the dessert."

Churchill was all too well aware of the sense of betrayal that had arisen within a Germany racked by deflation and unemployment followed by a catastrophic inflation, which had destroyed the middle class. Worse, he realised that following the First War, Europe had been carved up into a series of 'new' countries, or the old boundaries of countries had been radically altered. Each of these countries contained numbers of ethnic minorities, many of whom were German. In Hungary, Bulgaria, Yugoslavia, and Romania there were sizeable German enclaves. Poland was nearly five per cent German and Czechoslavakia was over 20 per cent German. For a resurgent Nazi Party, the campaign to 'free' their fellow Germans was compelling. Halifax turned to the group. "The Germans may well not succeed. Remember what happened to Napoleon? And rest assured, Stalin will fight to the last peasant. As for the Jews they are in some ways the author of their own demise. Hitler is right in thinking the Bolshevik revolution is in many ways a Jewish revolution, not here of course but at its heart. They are the brains of the movement."

Chamberlain picked up his fountain pen and reflectively unscrewed the top. "Why don't we convey our conditions to Canaris and see how he responds? Stewart, what do you think?"

"There is theoretically no harm in doing so but I fear time is not on our side. Also, our information is that the German High Command may see it the other way round. He hesitated. "I know this is a delicate subject Prime Minister, but our information from Berlin is that the German military were about to remove Hitler when we and the French accepted the German occupation of Czechoslovakia. As a result, Hitler became an instant hero in Germany and the military pulled back." Chamberlain's cheeks flushed but before he could say anything Winston rounded on them.

"Try to do a deal if you wish but you are deluding yourselves. This is about character. Hitler has no morals and knows no half measures. If the German High Command had any guts they would have removed him long ago. They haven't, and so we shall have to fight. And by the way I vote for assassination. Perhaps Douglas here could help us arrange it."

Chamberlain swiftly changed the subject and the four

politicians plus Sir Stewart agreed to reconvene first thing in the morning. Harry was thanked for his contribution and he and Rupert were excused from further attendance.

On the way home in the car, the two were silent for some time. Finally, Rupert spoke. "Do you realise we have just attended a meeting at which the final decision may result in the life and death of thousands of our countrymen? I'm not sure I quite know what Churchill's position is. He changes his spots, so we have to be careful. He was a great supporter of that mindless dill, the Prince of Wales, and he and that woman Wallis Simpson he's so desperate to marry are avid admirers of Hitler. It's the small changes. If Edward VIII had become King and Halifax somehow Prime Minister, we would be the greatest of pals with Hitler. What a responsibility they have hanging over them. What would you do if it were you?"

Harry thought briefly. "I can't be sure but I think we have to fight. I believe Hitler and his like will be made drunk by success. It has already happened. If you attended one of the Nazi rallies you would see it. Should we decide to stay on the sidelines, and if they then defeat the Russians, they will turn and come after us. They will not be content to share power with anyone."

Rupert took a while to digest the implications. "Maybe Winston is right, we should assassinate Hitler."

"That makes us as bad as them doesn't it? Just a bunch of gangsters; fighting a legally declared war is one thing, murder another."

"I don't think it does make us as bad as them. We can see war coming and maybe millions will die. Are you telling me allowing millions to die if there is any chance of preventing it is not murder by another name? Hitler is a deranged madman. If we kill him I think his minions will settle. They are thugs but they are rational and being rational we would be able to negotiate.

None of them has that suicidal will to war. They have objectives that could possibly be met. Every now and then the world throws up these deranged men who manage to exert a hypnotic control over their fellow men. Caligula, Nero, Ghengis Khan, Attila, Napoleon, even Stalin. You remove them and their movement is deprived of its vitality, of oxygen if you like. If you want to kill a snake, chop its head off. I would do it."

"Why don't you do it?" asked Harry, interested to see how Rupert would respond.

"I can't shoot straight, I'm as blind as a bat, but believe me if I could I would. How about you? You're a dead shot."

Harry laughed. "How do you know that? I've never said anything."

"It's our job to know."

"We use professionals to do professional jobs. I'm an amateur at killing anything but rabbits. It's an absurd idea."

"Is it?" replied Rupert, "you're a crack shot, you speak perfect German, you have friends in high places, and you're always visiting Germany. Perfect I would have thought."

There was a light drizzle of rain. Harry looked at the traffic around Marble Arch, people going home, in buses, in cars, in taxis. Some would be worried about what might be about to take place, some excited and some oblivious. All would live with whatever the politicians decided. He was glad it wasn't his decision. "If we did it, it might provoke war instead of peace; the tragedy of unintended consequences."

"We would be no worse off if it did. At least we would have removed their Commander-in-Chief. If we don't, and war starts, our opportunity is gone. We might bitterly regret that."

Harry shifted uncomfortably in his seat. "They always said that beneath that polite veneer the English are ruthless. Well, it won't be our decision, thank God."

CHAPTER 14

Harry sat patiently to see who would take the empty seat next to him on the KLM flight out of Prague. He had been instructed to take the commercial flight from Amsterdam and informed that in mid-flight the plane would be diverted to Prague for a vital pick up. He was to on no account leave his seat but to wait for the seat next to him, which was empty, to be occupied. The time passed slowly as the plane sat silent on the tarmac before he glanced out of the window to see about a dozen men hurrying towards the plane accompanied by a luggage cart piled high with suitcases and boxes. They disappeared from view under the plane's tail. A few minutes passed before the rear door opened and the new passengers climbed on board. A tall man in a gaberdine raincoat sat down beside him. He had rimless glasses and his hair was slicked down on his head with some sort of gel. Small sprouts escaped, which suggested that without assistance his hair would spring up uncontrollably in every direction. From the acute angle at which they were seated, Harry could see through the thick lenses of his companion's glasses. The view behind was completely distorted. He must have appalling eyesight. Harry waited but there was only silence from his neighbour. The plane started its engines and headed down the runway towards take-off. As it lifted off, his companion turned to him.

"Aardvark?"

"Correct," replied Harry.

"And you?" "Rum and Black." They both laughed and sat back in their seats as the suburbs of Prague disappeared below the airliner's wings.

"So, what have you to tell me?" asked Harry. They spoke German.

"It's an unmitigated disaster. We have been informed by our mutual friend that the Germans will invade Czechoslovakia and that the invasion will take place at dawn on the 16th. The Germans will not be resisted. This plane contains most of our Intelligence staff and all our secret files that matter. We needed to rescue something. I hope we make London. It is a tragedy for us but we have too many Germans within our borders to offer any resistance. Chamberlain left us defenceless when he backed down in '38." Harry could think of nothing to say that would defend the decision at Munich, which they were now living with.

Barely a week later Harry and his travelling companion, whom he now knew as Alois Frank, met in the offices with Rupert and the newly arrived Captain Fryc. Fryc had somehow squeezed himself out of Prague on a local flight and then to Croatia and to Paris and at last London. He was in despair at the state of his country; their failure, notwithstanding an army of nearly 750,000, to offer any resistance but, as he explained it, the Czechs had quickly seen that they would not get any assistance from Britain and France. Hitler had been correct in his estimation. He laughed bitterly. "We had a report from our German friend of a meeting he attended with Hitler. Hitler was ranting, apparently. He called the English decadent and Chamberlain a doddering old idiot and then went on to label the French Latin dogs, parasites and Daladier, the French Prime Minister, nothing but a pastry cook. Then he launched into the Hungarians, who we had assumed were his allies, but Hitler called them cowards, pigs and effeminate Slavs. He raged at all his perceived enemies but none of the German officers stood up to him and now he has succeeded beyond his wildest dreams without a shot being fired. Truly Churchill is right, 'His Majesty's Government had the choice between shame and war. They chose shame, and they will have war.' "

Rupert rose from his chair, and walked to the window where he gazed out at a grey London day. "What about the Admiral? Do we know what he is thinking?"

Fryc replied before Harry could speak. "We had a meeting with Oster, the Admiral's right-hand man. Afterwards he and I had a drink. He told me Canaris thought Chamberlain was a blockhead. Oster then went on to say Canaris had come back from a meeting with Hitler and stormed into his office saying, 'I've just seen a madman. He is mad, mad, mad. Do you understand? He is mad.'"

Fryc laughed, "Mad, but winning unopposed, it seems." Oster reflected for a moment. "You know," he said, "when Canaris took control of the Abwher, he adopted the motto of his predecessor Colonel Nicolai: 'The Intelligence Service is the domain of gentlemen.' He hates cruelty and respects the rule of law, but we need to persuade him. For us all to survive he needs to change."

Stalin sat silently behind his desk. Not a paper or pen cluttered the top and the room was silent, save for the ticking of the wall clock. It was after midnight. He had been sitting hardly moving for some time when the door opened and Molotov strode into the room clutching a battered briefcase. "We've won. I have the Treaty in here. Ribbentrop signed it an hour ago. They've completely capitulated. We have everything we asked for."

"Being precisely?" asked Stalin.

"Everything. Latvia, Lithuania and Estonia, the ports of Libau and Windau, our claims in Finland and Bessarabia. The whole of Eastern Poland and, finally, neutrality in case either of us is engaged in war with a third party."

"Why did they capitulate so quickly?"

"Because they are on the brink of invading Poland, and the British and French have just affirmed their commitment to Poland. The Germans want a free hand. To think we were worried about the German, Japanese, Polish and British all aligning against us. This will cause despair in the West."

"Better than that, Comrade. The Germans will fight the British and French until the land is littered with their dead. They will be much more efficient at killing than last time and when they collapse exhausted we will call our Comrades to arms all over Europe and this time the Revolution will not fail. We came close after the last war but this time we have time to build up the Party whilst they slaughter each other. Europe will be communist and so will Britain. This is the pivotal moment in the internationalisation of our Revolution."

He reached into the drawer in the desk and pulled out a bottle of vodka and two glasses. "To a Europe drenched in capitalist blood."

In both Britain and Germany, the momentum towards war increased by the day whilst in the background peace feelers were surfacing from an impenetrable cloud of rumours and clandestine contacts, to be unscrambled by Sir Stewart Menzies and his team, including Harry and Rupert, at S.I.S, or MI6 as it became known. The contacts with the German Catholic right via the Vatican were growing and were to continue for some years. The Swedish businessman Dahlerus, with his high-level contacts, was constantly liaising between Goering and the various members of the Government in Britain, bypassing, much to their annoyance, normal diplomatic channels. Various Tory peers supported by Government members like Rab Butler and Sir Samuel Hoare, seeing Halifax as an ally, tried to persuade him that peace with Germany was for now the only logical policy. Then came Venlo. Two MI6 officers in Holland embarrassed the entire British Government by allowing themselves to be arrested by the Nazi security organization, the S.D., on Heydrich's orders, again complicating relations. The arrests had come hard on the heels of an abortive homemade bomb attempt on Hitler's life and were timed to suggest that MI6 had been behind the attempt. Sir Stewart stormed out of his office muttering about 'bloody amateurs'. Sir Stewart was effectively running MI6 although his official appointment was not to be announced for another month.

Canaris returned to his villa in Schlachtensee on the outskirts of Berlin. For once it was early in the evening. He entered to find his wife Erika practising on her violin. He had met Erika at Kiel in 1917 but had kept his interest in her to himself, wondering what sort of life they could have whilst the war continued and the life expectancy of a submariner was not much. Finally, though the war was over and they became engaged in January 1919, when perhaps Canaris felt his fighting days might be behind him. Here they were, married with two beautiful daughters and now he was involved in what might be an even bloodier struggle than the previous affair. He paused at the threshold listening. Erika loved that violin, a rare Stradivarius, and she loved to play. She stopped to welcome him but Canaris waved for her continue. He slumped in his chair whilst the Dachsunds tussled with each other for attention. His daughters were upstairs in their rooms. He wondered to himself about the increasing intrusion of their mutual friend, Reinhard Heydrich, into his life. Heydrich was an accomplished violinist. He had been invited by Erika to play at her Sunday musical parties, mainly recitals of Haydn and Mozart. Canaris had to admit he was very accomplished. He and Heydrich had been old friends since the navy and Canaris had been a mentor to him. But now he wondered. He had seldom seen a more ruthlessly ambitious character. He had felt at first that Heydrich might mature and soften but in fact he had become worse, driven by his fanatical support for Hitler. He would have to watch with extreme care.

On the 3 September 1939, Harry and Rupert sat listening to the radio in their office in Whitehall. Chamberlain was addressing the nation. "This morning the British Ambassador in Berlin handed the German Government a final note, saying that, unless the British Government heard from them by eleven o'clock that they were prepared at once to withdraw their troops from Poland, a state of war would exist between us. I have to tell you that no such undertaking has been received, and that consequently this country is at war with Germany."

Rupert looked at Harry. "Christ, what a bloody disaster. Winston warned us and now it's happened, a reward for pusillanimity on a grand scale. This could have been avoided. What are you going to do Harry? Do you want to do it all again?"

"I'll call my family in New Zealand first. We're bound to be in it with the Aussies. This time I'm in no doubt though. Hitler must be stopped."

"Stand by anyway," replied Rupert, "Sir Stewart will want a meeting immediately. There goes my weekend's grouse shooting."

France, Australia and New Zealand joined in the Declaration of War within 24 hours.

At first nothing seemed to change; a phoney war as it was called. Whilst the war was taking place in various theatres, including on the high seas, a strange quiet existed for a long seven months to May 1940. One hundred and ten British and French Divisions remained inert on the western front, notwithstanding there were only 23 German Divisions opposing them. For people living ordinary lives in England, there was little sign of change. But despite the quiet on the western front, Russia invaded Finland and was expelled from the League of Nations for its troubles. The British aided Finland with electronic equipment but not with men. Sir Stewart passed on certain information of interest to Canaris, thinking perhaps that Germany might prefer to see Finland succeed in defending itself against Russia, a view that for a time at least appeared to be correct. Then Germany attacked Norway and this time Britain did intervene, sinking a number of German ships in the Baltic but was quite unable to prevent a German victory and the surrender of Norway together with its invaluable access to Norwegian iron ore.

In May 1940 the Germans invaded Belgium, Holland and Luxembourg. Churchill was appointed Prime Minister and announced to Parliament and the British people, "I have nothing to offer but blood, toil, tears and sweat."

The war started disastrously. The Germans swept through the Ardennes, through Belgium and into France. The Maginot line, the line of forts constructed from Italy to Belgium along the German border and which the French believed would make them secure against any German attack, was simply bypassed. The Germans ran their powerful panzer tanks around the northern end through Belgium leaving the French forts useless. The threat to England's shores saw the pacifist strain in the English character, which Hitler believed he could rely on, suddenly change. The English decided they would fight. On the day Eden appealed over the radio for Local Defence Volunteers, a quarter of a million men responded followed by another million soon after. And in the miracle of Dunkirk, Churchill managed to present the evacuation of 333,000 men from the beaches as a victory which in a sense it was. Paris was taken in June and a few days later a totally demoralised France signed the Armistice.

Sir Stewart called a meeting which Rupert and Harry attended. The question everyone was concerned with was whether or not Hitler would order the invasion of Britain. Sir Stewart hesitated. "We have some comfort on this score. We have received intelligence that Hitler has reservations and still hopes for peace negotiations, although he will not be comforted by Winston's latest speech. There are some in Germany who wish to see Britain survive. We have a remarkable insight into the plans for Operation Sealion; not only that, we are using every deception to persuade Hitler that our defences are stronger than they are." He laughed. "We think he has been informed we have 39 divisions available. If only it were true. This, with the Luftwaffe's inability to command the air space over the Channel, may just save us." No-one said a word but the question hung in the air. How had Churchill achieved this invaluable insight into Hitler's plans?

Afterwards Rupert turned to Harry. "Your German friend's prints are all over this. Pray God Hitler never finds out. In any event it appears he hasn't, since Canaris has been made a full Admiral. Remarkable."

For the moment Britain was saved.

From time to time it was clear to Harry and Rupert that Canaris's hand was involved in some event. Information came via odd sources – the Vatican, neutral Sweden or Spain, the occupied states like Poland – but Sir Stewart was never prepared to confirm Canaris's role. At one stage Sir Stewart vanished for a few days and the rumour was he was in Spain meeting some vital source, but he simply reappeared and no explanation was ever asked for or given.

Harry and Rupert watched as the war unfolded. Sometimes in the early days it was almost impossible to see how Britain could escape defeat. Gradually things improved and victories began to occur. Harry paid close attention to how the Australians and New Zealanders were managing. There were the Australians helping to take Bardia in Libya and then capturing and holding Tobruk. The Kiwis getting belted in Crete. Harry's parents wrote, his father sounding staunch and resilient, his mother unconvincingly upbeat. There were letters from time to time from Jack and from Peter who was with the Australians in North Africa and had been in Tobruk at some point that Harry couldn't determine. Occasionally a colleague would arrive in London with an update on one or other of them.

One such visit was a short wiry Kiwi Lieutenant, Gary Melluish, a North Island boy, from the Kapiti Coast, who had been with Jack in Crete. He called Harry and they met in the usual spot, a convenient pub. He handed over a letter from Jack, which he knew would contain only what the censors would allow. Harry put it in his jacket to read later. "So now tell me the real story. What happened?"

Gary blew the froth off his pint, careful not to blow any beer out. "It was a bloody mess. What else? The Germans should never have been able to land paratroops. It was ridiculous. Anyway, eventually we had to get out. Jack and I were beating a retreat in our truck with bullets whizzing past our ears. We just got over a rise and out of the firing line when the bloody truck coughed and died. Anyway Jack was out of the truck with a pair of pliers and a coil of wire. A mortar nearly blew our heads off but Jack didn't blink. Next thing he gave the starter motor a thump with a spanner and I pulled the starter and we were back in business. We got ourselves to the port, Heraklion. What a mess. It had just been bombed for the nth time and troops were milling everywhere trying to get out. We pushed our way to the quay and eventually got ourselves on a destroyer, HMS *Imperial* with a group of Aussies.

"Typical Aussies, they had pilfered some booze, which they were happy to share with us. But it was 2am and we were buggered, so we found a corner of the deck and went to sleep just as the ship started out of the harbour. Next thing all hell broke loose. The steering had jammed. Even Jack couldn't fix that. The ship slewed sideways and nearly collected a caique full of soldiers travelling alongside us. The ship finally stopped and we all had to be transferred to another destroyer. It was pitch black and we had to jump as soon as she came alongside. Thank God it was calm and the Luftwaffe was nowhere to be seen. They got everyone off but then someone realised the Aussies, full of booze, had gone to sleep it off down below and no-one could find them. We couldn't hang around so we took off, but next thing our ship fired a torpedo at *Imperial*. Down she went. No more *Imperial* and no more Aussies. They couldn't leave her there afloat. Anyway we were only going half speed we had so many on board and of course as soon as it got light the Luftwaffe were out of bed and it was on. They just kept coming from the nearby airfield on the island of Skarpanto. Jack and I collared a Bren gun and we were all firing back, but the casualties were hideous. Some of the ships were badly damaged. A couple of bombs went through three decks on *Orion*, and *Dido* and *Hereward* were hit. It was a motley crew that made it to Alexandria. It was dark again by then and they trained a searchlight on a Black Watch Piper on the bridge playing a lament. The whole lot of us were in tears. We lost more men on the ships than we did in Crete."

They were silent for a minute.

"So how is Jack after all that?"

"Like the rest of us. Just shrugs and carries on. What's the alternative?" Harry digested it all and not for the first time felt a pang of guilt that he wasn't in the action.

CHAPTER 15

It was a few days before Christmas 1940 when Canaris called a meeting with colonels Lahousen and Oster. Canaris had been in a better mood lately. His strategy to keep Spain and Vichy France out of the war had indeed been successful. He had a deep affection for Spain and knew only too well its wretched condition following the Civil War. Spain was hardly in shape to become a combatant in the current war. He had held his breath earlier in the year when Hitler had scheduled a meeting with Franco and Marshall Petain. Canaris had had time to brief his close friend Franco before the meeting and had carefully run over every possible objection to Spain entering the war. The two dictators had arrived in their special trains just over the Spanish border in the little town of Hendaye and the meeting had been held in Hitler's carriage. The talks went on for seven hours. Hitler tried threats, bluster, promises – anything to get Franco to commit to enter the war and participate in the capture of Gibraltar. Franco stonewalled. Spain was bankrupt from the Civil War and its armed forces in disarray, riven by ongoing hatred between government forces and the socialists. Franco had limited weapons and no petrol, he was worried by the increasing support of Britain by the United States and, finally, his people were starving. He also demanded guarantees of French territory in North Africa, which he knew Hitler would never be able to agree since it would be an affront to Marshall Petain and to France.

After seven hours, Hitler, barely able to contain his rage, submitted and after an intended celebration in the Fuhrer's dining car at which the atmosphere became increasingly chilly, Franco departed and Hitler turned his attention to his meeting with Petain. Petain was equally elusive. Hitler tried to persuade him that Britain was the common enemy but Petain, the victor at Verdun in 1916 after appalling carnage, and the head of the Vichy Government that nominally controlled much of the South of France under German direction, maintained his cool. France was in no shape for more war. Its complete inability to defend itself against the German onslaught was demonstration of that, and then there was the issue of the two million French prisoners of war that Germany was holding. Without their release and return to their families Petain would do nothing. Hitler was defeated. He would arrive at what he had expected would be a triumphant meeting with Mussolini with nothing. To make matters much worse Mussolini informed him that, without a word of warning to Germany, his ally, his forces had attacked Greece.

All this was the cause of much amusement to Canaris, Oster and Lauhausen but they had more immediate issues to contend with. Canaris explained, "The Fuhrer, via Marshall Keitel, has ordered us to eliminate General Weygand. He regards the General as pro-British. Weygand is in North Africa and Hitler fears he will be the focal point for Free French forces joining up with the British to form a centre of resistance. Hitler wants him eliminated. Lauhausen was appalled. "He thinks we are no better than the Gestapo. I have no intention of carrying out this order." Oster agreed and suggested that Hitler should be the one eliminated. Canaris waited until they calmed down and then gave his assent that conducting a murder was out of the question. Canaris pointed out that Article 14 of the Military Code read: "It is a crime to execute orders given for criminal reasons." Lauhausen looked at Canaris and shook his head. Yet again they would obfuscate this order so that Hitler and Keitel would never know of their refusal to carry it out.

In April 1941 Harry had a call from Sir Stewart's secretary asking him to drop everything and go out to Aldershot to meet a special flight returning from somewhere in Europe with Rupert on board. Harry did as asked. Rupert was usually dressed immaculately but on this occasion he climbed out of the plane his brown double-breasted suit rumpled, his white shirt dirty, and for once not wearing a Club tie. He slumped into the car with hardly a word beyond a request to find the nearest pub. Harry found a tiny village with a pub backed by a sunny garden overlooking a pond with an ancient water wheel. Water gurgled over a small weir. Ducks tugged at weeds and chased each around the pond. No more peaceful scene could be imagined. He fetched two pints. "What on earth's up, Rupert? You look like you've been in a war?"

Rupert took a long sip and sat back. "You could say that. I'm just out of Belgrade. No-one thought the Germans would bomb it but they just did. No declaration of war and they chose Palm Sunday for a really Christian gesture. There are thousands dead and maimed, bodies all over the street, rubble everywhere and can you believe it, the bloody animals escaped from the zoo? There are lions and things roaming around. Christ, I'm glad to be home.

Those poor bastards when the German troops get in there."

Harry knew a rough outline of what had happened but it wasn't until a few days later, after Rupert had recovered, that he had him run through the prelude to all this. "Yugoslavia has always been a madhouse but we thought we had a good thing going. Prince Paul, who was fundamentally running the place, was Oxford and an Anglophile, our best friend in the Balkans. For God's sake, our King was the best man at his wedding. He's practically one of us. He was supplying us with all sorts of stuff but then things got a bit out of control. We think Hess, with Hitler's and your friend Canaris's knowledge, had engineered a contact with Sir Samuel Hoare, our ambassador in Spain. Prince Paul was in the middle of it. The idea was to engineer a coup to replace Churchill with Hoare, Eden with Rab Butler and make peace with Germany, allowing them a free hand in the East but preserving the British Empire intact. We know that Prince Hohenlohe and particularly his wife, Stephanie, who's still very influential with Hitler, has very good connections with the aristocracy in Britain and some of our barmier politicians. Before the war she was as thick as thieves with Lady Asquith and Halifax and she was even on Rothermere's payroll. Did you know she's of course Jewish but has persuaded Hitler to declare her an 'honorary Aryan'? Can you imagine it?

"In any event these so called aristocrats are the mainstay of the 'why are we fighting?' movement, which thinks some of the Nazis' right-wing activities might be just the ticket for Britain. They have never really gone away; the links are still open. Everything we know confirms that there are a lot of Germans who believe that war should not have broken out with Britain and that Churchill is the warmonger who has prevented peace happening. We've heard all these plots before so we just had a watching brief. Then Prince Paul signed the Tripartite Alliance with Germany to get them off Yugoslavia's back. We thought it would help this peace process, as if a piece of paper signed by Hitler is worth anything. Either that or he was scared of his own communists. Anyway it was disaster for him. Unbeknown to us those treacherous bastards in the Special Operations Executive had been talking to the Serb nationalists behind our back. We had Julian Amery confined to Istanbul but his father Leo has been up to his neck with the Serb opposition. On the night that Paul signed the Tripartite Agreement Leo somehow managed to broadcast a speech urging the Yugoslavs to rebel. He invoked the Battle of Kosovo against the Ottomans in 1389 when Prince Lazar was martyred. Lazar is a sort of King Arthur to Yugoslavs, the non-Muslim ones anyway. It was as if a signal had been given. Paul is actually a white Russian so he hasn't any real constituency in Serbia. Two days later the Serbs had deposed him, encouraged by the Russkies and our S.O.E. boys, and the Tripartite agreement's out the window. Bloody brave but bloody mad. Hitler's blown a fuse, bombed Belgrade, even though it was declared an undefended Open City, and is invading Yugoslavia as we speak. They won't hold out long. But here's the thing – the Russians are Serbs. They're supporting the nationalists, half of whom are communists and have been funded by the Russians anyway. The majority of Serbs are in the nationalist, communist camp. Now it's caused a massive rift between Hitler and Stalin."

"Have we just been out manoeuvred by S.O.E?" Harry interrupted. "But maybe this is actually pretty good for Britain. None of us would want peace on Hoare's terms anyway and now we've at last got Russia and Germany at each other's throats. Good result, except for poor old Prince Paul, wouldn't you say?"

"Quite. Good result and I was just pointing it out to Sir Stewart and he just gave me that death stare. So what I would really like to know, but we're never going to find out, is what he has really been up to and whether or not your Admiral has been in the middle of it."

"But Canaris would have wanted the peace even if Churchill had to go."

"Yes, he would, but he must have realised it was a very long shot. What's a great second prize for Canaris?"

"Germany smashes Yugoslavia, Russia comes in to aid the Serbs, gets pulverised by the panzers and the communists are finally obliterated from Europe. Then from a position of strength Germany makes peace with Britain."

"Exactly."

"And Prince Paul?"

"We had four hours to get him out. He's somewhere in Africa, as they say."

The MI6 team were still digesting events in Yugoslavia when Rupert barged into Harry's office. "You're not going to believe this. We've just been informed that Rudolf Hess has parachuted out of a Messerschmitt 110 over Scotland. He's demanded to be taken to the Duke of Hamilton. This is insane. After all, he's Hitler's Deputy, probably number three in the Nazi Party. We will be conducting the interrogation for sure. This was no accident, he's picked a plane with the range and speed to deliver him to Scotland. It was equipped with drop tanks and we think it was unarmed." Harry was told Hess was going to be held in the Tower of London and then taken to Aldershot. He was put in touch with the interrogation team and told to report in as soon as possible for a briefing.

As he was about to leave his office, an envelope was delivered. He tore it open. It contained a single sheet of paper containing the words, 'Take Hess seriously. Rum and Black'. Harry went immediately to Menzies and Rupert.

"So," said Menzies, "Canaris knew about Hess and that means, I think, that Hitler must know. All the bluster in the Nazi press is just cover in case, as they would calculate is likely, Hess's mission fails. We think Hitler would still like peace with Britain so maybe he is going to attack the Russians? Even Hitler would need to think twice about a war on two fronts. If he could persuade us to come to terms he could obliterate the Russians. We know both Hitler and Canaris hate the communists; the Yugoslav thing has brought all that to the surface. The peace feelers through Prince Paul are completely dead and all those activities around the Vatican and through the Swedes are too slow, so he had to find another way to reach us. But does Hess think the Duke and his friends could persuade Halifax and Hoare, and all the others who have doubts about the need for this war, to dump Churchill? Or does he think Churchill will negotiate a peace with Hitler. No, he could not be that stupid."

Rupert interrupted, "This is a huge gamble by Hess and he will lose, but why would he even try it if he didn't have authority from Hitler? Hitler and the Admiral have nothing to lose. If Hess fails nothing changes. But if he succeeds!"

Sir Stewart smiled, "Perhaps we did allow the Admiral to think there was a chance of a peace agreement and perhaps the Admiral persuaded Hess. As you say, Canaris had nothing to lose if he had authority from Hitler."

There was little point in speculating further on what the Hess incident was really about. Hess would be thoroughly interrogated and then locked up out of harm's way. Hitler had disowned Hess and his name would be erased from the records as far as Germany was concerned. In any event there were far weightier matters to consider.

Canaris and the Abwher were fully engaged in the plans for Operation Barbarossa, Germany's planned invasion of Russia, but Canaris could see potential problems that were apparently not yet causing concern to the military or indeed Hitler. The disconnection with reality was marked. Just before the invasion Heydrich remarked to Canaris, "The Fuhrer's words show that he himself is much less optimistic than his military advisers. General Halder assures the Fuhrer that the Russian armies will be destroyed in six weeks. Keitel and Jodl calculate that it will take eight weeks, but the Fuhrer has told Himmler that he himself reckons on ten to twelve weeks. I believe it will take two or three months. What do you think Admiral?"

The Admiral shrugged his shoulders and was silent but Heydrich insisted. Canaris could see the danger of this loaded question but eventually he replied. "First, I am worried about seeing us engage in a war on two fronts, which is very dangerous. I do not share the General Staff's view that, with our overwhelming superiority in men and material, the war will be over in a few weeks. It is just possible that a military defeat, rather than the annihilation of the Red Army, will have the contrary effect of enabling Stalin to fortify his Party and Government by appealing to the ancient patriotism of the Russian people. A war of this kind on Russia may prove a source of strength to Stalin." Heydrich received this in a chilling silence. It was exactly as if he considered such an opinion as little more than treason.

After Heydrich had gone, Canaris pondered yet again how someone so totally without empathy could have been such a fine musician. He remembered Heydrich as a naval cadet, with his passionate artistic temperament and high pitched voice, the most unpopular cadet on their training ship, and now moulded somehow into an arrogant bully.

Schellenberg tried to lighten the mood. "Marshall Goring is more optimistic than any of us. He says the Luftwaffe will crush the Russian air force, flatten Moscow and pick off Soviet tanks like sitting ducks."

"Goring!" sneered Heydrich. "He said the same about England in 1940." Canaris was about to refer to Napoleon and the Russian winter but thought better of it.

Living in London during the Blitz was a special experience for Harry and Kathleen. Raids intensified during 1940 and they found themselves constantly having to evacuate to shelter. Fortunately, they were close to an underground station and they would make their way there trying not to hurry as the sirens wailed and the first crash of bombs could sometimes be heard. If life above ground was chaotic, often not helped by bad weather, life in the underground was mostly orderly. The sounds from above were muffled but as the Blitz continued organisation improved, stoves and canteen food trains began to operate. Harry noticed that morale was surprisingly strong. Although there were occasional scuffles over bunks or food, for the most part people were either quietly resigned to enduring or defiant over this Nazis outrage. The bombing of St Paul's Cathedral seemed to have been a seminal event. "Shocking, despicable," people muttered to each other; but St Paul's was still standing, defiant, for all Londoners to see. Eventually everyone would emerge to be confronted by the results of the night's raids. Fire wardens were everywhere, with vehicles and volunteers helping wherever damage had occurred. Buildings had toppled, fires were still burning and inevitably bodies were being recovered. The Red Cross and Salvation Army did their bit and there was no shortage of volunteers. Harry and Kathleen would return to their flat always with the small pang of anxiety that when they rounded the corner into their street the building would be gone. After one particularly heavy raid as they made their way through some debris, Harry laughed. "I know the only thing you're worried about." "What's that?" "The jolly painting. The Marc; you love that painting". Kathleen tossed her head. "It's not the only thing."

Harry of course new much about the extent of the raids and Kathleen and he would talk it over. The ports were of course hard hit. Plymouth, Bristol, Cardiff and tiny Hull, conveniently close, was raided 86 times. The provincial cities were equally badly damaged with cities like Manchester and Birmingham hit hard and Coventry hardest of all the latter paying for the munitions factories that surrounded it. Kathleen worried about her family as much as herself. Although they were out of the centre of Manchester Harry had not exactly helped by telling her how poor the Luftwaffe targeting was. "That's not much comfort really" she responded. "You wouldn't be that pleased if your family weren't in New Zealand. Every time they miss their target some little village is obliterated and women and children are killed." Harry decided changing the subject might be wise.

One morning a few weeks later when he was running late for the office, Harry was about to rush out the door when Kathleen reminded him it was his mother's birthday. She was less than impressed with a plea to come up with a suitable telegram which sounded like he had drafted it, a plea she refused point blank. "Your Mother will know in an instant it's from me not you. Harry, this one's for you." Grasping a wriggling child, she kissed him on the cheek and fled before he could argue. Later when he was at his desk thinking about how much he missed his family and the Southern Alps, a secretary interrupted his reveries.

"Sir Stewart wants us all in the boardroom. Don't ask me what for," she announced. Harry found himself in the company of most of the staff, both senior and junior. To his surprise, given it was mid-morning he noticed several bottles of champagne on ice.

"Gentlemen, and ladies, I believe Britain will now win the war. An hour ago I heard that the German Army has attacked Russia across a broad front. We know only that the military forces Hitler has deployed are enormous. Our preliminary estimate is that it involves more than three million men, maybe more than four. Russia is not well prepared even though we have actually sought to warn Stalin that this might occur. Nevertheless, attacking Russia is a monumental task, as Napoleon discovered. If they are not defeated before the Russian winter, and we will do all that we can to see that they are not, the Germans will rue the day they embarked on this enterprise. So, let us drink to our new ally, the Russian bear."

After the staff had dispersed, Sir Stewart took Harry and Rupert aside. "We think Hitler's attack on Russia was delayed by more than a month by his invasion of Yugoslavia. So it may just be that the events surrounding Prince Paul may have saved the Russians. The Germans are that much closer to winter." Sir Stewart was in an expansive mood. He poured each of them a drink and sat back in his armchair and toasted "to victory."

After the attack on Russia, the situation within MI6 became a lot more complicated. The department understood that the Russians were now Britain's allies and that they needed support against the greater enemy, Germany. But even so, the department believed that Stalin was just as untrustworthy as Hitler, as the Molotov–Ribbentrop pact had demonstrated. Many of them had sympathy with the views expressed by the likes of Hess and Canaris, that the Germans were natural allies of Britain whereas the world Stalin and the Bolsheviks believed in was totally abhorrent to everything England professed to stand for. Cooperation was not easy and Sir Stewart vetted shared information on a need-to-know basis as far as Russians were concerned. As the year progressed, Churchill kept up his efforts to persuade a much more compatible ally to join the war effort. He kept in constant contact with Roosevelt and enlisted the assistance of MI6 whenever he could to provide evidence of the hostile intent of Germany towards the United States. In August Churchill sailed to Newfoundland on HMS *Prince of Wales* and transferred to USS *Augusta* in Placentia Bay to meet with Roosevelt and announce the Atlantic Charter.

On Churchill's return, Menzies attended a briefing at Westminster. He returned to his office frowning. "Churchill's in a foul mood. He says every time he communicates with Roosevelt he comes away satisfied Roosevelt has promised all manner of support but when he tries to turn words into action nothing happens. He gets fobbed off with all sorts of excuses. He forgets Roosevelt has a domestic constituency to manage, and there are plenty of Americans who want nothing to do with a European war. It's easy to overlook how much help we've already had. There's another thing. He's being constantly harassed by Stalin. Stalin has followed the Hess case. He's suspicious that Hess was indeed sent by Hitler and that we will sign a peace agreement with Germany and leave Russia to fight alone. Exactly what he would do to us if he could. Harry, what is the latest on Hess?"

"We've very closely monitored him and we've come to the conclusion he's mentally very unstable. We think we have all the information we can get from him but we're still not sure how much of his flight was encouraged by Canaris and how much by the misinformation we fed him about our so called search for peace. Either way he's of no further use to us except for propaganda."

Menzies grunted, "Not much help to Winston. Stalin won't believe him whatever he says."

Even though Japan was not particularly high on Sir Stewart's agenda, as 1941 began to draw to a close, MI6 began to pick up more and more information pointing to an increasingly hostile Japan. Sir Stewart began to wonder if the Japanese might take leave of their senses sufficiently to actually attack the United States. It was a few weeks later on 7 December 1941 that the Japanese attack on Pearl Harbor occurred. Sir Stewart was ecstatic. More champagne was served in the boardroom when the Germans and Italians joined their Japanese allies by declaring war on the United States five days later. Sir Stewart understood only too well that an attack of the nature of Pearl Harbor would unite the whole of the United States behind their President and that their efforts would be all the greater thanks to the underhand theatricality of the attack. Americans were outraged that such an unprincipled event could occur. Churchill and Sir Stewart had long held that the capacity of the American economy, once it was on a 'total war' footing would, joined with the Allies, eventually overwhelm the Axis powers. A feeling began to permeate the organisation that sooner or later this war would be won whatever setbacks might occur, but few of them imagined that the struggle would go on in every corner of the globe for another hard, relentless and bloody four years.

Canaris found himself alone with Oster when he heard of the Allied invasion of North Africa. Only a few weeks earlier, Canaris had received a top-secret communication from one of his North African operatives, a Colonel Seubert. The colonel had been sent to Libya by Canaris and there he had met up with the Grand Mufti of Jerusalem. The mufti was a strange and unpredictable character but had dedicated himself to the support of the Nazis against the Jews and, by extension, the Allies.

He had visited Hitler in Berlin and participated in a bizarre charade in which he demanded coffee. The mufti's interpreter tried to explain that this was necessary Arab etiquette. Hitler, who didn't drink coffee, then left the room returning with an SS guard bearing lemonade. Having overcome this minor frisson, they found themselves in firm agreement – the Jews were the heart of all their problems. Moving on to a meeting with Himmler, the mufti and Himmler found themselves getting on famously. Himmler confided in him that the Germans had already got rid of three million Jews. The mufti boasted that he would support the Nazis "because I was persuaded that if Germany carried the day, no trace of the Zionists would have remained in Palestine".

In a demonstration of his support, the mufti showed Seubert a long letter, hiding the letterhead but proclaiming that it came from an impeccable source. It forecast an Anglo–American landing in "the first days of November, probably between the 5th and the 10th". And it continued, "it is an operation on a grand scale, its first objective being to penetrate the Central Mediterranean, then to destroy the Axis forces in North Africa and finally to prepare bases essential for the subsequent elimination of Italy."It went on to specify the initial objectives as being Casablanca, Fort Lyautey, Oran and Algiers. Seubert had pressed the mufti, claiming that the letter could have no credence unless he knew the source. Finally, the mufti relented on a promise that only Canaris could be told. The letter had come from Mohammed V, Sultan of Morocco, driven by a belief that somehow the Germans rather than the Allies would assist Morocco in its quest for independence.

Canaris had tried to warn Hitler of this impending assault on the soft underbelly of Europe, but the more difficult the war became, the less Hitler wanted to hear what he considered negative information, particularly from someone who seemed to be less than enthusiastic about the ultimate triumph of the Nazi machine. Nothing was done.

Canaris went quietly back to his office. Oster came in and tried to cheer him up but Canaris would have none of it proclaiming that the war on two fronts would be lost. Oster protested that there would be many twists and turns before any conclusion would be reached. Canaris turned on him. "As you know, we have some quite reliable sources within the United States. They have produced some very detailed data, which of course Hitler and the Generals refuse to listen to. Our people calculate the United States current military production exceeds the combined total of Germany, Italy and Japan. We believe they are rapidly achieving the capacity to build a plane every five minutes, 50 merchant ships a day and eight aircraft carriers a month. You need to sit and digest figures like that. All the grand speeches and parades, the bravado, the threats and propaganda count for nothing against statistics like that."

CHAPTER 16

It was in the summer of 1942 that Sir Stewart called Harry and Rupert to a meeting. Sir Stewart had long been concerned about the possibility that the Gestapo might be about to succeed in its long-held goal to take over the Abwher and remove Canaris. The extent to which Sir Stewart could do business with Canaris was a matter for conjecture, but Heydrich and the Gestapo were an entirely different matter. There could be no circumstances whatever under which MI6 could ever do business with the Gestapo. MI6 needed Canaris to remain in place. Sir Stewart looked at Rupert and Harry. "Time to take an active role, I rather think." Rupert agreed. "Harry and I will see to it. We may not have much time but all the pieces are in place. Sadly, though, it will not be good for our Czech friends. You have seen their comments on the likely German response." Sir Stewart frowned but made no further comment.

Heydrich was the current head of the Gestapo. Although he and Canaris had been in the navy at Kiel together and in fact lived next door to each other they had become bitter rivals in the struggle for power and for Hitler's ear. Sir Stewart had heard from his channels in Czechoslovakia that Heydrich had been assembling a case against Canaris and the Abwehr. Canaris and Heydrich had set up an agreement between the two organisations called 'the Ten Commandments', which would regulate their respective spheres of operations, but Heydrich considered it was restricting his operations and that the Abwehr was not performing. Worse he had been assembling evidence against one of Canaris's closest colleagues, Paul Thummel. Thummel had been arrested but, protected by an impressive party record, his long friendship with Himmler and after intervention by Canaris, he was later released. The cat and mouse game continued for some time, but the evidence was building. The SS, rummaging through the British Consulate in Belgrade, had come across a report detailing Luftwaffe plans to bomb the Yugoslav capital, information that could only have come from three sources, one of which was Thummel. Thummel was again arrested and Heydrich had now reached the point of denouncing Canaris to Hitler. It would be a disaster for Britain if this were to eventuate. Canaris was a 'friend', as much as that was possible, and Heydrich was just as definitely an enemy. But if Canaris were removed it was MI6's assessment that Heydrich would gain control of the Abwher, as well as the SD, and purge it of Canaris's men, many of whom felt as he did about the disaster Hitler was visiting on Germany.

On 28 December 1941 an RAF Halifax bomber left an airfield near London carrying seven Czech parachutists divided into three teams. The first team, 'Anthropoid', consisted of two specially trained commandos, Joseph Gabcik and Jan Kubis. The teams were to lie low in Prague until such time as an opportunity to assassinate Heydrich should arise, although the strategists in London were aware this might take some months. But it was known to all that the arrogant Heydrich, confident that his men had systematically crushed all opposition to Germany within Czechoslovakia, rode about Prague in an open-top grey Mercedes protected only by his bodyguard and driver. As the weather warmed up in spring this would surely present an opportunity. A furious dispute over the plan had occurred with the local Czech underground, who were grimly aware of the likely local reprisals from such an attack. But in London, MI6 and President Benes, the head of the Czech Government in exile, were determined to act.

On the morning of 27 May, as the flowers began to bloom in the gardens and parks of Prague, Heydrich kissed goodbye to his favourite daughter, waved to his two watching boys and his pregnant wife, and headed for central Prague. The car crossed the Troja Bridge and slowed as it negotiated the tram tracks and avoided the picturesque little red trams that the people of Prague were so fond of. As it turned a corner a man standing quietly nearby opened his raincoat and produced a submachine gun. He pressed the trigger but nothing happened. The gun had jammed. Heydrich turned and drew his gun, only then noticing a second man appearing from behind a tram. A grenade rolled under the wheel of the car and there was a blinding flash. The car swerved and crashed, a gaping hole in its bodywork. As it stopped, Heydrich and his driver, a huge man called Klein, leapt out with their revolvers. The two Czech parachutists ducked and weaved trying to find shelter behind the tram. Bullets whizzed past and they could see Heydrich firing, apparently unharmed. They spun and fired back as the locals dived for cover or lay flat on the ground as the shootout continued. Klein pursued them both, firing as he ran but, turning, Gabcik realised Klein had run out of ammunition. He aimed carefully and hit Klein in the legs. The two assailants, realising that the police and army would

ı

arrive any second, sprinted further up the hill and finding a tram crossing their paths they boarded as nonchalantly as possible and sat quietly until the tram reached Wenceslas Square. There they disembarked and made good their escape, devastated to think that the main object of the attack had not been killed or even injured. In fact Heydrich, running on adrenalin, had not at first realised that the grenade had blasted thin fragments of metal into his lumbar region and spleen. As the fuss subsided he began to feel the pain and he staggered over to the Mercedes and collapsed across its bonnet. The tram passengers stood and gaped until two Czech police took command of a passing baker's van and, draping Heydrich across the sacks of flour, ordered the driver to take him to the Bulov Hospital. At the hospital emergency surgery took place and the metal splinters were removed. Notwithstanding a broken rib, fractured thorax and punctured diaphragm the operation appeared to be successful. For five days, helped by the best medical practitioners from Berlin, Heydrich appeared to be on the mend. Then he suddenly worsened. Septicaemia had set in and, without penicillin available, the poison overwhelmed him. He died after spending the last few hours in agony early in the morning of 4 June.

Himmler was the first to arrive in Prague and his first move was to demand the Protector's clothes. He rummaged in the pockets and located a set of keys to Heydrich's safe in Berlin. Himmler was in no doubt the safe would contain information of great interest, deadly to himself should it fall into the wrong hands and just as likely to prove deadly to his enemies. He looked forward to looking at the file on Admiral Canaris.

The Nazi Party, among its other attributes, well understood the powerful effect of grand theatrical extravaganzas on an already cowed populous. A catafalque was erected in the main courtyard of the Hradschin for the funeral ceremony, with a huge backcloth bearing the silver SS insignia on a black background. An SS guard in dress uniform and steel helmets kept watch on the coffin. Two days later a funeral cortege took the coffin to the railway station accompanied by the sound of muffled drums and the thud of marching boots on the cobbled streets of Prague. In Berlin the coffin lay for two days in the Wilhelmstrasse palace. On the 8 June Hitler arrived by air for the service. The Fuhrer, flanked by his ministers and surrounded by the full apparatus of the Party, looked pale and drawn. Canaris stood next to SS General Sepp who had been heard to remark, when he heard Heydrich was dead, "Thank God that bastard has gone at last." Mourners were taken aback to see Canaris in tears but no-one could be sure whether they were shed for the loss of an old friend and colleague or in gratitude for the elimination of a mortal enemy.

Hitler was in a vicious rage, determined to avenge this insult in the most pitiless way. Chief of Gestapo Heinrich Muller put in charge and 60,000 auxiliary police were assigned to the case. The ballistic experts soon discovered that the grenade was foreign, indicating the likelihood of a foreign assassination team. The assassins could not be found, however, so a brutal campaign of terror and reprisals was instituted. It failed to find the two commandos but finally pointed to a connection with the village of Lidice just on the outskirts of Prague. The commandos tried to fight their way out but inevitably they, together with all 199 men from Lidice, were either killed in the shootout or summarily shot. All 184 women in the village were deported to Ravensbruck Concentration Camp along with all of the village's 88 children. Of these children 81 would be gassed in Chelmno.

When Rupert brought the news to Sir Stewart, including bitter rebukes from the Czechs, he bowed his head slightly then looked up at Harry and Rupert. "This war becomes more brutal every day. It's getting harder to remember that practically every decision we make is bad for someone we would rather protect. We simply have to live with the reality that to win this war we must do what we have to, whatever the cost. Fortunately, Winston knows that and, so I hope and trust, do all of us."

It was Harry's job to try to keep tabs on Canaris's movements, but he was unable to divine much about the consequences for him of the attack on Russia. Canaris, to all appearances, had genuinely grieved for Heydrich, his friend of so many years but with Heydrich's removal, things had settled down between the Abwehr and the SD for the moment. Canaris went on with his campaigns, the ultimate beneficiaries known only to him. Harry continued with his other work for Sir Stewart – translating endless documents, looking for tiny nuances to help piece together German intentions, interviewing captured soldiers, sailors, airmen or spies and, in between, making clandestine visits to Europe. He flew by Lysander at night into France to interview captured Germans and he had learned the lesson that Sir Stewart had imparted – that unfortunately someone would always be hurt. Harry had cross-examined the latest 'asset', apparently a Wehrmacht officer who had deserted to the underground. The more Harry questioned him, the more nonsensical seemed the man's exaggerated claims to be part of an anti-Hitler network. Harry cross referenced these claims, checked his own records and very quietly did an oblique check through 'German sources'. The French underground had its own sources. One of them, a female agent who had worked as a secretary in the SS offices in Reims, identified the man as a senior SS Officer. There was no doubt in anyone's mind that they had turned up a double agent. He was taken out and shot before he could betray them all.

A few days before Christmas 1943, with a dusting of snow

on the trees in Hyde Park and the Serpentine covered with a thin layer of ice, Sir Stewart called Harry into his office. "I need you to go to Istanbul to assist with a rather delicate operation. You'll be using a German passport, pick it up from Moira, and report to Nicholas Elliott in Istanbul as soon as you arrive. Moira will give you the briefing but come back to me if you have any queries. Background is we've been rather 'hands-off' with Abwehr but they still haven't recovered from the Yugoslav affair. Now we have a higher priority, so unfortunately we are going to have to do a few things that will not help the Admiral."

Harry settled down with the file notes. Erich Vermehren, as a young man, had been prevented from taking up a Rhodes Scholarship at Oxford because of his failure to join the Nazi Youth Movement at school, coupled with his trenchant anti-Nazi views. He was now a minor player in the Abwehr stationed in Istanbul but his wife was Countess von Plettenberg, one of the most glamorous women in Germany, a good Catholic, and far too openly anti-Nazi. Erich was desperate to have her join him in Istanbul but the Gestapo forbade it. Nicholas Elliott, station chief in Istanbul, had reported that he had had one of his men meet with Vermehren and it appeared that there might be a way of getting his wife out of Germany to Istanbul despite her being blacklisted by the Gestapo. If this was to occur Vermehren wanted to know if the British would be able to smuggle them both out of Istanbul before German intelligence could intercept them. Nicholas Elliott, after checking with Sir Stewart, affirmed their support.

Istanbul was an ants nest of competing intelligence services all trying to subvert the Turks or anyone else who could help their cause. Elliott guessed that most of the British operatives stationed in Istanbul would be known to their opponents. He needed backup but it needed to be a fresh face. Harry was ideal, with his faultless German and posing as a German traveller he would be completely invisible to the Germans and could watch the Countess's back until the deed was done.

Harry loved Istanbul on sight. To him it was a city to rival any he had ever seen with its rich history – a network of extraordinary Byzantine culture overlaid by its more recent Ottoman past in what appeared to be surprising architectural harmony.. It was agreed that he would come to an apartment owned by a sympathetic local Turk who was engaged in the trading of tea. Harry would stay with him ostensibly in the interests of selling tea, a scarce but essential product in Turkey, its supply lines disrupted by the war. The apartment was close to the Sea of Marmara, on Nakilbent Sok between the Kucuk Aya Sophia and the Bukoleon Sarayi. Before his meeting with Elliott, Harry was out as the sun rose, awakened by the Muezzin calling the faithful to prayer, walking the local streets up to the Blue Mosque and Topkapi, Aya Sophia and the Hippodrome. He stood for a while in front of the Serpentine Column and read the plaque describing how Constantine had stolen it from the Temple of Apollo at Delphi. It had been created to celebrate the defeat of the Persians at Palatea in 479 BC and was made from the shields captured as booty.

Harry was tempted by the smell of newly baked bread and coffee brewing, and would have liked to sit watching the locals getting ready for their day's affairs, but he knew he had to get back. People milled around everywhere as the city sprang to life and Harry felt at ease as he walked amongst them even though he knew it was possible he was being followed. If he was, he was happy that the last hour would have been of no value to anyone except himself.

The Countess had already tried to join her husband but each time had been intercepted. She was lucky to be still free, thanks largely to an impressive cast of influential friends. On her latest attempt to leave Germany, she and Erich caught the train to Istanbul but Erich soon realised there were Gestapo in the next carriage. As the train approached the Bulgarian border, their anxiety increased and it was almost with resignation that Erich saw Elisabeth marched off the train. She was told her papers were not in order and she was returned to Berlin. But Elisabeth had impressive connections. She was a cousin of Von Papen, Hitler's original Vice Chancellor and his Ambassador to Turkey, besides which, she still maintained her old friends in the diplomatic corps. Somehow she managed to cajole someone into finding her a seat on the twice-weekly diplomatic courier flight from Berlin to Istanbul and to evade her minders for just long enough to scramble on board at the last minute.

Istanbul was by now seething with spies and informers from each of the combatants. The Turks were desperately trying to maintain neutrality but the geographical importance of Turkey to both the Allies and the Axis nations meant that none of them wanted to see any sign of the Turks favouring either side. Each side spied on the other, and on the Turks, and any foreigner was, with justification, suspected of having intelligence 'connections'.

Elliott caught up with Harry in a small coffee shop in the Grand Bazaar. Harry negotiated the tattered map of the bazaar's endless passageways, dodging the numerous carpet vendors and the sellers of icons, brassware, endless items of jewellery, clothing and food of every kind, until at last he found the designated shop. He walked in the front but before he could sit down he was escorted by a bowing Turk through a curtain at the rear which covered a doorway into another shop facing another passageway. Elliott was seated at a table drinking a small cup of Turkish coffee. Having offered Harry a cup and a warm if brief welcome he explained that the Countess had arrived and they had her in hiding but that the Germans were furious and had mobilised all their resources to find her and her husband, who was also in hiding. "We have him covered, but I need you to go to a location tomorrow morning and pick her up in a car. The driver will know where to go. He will bring you to the Blue Mosque just before prayers and let you out. Mingle with the crowd and then slip away as the crowd moves into the mosque and make your way down to the edge of the Sea of Marmara. This map will show you exactly where to go. It is near where you are currently staying so you can walk the route tonight." Elliott unfolded a map and pointed out the route they were to take. "See here, this street has houses along each side but just here is a passageway which you will go down until you come to a large square. On the other side the passageway continues until it comes to a stone jetty jutting into the harbour. You must be there exactly at 11am and there will be a Gulet alongside to pick you both up. Vermehren will already be on board. Now take this," he produced a small pistol. "It's a last resort. If you need to use it, it's probably already too late but just in case. Any questions?"

Harry had only one. "On myself, or the enemy?"

Elliott looked steadily back at him. "Well my friend, that has to be your choice, I rather think."

The next morning, Harry found himself in the back of an ancient Renault winding through a series of alleys down near the Galata Bridge. They pulled up outside a three-storey house with arched windows, ornately decorated with what appeared to be cherubs, looking down over the street. The driver managed to wedge the car into a space that appeared far too small for it by dint of nudging the car in front in the rear. They waited impatiently for the Countess to emerge but nothing happened. This was not in the plan. Time was critical and Harry's advice was never to hang about in the same spot for longer than absolutely necessary. He was about to jump out and bang on the front door when it opened and a slim figure dressed in a cape and head scarf, and carrying a large valise, stepped out and squeezed herself as elegantly as possible into the back seat. Harry reflected that she had probably dressed to make herself as inconspicuous as possible but it was impossible not to notice her natural grace and the elegance of her clothes, however nondescript she might think them. The driver bumped his way back into the lane. Harry apologised for not giving up his front seat but the Countess simply gave him a little wave of her hand. "It's of no importance." She addressed him in German. "Thank you for helping me. What excitement, a real drama in Istanbul; such a romantic city. Now, can you brief me?" Harry did so as she listened, betraying her nervousness only by twisting the gold band on her finger.

Then Harry asked, "One more question. Didn't you think it odd that, after having been removed from the train by the Gestapo on your previous escape attempt, you managed somehow to hop on a flight to Istanbul without being stopped?"

The Countess looked at him sharply. "As a matter of fact I did, especially as I am almost sure I was being followed."

At the mosque the crowds were as large as Elliott had predicted. The car nosed amongst them until the driver said, "Now, out." They pushed their way through until they reached the other side of the Mosque's courtyard, found their way to a row of stalls filled with the usual bric-a-brac and turned into the side street Harry had scouted the night before. Harry glanced quickly at the map then dived down the street following the map's guidance towards the water. They found the passageway easily enough. Harry stopped and looked around. For the first time since he had arrived in Istanbul, there seemed to be no-one about. He listened intently but there was no sound except the distant noise of traffic and a jumble of voices and rhythmic chanting from the direction of the mosque. Finally, taking the Countess gently by the elbow, he stepped into the square. They stopped to catch their breath as Harry checked the location of the exit to the jetty. It led out of the far corner of the square. Still holding the Countess's elbow, he began to walk towards the exit, breathing more easily as again there seemed to be no-one about. The cobbled surface of the square was slippery and still carried a sheen of water left over after an early morning shower. As Harry lengthened his stride, the Countess stumbled and he caught her elbow and steadied her. "Perhaps I should have worn more sensible shoes," she remarked, looking reproachfully down at her gold sandals. They had almost reached the shadows of the buildings on the far side of the square when two figures stepped out of the passage in front of them. Both were pointing revolvers at them.

"Get your hands up," shouted one of them in German. "You," he waved the gun at Harry, "on the ground, face down, hands behind your head. Countess, walk slowly towards me." Harry thought about resisting, about the pistol inside his jacket but on the whole the odds seemed worse than poor. He slowly stretched himself on the wet cobbles. He wriggled onto his side and could see the Countess hesitating to move away from him. There was the sound of a shot and a bullet whistled off the cobblestones close to his head. "That was a warning. Just one." The Countess took a few hesitant steps towards her captor whilst the other German moved forward and quickly trussed Harry's ankles. He was forcing Harry's hands up behind his back, preparing to tie them when Harry heard two almost simultaneous shots, followed immediately by two more. The shape of the square meant that the shots echoed around him and Harry had no idea from which direction they had been fired or at what target. As he raised his head, he heard a grunt followed by a sigh as if someone had been punched hard in the stomach and saw his captor sink slowly to his knees and fall forward beside him. He looked up and saw the other German spread-eagled on the cobblestones, a pool of blood seeping out from under him. Two Turks each carrying a black Mauser were standing at the entrance to the square. One of them ran over and quickly untied Harry's feet while the other grabbed the Countess by the arm.

"Get up and go. Quick. You too, Lady. Go. Now. Move it."

They needed no encouragement and, grabbing her hand, Harry dragged the Countess down the passageway towards the sea. As promised a wooden Gulet was bobbing up and down at the end of the jetty, the swell bouncing it against the wooden wharf where two sailors, aided by large fenders, held it off as best they could. They grabbed the Countess by the arms and almost threw her over the low sides of the boat. Harry waited until the boat rolled towards him on the top of a swell and then leaped across the gap, crashing into the cabin top and gripping the cabin rail while the two sailors steadied him. Not a word was said as the skipper gunned the engines and they bounced away from the wharf and out into the stream. As they turned seaward, two figures emerged from down below, one of whom was Elliott and the other, it soon became obvious, was Vermehlen. He grasped his wife in a huge bear hug and they danced a sort of jig of happiness as the dome of the Blue Mosque and an array of minarets disappeared behind them. Elliott pointed back at the wharf and Harry turned to see the two Turks each carrying a body, which they hoisted high above their heads like Turkish wrestlers before tossing them into the sea. One of them saw them watching and gave a little half wave before disappearing back up the passage. Elliott looked at Harry. "So far, so good. I always think backup for the backup is advisable."

The Gulet headed downstream away from the Bosphorus

and into the widening expanse of the Sea of Marmara. Ships large and small were heading in each direction, fishing boats crossed the sea lanes at right angles, with a few dinghies and sailing boats threading their way amongst them. Some of the ships were headed up to the Black Sea but the Gulet joined the procession the other way as they headed down towards Canakkale and Gallipoli, where the Bosphorus passes the ruins of Troy perched high above the Dardanelles and finally exits into the Mediterranean. To Harry's disappointment, after a couple of hours, and before they reached the Dardanelles, they sighted a rusting freighter flying a Turkish flag, plodding along and emitting noxious clouds of black smoke from the top of a tall funnel. "That's our ship," said Elliott, peering through his binoculars. They soon caught up and manoeuvred up against the starboard side, out of sight of other passing ships, where a ladder awaited them. It took several attempts before they managed to get the Vermehrens onto the ladder, the sailors lifting from below and the crew of the steamer reaching down to give assistance.

As Elisabeth was about to step up, she turned to Harry. Pulling back her hood, she gave him a small kiss on each cheek. "Thank you again and to you all. May our next meeting be in the cocktail bar at the Parc. It will be our great pleasure to buy the champagne."

Harry gave her a smile. "It will be our pleasure to drink it. Good luck".

The trip back to the city was uneventful. Elliott and Harry chatted. "We'll have you out of here as soon as we can. 'C' wants you back in London and I don't want you around while the SID are looking for revenge. They are extremely agitated. I'm afraid there will be no celebrating on the town tonight."

The Vermehrens were taken to Egypt where the British played up Erich Vermehren's importance. They claimed that he was the Abwehr station chief in Istanbul and had defected with the Abwehr code books. The news was leaked to major wire services and soon the suitably dramatic escape story, complete with beautiful heroine, was thrilling the readers of a number of newspapers.

Hitler, prompted by Himmler, exploded and it was the final straw for the Abwher. Hitler summoned Canaris and accused him of allowing his service to disintegrate. Canaris stood his ground but it hardly helped his cause when he responded that disintegration was hardly surprising and added, "given that Germany is losing the war." That was it. Canaris was dismissed as head of the Abwher. To his own surprise, he was not arrested but only 'retired' and banished to Lauenstein Castle with his family and the dachshunds. Heydrich's dream of a unified service under his sole control was now to be achieved, but with Himmler in the role that Heydrich had coveted.

Back in London, Harry was debriefed by Sir Stewart. "Good result Harry, but it is rather interesting that the Vermehrens escaped so easily. The whole episode has an almost Heydrich-like feel about it. Himmler is just as duplicitous as Heydrich was. I suspect he may have allowed the escape knowing Hitler's likely reaction would be to dismiss Canaris, and that this would leave him on top of the pile. After all, the Vermehrens were of no great importance from an intelligence viewpoint. I'm afraid we've rather ditched our friend by going along with the plan, but there was no other option. Fortunately, the result is as we hoped. Without Canaris's guidance, the Abwher has actually disintegrated and just when the Germans need their intelligence service to be at its most effective. We hope we've struck a telling blow for the war and we expect it may help our men when the invasion of Europe takes place. They are going to need every bit of help we can give them."

"What about the rescue attempt?"

"Exactly, very amateurish, not the Gestapo's style at all."

CHAPTER 17

It was September 1944 and the Allied invasion force had finally established a foothold inland from the Normandy landings. It had been a bloody exchange. However, thanks to the tenacity of the Allied forces and the campaign of disinformation that persuaded the Germans the invasion would be targeted further north along the coast, they were now past any immediate danger of being pushed back into the sea. Harry had been put on a corvette and sent across the Channel to join other security officers in the task of debriefing German prisoners. Information was vital. What was the state of German morale? How many casualties were they suffering? Were they getting reinforcements and, if so, what sort and how much? And, most importantly, where were the panzer divisions?

Harry had just left the large tent that served as their interviewing area when a sergeant hurried up and saluted. "Morning sir, can I speak to you for a minute?"

"Certainly, what have you got for me?"

"It's like this, sir. We were just in the village up the road when we saw a white flag poking out of the cellar of one of the houses. We kicked open the door and this German officer was inside all dolled up in his uniform. Pretty cocky he was too, considering Reg wanted to shoot the bastard on the spot. Anyway he had some English and he said he wanted to be taken to an officer, someone in Intelligence. He has some vital information, so he reckons, though Reg and I reckon something's funny when you find just this one guy all dressed up on his own in a cellar. They usually fight to the death."

"Okay, bring him to the tent. There's a sealed-off area and I'll see him there. And sergeant, just make sure he's completely disarmed will you?

"Right sir, be back in a tick."

The sergeant ushered in a very sprightly looking German dressed in the uniform of an Oberst, his cap clasped tightly under his arm and his hair neatly brushed. Harry motioned him to a canvas chair and watched him in silence for some time until finally the German responded in English by asking for a glass of water. Harry poked his head out of the enclosed area and arranged for some water. Switching to German, he began by asking for the usual information: rank, unit, and general details relating to the current fighting. "So," he finally said, "what do you have to tell me and why did you surrender in such unusual circumstances?" The German, whose name was Gerchek, shifted in his seat and then began to talk.

"I am a good German, a patriot and a believer in the destiny of the German people. Hitler is destroying all that I love and believe in. He has gone mad. His decisions are suicidal and his strategies a disaster. The panzers could have pushed you off the beaches but they were in the wrong place, thanks to Hitler. Your tanks are no good. So. You perhaps know that there was an attempt to kill Hitler. A high-level plot but it failed and one by one the conspirators are being caught and hanged. But many of them are still free and the trail is being obscured. It is strongly rumoured that one of the plotters was a very senior officer in the Abwehr, I'm not sure who, but I know he is very senior. I don't dare to think it could be Canaris but maybe even that is possible. This man and his co-conspirators in the army still have the objective of ousting Hitler. They believe they can then make a separate peace with the Western allies and combine to defeat the Bolsheviks before they rot all our civilisations with their nonsense. But the thing is, some of the senior generals won't cooperate while ever you demand unconditional surrender. They understand any need to ensure Germany can never repeat this bloody fiasco but they need to know that Germany will survive as an entity. They fear it will be dismembered or, even worse, occupied by the Soviets.

"Our group cannot understand why you do not see the risk with the Soviets in the same way we do. Do you think they are your friends? Have you completely forgotten the Molotov–Ribbentrop Pact? Hitler is an aberration, a product of the betrayal of Versailles and the Great Depression but fundamentally Germans are like you British, we believe in many of the same things you do even though these common characteristics have been obscured in this holocaust. But the Soviets are out to destroy you just as much as us. Read Marx, listen to Molotov and Stalin. Their goals are quite clear. So, you must find this man and make contact and I can help you do that, but Churchill must also persuade Roosevelt that the word 'unconditional' needs to be removed. Then we may have peace."

"Why do we need to do this? If we made such a move and the Soviets got wind of it, and they will. I must tell you your internal security is full of leaks, we would cause a dire response from

Stalin whose goals I assure you, we, in Britain at least, are very well aware of," responded Harry. "I think even the German High Command realises Germany is going to lose the war regardless and this suggestion could be a very devious way of splitting the Allies.

"I repeat, because you need to understand that Russia and the Bolsheviks are your real enemies and Germany, the real Germany, is your natural ally in containing them. Though Hitler is now insane, way back in 1922 he saw the truth of this and he said so. Nothing has changed." Harry sat back and as he did so the air was filled with the deafening roar of a flight of fighters heading for the front. The two men looked at each other and before Harry could speak his prisoner resumed speaking. "You command the air so now you can command the panzers. It's lucky for you." The interview continued into the afternoon. Harry brought in one of the other officers to help note everything down. There were names and places and information which, bit by bit, could be pieced into place to allow them to see what had really taken place so dramatically on 20 July 1944, the day of the assassination attempt.

Harry had just instructed the guards to remove Gerchek when he asked Harry where his accent came from. "Your German is excellent but there is very strange accent. I am good with accents but it is strange."

"I'm from a long way away. I'm from New Zealand," explained Harry. Gerchek's face split into a wide grin.

"I only know of one New Zealander. I was at the 1936 Olympics. I saw Lovelock win the 1500 metres and break the world record. What a run. He beat the favourite Cunningham from America. What an athlete. Your country must have been very proud."

"I was there myself and indeed we were proud," replied

Harry. "He was one of the best."

"Even Hitler was impressed. Everyone thought Lovelock looked Aryan. It was a relief after Jessie Owens. So tell me, New Zealander, what are you doing fighting on the other side of the world? It's not your fight."

The guards had listened without comprehension to this exchange. As they escorted Gerchek out, Harry replied, "We need to rid the world of Hitler. Could it be, exactly as you do?"

That night Harry spoke for a long time to Rupert and was not surprised when he received orders to complete the interview as quickly and possible and return to London. They would send a plane to fetch him.

Harry and Rupert met with Sir Stewart the next morning and Harry recounted all that Gerchek had told him. When he had finished, there was a long silence. Rupert finally spoke, addressing Sir Stewart. "What's our most up-to-date information about our friend Canaris then?"

Sir Stewart leaned back in his chair. "Ah, it is complex. He was arrested soon after the assassination attempt and sent to Lauenstein Castle, as we know, but he seems to have been allowed to behave as if he was free. It was announced that he had retired and then one by one the conspirators have been rounded up and most of them shot after intense interrogation. But Canaris has remained untouched. We had an approach some time ago through the French Intelligence heads. It seemed to be another message suggesting a credible German plan to capitulate to the West provided the old chestnut about 'unconditional surrender' could be dropped by us. Of course that was not going to happen but still, Canaris has not been harmed. We believe that Canaris is being protected by, of all people, Himmler, who should be his sworn enemy. Why? It seems the most plausible explanation is that Himmler knows the war is lost and also knows that his only chance of surviving and perhaps even replacing Hitler is to negotiate with us. Who has the best links to the West at a senior level? Canaris, of course. So Canaris is safe for now but three things could wreck his peace of mind. If he was connected to the bomb plot and one of his co-conspirators cracks under interrogation, or if there is something in Abwher records to connect him, or finally if Himmler decides Canaris is more of a threat than an ally then Canaris is doomed. These are very high risks and frankly we can't do much about it."

Harry responded "Is it too far-fetched to consider springing him free?" Sir Stewart contemplated the question gravely for a few seconds.

"You see, old chap, he's not really much more use to us. Risk is too great for the rewards."

Rupert laughed. "Have you seen the latest effort to destabilise the Nazis? We've dropped all these stamps on Germany with Himmler's face on them. Well you never know, Hitler's mad enough to take it personally." Harry smiled but in reality it seemed to him abundantly clear that Canaris, whom he had come to like and trust and whom he believed was in his own way a friend to Britain, was doomed – just another brutal casualty of the realpolitik of war.

Sir Stewart had considered the whole matter in silence for some time before he arrived for his meeting with the Prime Minister. Churchill was predictably to the point when Sir Stewart was finally invited to take a seat. "So, what do we have to go on?"

"We believe Douglas's interview is a genuine statement of the situation in Germany at the moment, Prime Minister. We have a number of other confirmations of the assassination attempt and also of rising disaffection within the military. On top of that many Germans know that now they will lose the war and they certainly don't want Germany to be run by Stalin and his minions. We also believe that Roosevelt's call for unconditional surrender has complicated the issue. This is consistent with many other approaches, but the circumstances now make the opportunity for a separate peace better than they have ever been; better, but in our judgement, still not good enough."

"Who is this senior member of the Abwher who is involved? Is it Canaris himself?"

"We can't be certain, Prime Minister"

"But you believe so?"

"Yes."

"What game is he playing? I don't trust him. He foxed us in the Falklands and caused embarrassment to Jacky Fisher and me. And he cost us millions bribing the Spanish Generals to stay out of the war. What's he really after? You know him."

Sir Stewart deftly avoided confirming whether he did or he didn't. "I believe it's as Douglas says. He's a patriotic German, who likes and, I have to say, has helped Britain, and he hates the communists. So I think it's true."

"It's an impossible situation. Roosevelt will never agree to a separate peace. The Germans know they will lose and are now trying to dig themselves out of the hole. They have invited this and now we should smash them to pieces. We gave them an Armistice the last time and they've been claiming they were betrayed ever since. So this time let there be no doubt who won. Do you agree?"

"Yes, you know our thinking. We think Roosevelt has been seduced by Stalin's 'Uncle Joe' routine. He agrees with Stalin that the USA and the Russians are the only people who count at the moment and he is being strongly influenced by Stalin's anti-imperialist stance, which is aimed squarely at us. Stalin knows that if he can persuade Roosevelt of the evils of Imperialism he can push us out of India and the Middle East and Russia will have a free hand there. It's the Great Game all over again."

Sir Stewart was referring to the hundred years of rivalry between Russia and Britain that had lasted most of the nineteenth century and had led, in 1842, to the British retreat from Kabul, memorialised by Rudyard Kipling, which resulted in the death of every European soldier bar one. "All along it is clear Roosevelt has gone out of his way to keep Stalin happy and he won't hear of betraying the Russians by a separate peace; not only that, we also know that Stalin is deeply paranoid about exactly that eventuality. Finally, we still have no-one to make peace with until Hitler is removed and once again that outcome has been thwarted. But there is now another side to this."

"Meaning what?"

"Since the defeat at Stalingrad, we have been noticing that Hitler is increasingly erratic. He interferes more and more in the strategic decisions and gets them wrong. We believe he was convinced by Plan Fortitude that Normandy was a diversion from the real invasion in the Pas-de-Calais. As a result, he refused to release the Panzer Groups until it was too late. We think Canaris and some of Hitler's Generals, including Rommel, may have suspected it was a feint but luckily for us Hitler is now beyond listening to his own advisers. We believe his continued involvement can therefore only help us shorten the war. Under the circumstances we should act only if Kluge, Rommel and whoever else in the Wehrmacht remove Hitler themselves and can deliver on any agreement we might impose. This has been going on since before the war started, as you will remember, and all to no effect, as the latest fiasco demonstrates. For the moment, we should not reveal this alternative under any circumstances."

Churchill reflectively swirled the brandy around his glass. "Hmm, they betrayed us at Munich. I warned Chamberlain and I warned Britain. We have no alternative but to continue, but it is imperative we get to Berlin before the Russians."

Sir Stewart nodded his agreement and rose to show himself out.

The consequences of the failed attempt on Hitler's life on 20 July 1944 took some time to permeate the ranks of conspirators but gradually they were rounded up interrogated and either gaoled or summarily executed. Those at the top of the Abwher had either been arrested or waited in resigned expectation that either documents they had somehow failed to destroy, or the results of torture, would eventually implicate them. By September the prisons of Berlin contained thousands of prisoners waiting to be tried. The principal accused were kept in the cellars of Gestapo Headquarters in the Prinz Albrechtstrasse, or in Lehrstrasse prison. The cells were tiny, barely five feet by eight, with a folding bed, a table and a stool. Canaris had been arrested three days after the bomb attempt. He was in the garden of his villa at Schlachtensee playing with his two dachshunds when a black Mercedes drew up and two SS men sprang out. The more senior, Schellenberg, was almost regretful in his explanation that he had come to arrest Canaris. He attributed the order to SS Group Leader Muller and to Kaltenbrunner but did not mention Himmler. As Canaris was escorted to the car, his family and friends watched. It was as if he was being chauffeured to an important dinner or perhaps a theatrical performance.

Canaris tried to discover Himmler's role in the arrest and quickly realised Schellenberg was wary of his well-known relationship with Himmler, and the possibility that Himmler may not have authorised it. He must try somehow to arrange a meeting with Himmler as quickly as possible if he was to have any chance of escaping the SS.

Notwithstanding the mild manner of his arrest, and subsequent appeals to Himmler, by September Canaris was imprisoned in Gestapo Headquarters and accompanied in the prison by a clutch of Generals, Pastor Bonhoeffer, former Ministers in the Government and by many more of the regime's most prominent citizens. They received little food and only water with an occasional ersatz coffee. The deprivation from proper coffee was only a little thing, trivial compared to what was taking place around them, but it seemed in a way to be the last straw.

There were many air raids and during these they were escorted to a concrete bunker in the courtyard nicknamed the 'Himmler' bunker. Canaris, Oster and Dr Josef Muller were manacled, restricted to one-third of food rations and subjected to taunts and insults and made to perform menial tasks. As Canaris, down on his knees, scrubbed the floor of his cell, an SS guard sneered, "Well sailor, you never expected to come back to scrubbing the deck."

On the morning of 3 February, the prisoners discovered that another round of death sentences had been proscribed by the so-called Peoples Court against yet another bunch of miserable conspirators. The presiding Judge, Roland Freisler, had already condemned a whole string of prisoners and seemed to relish the task of ridding Germany of such undesirables as expeditiously as possible. As the Judge briskly worked his way through the death sentences, a low buzzing sound, faint at first but building into a crescendo of sound, filled the air over Berlin. The heaviest daylight raid ever carried out by the allies against Berlin had commenced. Wave after wave of allied bombers swept out of the blue sky of a freezing winter's day and, virtually unopposed, unleashed an inferno. Buildings toppled over or collapsed in on themselves and delayed-action bombs and incendiaries added to the chaos. Flaming phosphorus ran along the gutters and into the cellars where Berliners were cowering. Men, women and children, war criminals and the innocent alike, were buried or burnt alive and, as if to underline the randomness of the bombing, the butcher Freisler, the all-powerful President of the Peoples Court, was mutilated by a nearby explosion.

Records were destroyed and the prisons damaged to such an extent they could no longer be used. After the chaos had died down it was decided to evacuate the prisoners to Buchenwald concentration camp in Thuringia or to Flossenburg in the Palatinate. Canaris, along with Generals Oster, Thomas and Halder plus Judge Sack, and along with Dr Schacht, the economic genius who had rescued Germany from inflation, Theodore Strunck and the ex-Chancellor of Austria, Dr Von Schuschnigg, were bundled into a van for the 15 hour drive to Flossenburg.

CHAPTER 18

In the summer of 1945, Douglas had been transferred from the main intelligence centre in France to join the British Army near Bremen on the Aller River. The push towards Berlin was continuing but a message had been received from the local German command that they would consider negotiating a local surrender. An officer had come across from the German lines on the Eastern side of the river. The British wanted to know if this was a genuine approach or just another ploy to slow them down as they approached the crossing of the river. So it was that Douglas found himself sitting at a school desk in a small hut, watched carefully by two soldiers acting as armed guards, whilst he interviewed yet another well-turned out and well-fed representative of the German forces.

Outside could be heard the continuing sounds of rifles interspersed with the boom of bigger guns and the occasional rattle of machine guns. Gradually Douglas pieced together the story. It turned out that across the river at Bergen–Belsen there was a large concentration camp containing a mix of criminals and enemies of Germany, mainly Jewish people. The problem for the Germans was that typhoid had broken out and they had no resources to deal with it. All inhabitants of the camp were at risk and of course so were the German forces attached to the camp. Douglas's informer was regular Wermacht and it was easy to discern that he thought that Germany would lose the war and that surrendering, for whatever reason could be manufactured to sound honourable, would be a relief. Douglas told the soldiers to maintain the guard and set out to find his commanding officer. As he did so, a jeep appeared. "Hop in, sir," invited the driver. "You're wanted urgently at HQ. In the meantime I'm to give you this envelope." As they bounced along, Harry read the brief note, which was from Rupert. It read, "Harry, hope this finds you well-and in one piece. We have some intelligence that Canaris and several other high-ranking opponents of Hitler are being held at the concentration camp of Flossenburg near Bayreuth. We know he was arrested some time ago and also that some of his people have already been executed. We need him alive if we can find him. We've arranged for you to join the US 90th Infantry Division which is heading for the area. We are hoping that if they can overrun the camp quickly enough we can save him, so you'll be right in the front line I'm afraid. We owe him, and he would be invaluable as a source after the war so good luck. Rupert."

Having delivered as succinct a report as he could manage on the Belsen proposal to the colonel in command of the British troops, Harry was taken to a paddock behind the barracks. A small, army single engine Westland Lysander was waiting, the propeller already turning. He was helped into the cockpit alongside the pilot who gave him a cheery thumbs-up as he strapped himself in and pushed his bag behind the seat. "We're heading south towards Bayreuth to hook you up with the US

90th Division. Shouldn't take too long but we'll be flying low so you'll get a good view of a war going on. Hope they don't use us for target practice."

He was true to his word and as they bounced around in and out of the low cloud, Harry could see the ground below covered by columns of men, trucks and tanks. Every variety of civilian transport was heading west, as the armies moved east. Among them there were columns of civilians with family possessions, trailing children and using horses, bicycles and even wheelbarrows to help them on their journey. At one point, a squadron of tank-busting American Typhoons roared across the horizon in front of them heading east and he saw other aircraft in pairs or tight formations above his head, leaving wisps of vapour trails. From time to time a cloud of smoke was thrown into the air and the sky was full of smoke or fragments of cloud, it was hard to tell which. They crossed towns and small cities and Harry could see gaping holes where buildings had once stood, or piles of rubble where bombs or shells had landed and the holes they had left behind showed fresh earth or were filled with water from recent rain.

They landed in a sloping field between rows of pines and Harry was whisked away again in a jeep without ceremony to a nearby Inn which turned out to be the temporary accommodation of his host, a tall gangly Bostonian who was with US Military Intelligence. His name was also Harry, Harry Goerdeler, and he seemed pleased to see Harry. "I understand the mission," he explained. "We're anxious to get into Flossenburg as soon as we can, maybe even tomorrow. We are hearing some really bad things about what's happened there. By the way my friends call me 'Boy'. They say I never grew up, so call me that if you don't mind. It will save a lot of confusion." They spent a congenial evening together during which Harry 'Boy' explained to Harry Douglas the intricacies of the Boston Tea Party and why, although his name was Goerdeler, he was American through and through and Harry Douglas explained to Harry Goerdeler where exactly New Zealand was and the virtues of Romneys over Merinos. They talked about the war and when it would end. Boy hesitated, "It's funny, really. Half our armed forces are like me. They have German ancestors. As I said, we're all American now but it seems strange that we log the details of all these German soldiers surrendering and a lot of them have the same names as us. My family came from around Cologne originally. There are lots of cousins still there. The colonel says we should never have joined in. Reckons we'll get to Berlin and next thing we'll be fighting the Russkies."

Harry replied, "When the whole thing started, I had moments when I thought like your colonel. I wasn't alone by any means. The view was we should do a deal with Hitler and at least buy some time. But now I have seen what the Nazis really stand for, believe me, we made the right decision. You'll see tomorrow firsthand. The Nazis are different. It's hard for me to believe, but this is my second World War. In war, terrible things happen in the cauldron of the battle when the blood's up and we forget who we are. But these Nazis have planned the killing in cold blood. The extermination of a race, the elimination of towns and cities, the rounding up of families, grandparents, husbands and wives, children of all ages, and then killed them in the most cost-effective way. This is something the world has never seen before; the planning of murder down to its finest detail. This war had to be fought, there was no other way. Even in New Zealand, as far away as you could get from reality, we had to face it eventually. So you Americans have also made the right choice."

"The Colonel says if you guys had any guts you would have just bumped Hitler off before it all got out of control."

"We thought about it, but when we considered it carefully

there were four problems. One, we didn't want to set a precedent. Once you start bumping heads of state off you don't know where it's going to end and Democracies are the most vulnerable. Two, unknown consequences. We thought we could have started a war and Hitler would have been replaced by a Heydrich or Himmler who would have been just as bad. Three, we actually worried about the morality; seems rather quaint with hindsight. Four, it actually would have been an extremely difficult project. Hitler was very well protected, even then. Food tasters, unknown schedules, visitor body searches and so on. We were not sure we had the means. We even considered an eye in the sky operation, to try bomb one of his public appearances. But we didn't have the right aircraft or an accurate enough delivery system and on the ground probably would have been a suicide mission. The longer we left it, the harder it became."

"What about Canaris then? Is he worth rescuing?"

"Canaris is an enigma. We know a lot about him but he never dropped his guard. Personally I think he thought, like many good Germans, that Hitler was restoring German jobs and German pride and it was worth putting up with a little brutality to achieve that. He has plenty of blood on his hands but how could he not, given his role? But then I think he saw the Gestapo in action, his colleague Heydrich, the others, Hitler's cabal, and then he knew this had to be stopped. He thought if he could enlist us to get rid of both Hitler and the Bolsheviks then Germany would be saved. So he helped us to the best of his ability consistent with staying alive. We should find out tomorrow if he succeeded. By the way, Canaris is a personal friend of mine, a man I greatly admire, so I very much do want to rescue him."

Boy was astonished. "Far as I'm concerned he's part of Hitler's team so he can share the blame." Harry gave him a very hard look. "You might want to sit in a corner for a while and give some thought to what you might actually have done had you been surrounded every hour of the day by the Gestapo, by Hitler's murderous acolytes, trying to maintain the standards you had been taught, trying to save the country to which you have devoted your life, and with a wife and two daughters to protect." Boy paused. "Well he's still just another Nazi as far as I'm concerned." Harry stood up, shaking his head in exasperation. "If he was he wouldn't be in a concentration camp with a death sentence over his head."

Boy fossicked behind the bar and discovered another bottle of red wine. He refilled their glasses.

"Well, whatever happens, I'll be glad to get back home to Ohio. See the family, do a little hunting, drink a little hooch. I guess you're busting to get back to New Zealand too. Get as far away as you can from all this."

Harry paused. "I was definitely going to stay in Europe. I probably still will but then I look at all that's happened. Two World Wars, a catastrophic depression in between. They say England, Europe, is the centre of 'Civilisation', of 'Culture'; a sophisticated world of art, politics, the enlightenment and so on so on. But when I look I see something else; rampant Nationalism, and this war will leave a legacy of incredible hatred, and not just for the Germans. When you dig a bit deeper the nation states of Europe can barely tolerate each other, different languages, different customs and, worst of all, different religions; and now Stalin looms over everything. So I wonder, will they just be back at war again before we even know it? Well if they do they can leave us and the Aussies out. You wouldn't know but in the First World War they reckon we had a higher rate of casualties per head of population than England and I wouldn't be surprised if it isn't the same this time. What inbred European squabble would cause us to join in yet again?"

Boy tried the wine and grimaced. "God, we have to be desperate to drink this." He paused, "I agree, and we won't be bailing them out again. As you know half the country didn't want to this time. That cunning old bastard F.D.R. manipulated us in."

"New Zealand's far enough away we don't worry about wars normally. We had a vicious war with the Maori. They can fight I'm telling you. Scary. But we signed a Treaty, reached a settlement of sorts. The sophisticates in England snigger at us but when things get tricky we all go off and play rugby together, take it out on the opposition, and forget about it."

Harry paused, took a tentative sip of wine and grimaced. "You know Canaris once sat me down and told me about 'Culture'. He talked quite a bit about Heydrich, described him as a man of the highest 'Culture', of excellent good taste; the only trouble was Heydrich was utterly ruthless, a sadist and a coldly calculating mass murderer, not afraid to exterminate a whole race, the Jews especially, but he was not that particular whom he murdered. We should all thank God the Czechs assassinated him. So what so called 'Culture' do I want to put my family through?"

Boy laughed. "Seems pretty damn clear to me. You should jump on the first boat home."

"You would think so but I'm torn between doing that and staying to see what happens and perhaps even have some influence. The thing is I've been immersed in the life of Europe for a long time now. My skills are European skills and my thoughts European thoughts. My wife's English and so are most of my friends. Do I really want a sort of second-hand life, find out how the World is going from old copies of The Illustrated London News? Good people can make a difference even in the worst of circumstances. Canaris is an example. Culture has bugger all to do with it."

The next morning it was drizzling, a cold sideways sleet that found its way down their necks and inside their jackets as they bounced along just behind the frontline troops. There was only spasmodic resistance and they were able to follow local roads until finally they all came to a halt at the edge of a village. To their left, on top of a hill was what Harry at first sight thought were the ruins of a medieval castle. He peered through his binoculars. It was in fact a stark outcrop of granite, towering over the countryside like a piece of bleak modernist sculpture, a visible sign of the original purpose of Flossenburg, a granite quarry. A sergeant came up to the jeep. "That's the Flossenburg camp through that path through the trees. The scouts say there's not much going on. We think it's been abandoned by the Germans, so we're going in. Follow the half-track up there but watch out." They moved cautiously along the road with the trees hanging over them, dripping fat drops onto the jeep. Around the corner they came to a halt. There in front of them were several quite elegant stone buildings, looking like an abandoned spa or hospital. They edged forward towards an imposing two-storey building with gabled rooms adding further accommodation in its steeply sloping roof. It was a rust colour with a central arched entrance way protected by an iron barred gate. Through the gates they could see barracks and, behind the first row of barracks an electrified fence with watch towers and another smaller gate leading to what were clearly the prisoners' barracks, around twenty of them, mostly flimsy wooden structures but including a couple of solid stone buildings. As they moved slowly through the main gate they could see a gate post on which were displayed the words "Arbeit Mach Frei."

"What's that mean?" asked Boy.

"Work makes you free," replied Harry. Behind the fence the huts were splayed across the hillside and terraced down the hill. It looked like a substantial camp; their intelligence was that it held around 4000 prisoners and had been the site of many executions, 'sub-human' Slavs, gypsies, Jews, homosexuals and German traitors – all enemies of the Reich.

A small boy, quite neatly dressed, ran towards the troops and, after he had been welcomed by them, people started to emerge from behind the buildings and trees. Some looked like civilians, staff or inmates but then there emerged slowly, hardly walking, crouched over or crawling, clothed in rags or barely clothed at all, a bunch of emaciated humans their ribs sticking through their parchment-like skin, heads shaved and eyes staring either without comprehension or in fear. The troops hesitated as they looked with horror at this wretched apology for humans. Harry looked at Boy. "Now you see why we had to fight." Just as Harry and Boy were wondering what to do next, a soldier came over to them.

"The captain sent me to find you. They have a prisoner who has been hiding in the trees. He says there's a special prison section for important political prisoners. He'll take you to the place. He doesn't know if anyone's alive there. He says the Germans marched most of the prisoners out a few days ago, thousands of them. They've left behind a pile of bodies and some have been shoved into a mass grave." They could all smell the stench of rotting flesh as they followed him, and Harry found it hard not to retch. He put his handkerchief to his mouth as he looked about. They followed a path between crammed rows of single-storey barracks overlooked by guard posts up on the hill next to a cluster of log houses built on sturdy stone foundations, looking for all the world like some cute Austrian ski resort. Harry asked the guide what these were. "For the SS, sir" he explained. "No-one can go there."

They came to a corner and rounding it found a low white-washed building with a walled courtyard. Entering the courtyard, they couldn't see any sign of life. There was nothing but a single wooden bench seat. They both stood there in silence while their guide waited behind the courtyard gate until Harry walked forward to the rear wall and found a small door leading into the building. He pushed it cautiously and it swung back on its hinges. Harry stepped in and poked his head around the corner feeling protectively for his revolver in his belt holster. Inside the building, there were rows of closed cells, some with their doors open and empty and some with doors still locked.

Harry called out in English "Anyone here come out if you can. Come out slowly." From the end cell a voice replied. "I'm in here. Let me out." Harry and Boy kicked the door in and from the gloom within emerged a tall, stooped emaciated male in tattered prison overalls.

"Thank God. I don't believe it. Americans." He sank slowly to his knees with his hands on the ground whether to feel the reality of his freedom or simply out of weakness it was impossible to tell. "Captain Lunding. I'm Danish secret service. They left me. I don't know why." He sat still for a minute reflecting. "Why? How is it I am alive?"

Boy gave him some water and a dry biscuit. Lunding swallowed the water and chewed the biscuit and immediately vomited.

"Were there others in here?" asked Harry. "What happened to them?"

Lunding looked up from where he crouched on the floor. "All dead. Almost all."

"Do you know who?" asked Harry, but Lunding only shook his head. They carried him to the jeep and found a medical orderly who promised to look after him. Harry and Boy went with him to the infirmary, which had been set up in one of the prison barracks. They sat outside until eventually they were told they could speak to him for a couple of minutes only. He was on a stretcher at the end of the room flanked by the starved and dying residue of prison inmates, draped in blankets and stretched on stretchers, the floor or any place the staff could find for them. The stench was appalling. Lunding had regained some colour and tried to sit up as they came in but flopped back on his pillow.

"Sorry to do this, old chap," said Harry "but do you know who's dead? We need to know."

"I'm not sure, but the Admiral definitely. And Bonhoffer, and Oster. Lots of others. Not Mueller. I don't think so."

Harry's heart sank and he felt like throwing up himself. "The Admiral? Canaris then. You're sure?"

"Sure. Yes, I saw him dragged out naked. I'm sure. A great man you know. Our friend. All of us." The orderly came in and shooed them out.

"Come back tomorrow morning. He'll be a bit better then." They left the barracks and turned further away from the entrance down the hill. Alongside them was a ramp with rails leading down to a brick building with a chimney. Harry pushed the door open. He looked around, with Boy close on his heels. It was not hard to see the purpose of this small room. It contained bench clearly set up for dissections and beside it an incinerator. They backed out, gently closing the door behind them.

That evening was a quiet affair. As they sat toying with their food, Boy suddenly asked Harry, "Who were those other names he mentioned?"

"Oster and Bonhoeffer? Oster was Canaris' deputy. Bonhoeffer? If ever a man deserves to be made a saint, it is Bonhoeffer. He is, was, a Lutheran Pastor. He openly opposed Hitler from even before the war started without regard to his own life, which he has now sacrificed. He has continued to defy Hitler no matter how dangerous it was for him. Perhaps the Pope will make him a saint. Does the Catholic Church allow non-Catholic saints? Probably not."

In the morning, Harry and Boy made their way back to the infirmary. Again they waited outside until Lunding, a little more colour in his face and able to manage a shuffle came out, assisted by an orderly. They seated him in old armchair someone had purloined. "How are you feeling this morning?" asked Harry.

"Better than last night," was the reply. "I kept some liquids down and got some sleep."

"We wanted to ask you about what happened in there. Do you feel like you can tell us? Take your time but try not to miss anything, especially about Canaris."

Lunding sighed. "They put him in the cell next to me, number 22. I was 21. I could see through the crack. He was small, pale but well dressed and still with a soldierly bearing. We soon set up a simple alphabetic code system by tapping on the wall. He had baffled the SS for so long that he still thought he might make it out. First he was taken to some sort of sham trial before an SS Judge, no defence lawyer and no evidence, where they tried to get him to confess. He was too clever for them, but somehow they had found his diaries, all five volumes of them in Zossen. These detailed his contacts with London and his attempts to broker a peace. It was impossible after that. The Nazis had broken Oster and he admitted everything and completely implicated Canaris. They confronted Canaris with Oster and then he knew the game was up. When Judge Thorbek asked him if Oster was lying he simply answered 'No'. After that, things got much worse for him. New interrogators arrived. After a few days he tapped out, "That will have been the last.....I think....Badly treated...nose broken." There was a long silence.

Harry finally asked, very softly, "And then?"

Lunding looked up. "And then this message 'I die for my

Fatherland. I have a clean conscience. I only did my duty for my country when I tried to oppose the criminal folly of Hitler leading Germany to destruction. Look after my wife and daughters.' The next morning, I hear the guards and looking through the gaps I saw naked bodies being dragged out of the cells. Several of them. I'm not sure how many. But Bonhoeffer definitely, and Oster, some others too."

"What can you tell us about Oster and Bonhoffer?" asked Boy.

Lunding hesitated, "Oster was really Canaris's right hand man, I think. He was badly tortured and just gave in. Who can blame him? And Bonhoeffer was a Lutheran Pastor. He knelt in prayer before they hanged him. They had hanged his brother only a few months before. There were at least four others too. They hanged them with thin wire. It strangled them to death." There was silence. Lunding's face crumbled. Harry and Boy waited until he had regained his composure. "Then I was sitting in my cell awaiting my turn. It must have been a day or two later, this overpowering smell of burning flesh. My cell had only bars over the window but no glass. Ashes started to drift in. They floated in like grey snow and settled everywhere; they were the final remains of the burned bodies."

These events had occurred exactly ten days ago.

Boy and Harry looked at each other as Lunding subsided into a world of his own, oblivious to the pale sun and white clouds that drifted impassively above them on this pleasant spring day in Bavaria.

In 1965 a tablet was placed in Flossenburg Concentration Camp to commemorate Admiral Canaris. It read:
'Without sentence and without reason murdered by the National-Socialist Government'.